The Liquidator

FERDINAND MOUNT

The Liquidator

A Chronicle of Modern Twilight

HEINEMANN : LONDON

First published in Great Britain 1995
by William Heinemann Ltd
an imprint of Reed Consumer Books Ltd
Michelin House, 81 Fulham Road, London SW3 6RB
and Auckland, Melbourne, Singapore and Toronto

A CIP catalogue record for this title
is available from the British Library

ISBN 0 434 47995 0

Typeset by Falcon Oast Graphic Art, Wallington, Surrey.
Printed and bound in Great Britain
by Mackays of Chatham Plc.

... in spite of the tennis the labours abandoned
left unfinished graver still abode of stones
in a word I resume alas alas ...

Lucky in *Waiting for Godot*

I begin the story in the middle, because that is where I began. The real beginning – a romantic one – came later, and the end (which is violent) will turn up in its proper place. I could have told the story in a different order but that was not how it happened to me and it would not have turned out any happier.

The real beginning I owe to my cousin Theo Hale, a waspish solicitor of Nailsworth Glos., recently deceased (in 1993, I think). When I last saw him he had retired to the end of one of those narrow valleys once humming with cloth mills but now abandoned to the sheep and straggling orchards of unpruned apple trees. On that steamy afternoon, the long rutted track which led to his farmhouse seemed to be drawing us into a realm of unutterable neglect. On either side, an erratic electric fence kept the sheep in their steep thistly fields. The house itself appeared to be sliding down the hill into the stony stream at the bottom. The sheds around the muddy yard were filled with dilapidated cars gathering dust and chickenshit. A dusty hen was crouching on an old black mudguard. Inside the house: mouldering books, the smell of an elderly bachelor and his cooking. Piles of newspaper clippings on a chair suggested that our arrival had interrupted some complex research project. I had scarcely met Theo before (he was a quite distant cousin). In old age he had grown immense in his stained cardigan, his nose a great purple wedge. He had cooked the stew himself without bothering much with the chopping. Whole

1

mushrooms bubbled alongside meat chunks the size of builders' thumbs. The ivory knife handles coming away from their blades shook a little rust on our cracked plates. Amid this titanic disorder his voice came as a surprise: thin, sharp, absurdly precise. His reminiscences were malicious, operatically so. Our shared relations, respectable and stiff in the cold dark pre-war photographs, stirred again with all their old lusts and snobberies and meannesses beautifully preserved in the formaldehyde of Theo's resentment: 'But my dear, you can't imagine what she was like when she was twenty-five, so *acrobatic*.'

Then there was apple pie. The pieces of apple were as big as wheel-nuts with a metallic taste to match. My slice of the pie was like a cross-section of gash breccia in a geology book. As the bent spoon hacked at the pastry, my elbow caught the pot-pourri bowl at the end of the table. Inside the bowl there were crumpled butcher's bills, somewhat bloodstained, and pieces of cereal packets cut out to take advantage of special offers but presumably never dispatched. The bowl did not budge. Glued, Theo said with some complacency, we glue down everything here, saves a fortune in breakages.

'They never liked us, you know, never really accepted us.'

'Who didn't?'

'The family, your lot. We were different. Coffee?' He pulled a string dangling from the ceiling and the kettle began to sing. I expected the coffee to be tepid and gritty, but it was hot and full of flavour, and as we sat over it some of the loneliness and distress seemed to ease out of him. His melancholy gave him a kind of dignity, so that even his reminiscences about the sexual appetites of our shared relations seemed a little bit epic.

Then he got up and began to move around the room, his great cardigan belly nuzzling the backs of the chairs as he looked for things to show me, pulling open screechy cupboard doors and reaching into the back of shelves: his aunt's autograph album, consisting solely of the signatures of clergymen in the diocese of Chichester between 1870 and 1898, including a bishop and two archdeacons, a pamphlet on the history of bleach-and-dye works

2

in the Whitstable area – a subject not much talked about these days, Theo said with a sigh – composed by the same aunt who used to keep a small hotel in the area, a hollowed out horse's hoof in which he kept collar-studs and shirt stiffeners, he had owned a half share in the horse as a young man and it had once finished third in a nursery at Fontwell but broke down in the box on the way home and had to be shot in the car park of the old Wheatsheaf and the landlord refused to serve them afterwards, a lock of his wife's hair in a chipped enamel box with a coaching scene on the lid – not her best feature her hair, it was thin and wiry, she had lovely hips though but did not like to have them spoken of – ah this will amuse you, the plumed hat I wore at the carnival in Munich in 1927, I went as Bonnie Prince Charlie and was much fondled, Bridget came too as Flora Macdonald and had no success at all, we were getting on quite well then, it was several years before she took against me, don't blame her, she went off, you know, in every sense, became blowsy and wanted to get in with the smart set what there was of it in these parts then. I was dull, you know, dreadfully dull, always worrying about doing the right thing. At least I've got over that. But I suppose in our position, or lack of position rather, it was hardly surprising.

Then he began to speak of relations we did not share – his father's side which I knew nothing of – and there he carried me into a country that was strange, quite unsuspected.

By comparison, the middle section – with which this book opens – is set in territory which is familiar to me at least, my own early days in north London. It can be read if you like as a rather furtive chapter of autobiography. The connections with the peculiar family history relayed by Theo were hidden from me at the time and have only risen to the surface as the story has moved on to the present and other sources came my way, more reliable, less malicious sources. To these sources I must hasten to pay tribute and thanks: to Mr Timothy 'Captain' Oates, although reliable is perhaps not the *mot juste* for him, to the late Mrs Elizabeth Allenby, of whom much will be heard, to my old companion Mr Richard Shay (Rickshaw), to Mr G. H. Withers, formerly

3

Honorary Secretary of the North-East London Lawn Tennis Federation (Nelltef to its many friends), to Professor Heathcote Turner of the Centre for the Study of Middle East Conflict who so generously gave me the run of his card index, to Miss E. L. Sturdy, retired Assistant Librarian to the Commissioners in Bankruptcy, for much valuable guidance and information and, of course, to Miss Wendy Torrance, director emeritus (emerita?) of the Sinden Theatre, Ormouth, for what? Oh, for being her indomitable, intolerable self.

The last section can be left to speak for itself. A few names and circumstances (geographical, financial and so on) have been altered, but everything that matters has been as carefully recorded as possible. I do not think that readers will find it easy to identify from the text any specific firm of chartered accountants, lawn tennis club or group of terrorists. But I may be wrong.

Then

'There's something dreadful going on in them there woods.'

'Foul play, do you think?'

Through the pear-shaped hole in the chain fencing he had slithered, round shoulders and flat bottom, still as slippy as an amoeba in his long white shorts. And now from the tangle of bramble and bindweed came beating sounds, a dull thrashing mostly, once or twice a clattery rattle as the neglected bamboos by the wall came within range of his racquet. Peering through the dull green links of the fence, I saw the heavy September dewdrops hop and shudder at his flailing.

'It's only an old ball.'

'That's not the point.'

I looked up at the tall dutch-gabled house beyond the fence, long untenanted, occupied by squatters six months past: the black and ginger mongrel pacing up and down the balcony, the torn sheets not quite covering the windows instead of curtains, the bare light bulb swinging in the breeze of the broken pane. The club had complained, twice, three times, would complain again after the next committee meeting. The players were unsettled by the squatters strolling about the garden, peering through the fence with their quiet wolfish smiles. We felt spied upon, mocked. Our normal jocular calling died to a mutter.

'He's gone quiet.'

'Suddenly in the shrubbery.'

'As he would have wished.'

The beating began again, but more sedately now, the passion gone out of it.

The squatters had come round with a petition. We are professional-class homeless, they said, one of us is training to be a solicitor. Nobody at the club signed the petition. But they went on smiling their wolfish smiles. We would have preferred it if they had jeered, shouted, Anyone for tennis, done grotesque take-offs of our shots as passing teenagers did when we were playing on the public courts. The silent smiling in the brooding weather made us sweat. From the way they stared and ambled about the overgrown garden, they seemed to possess a more ancient right of residence than we had, some sinuous connection with the land which outdated by centuries the rectangular blocks of houses and tennis courts which now squatted there. We were puzzled by the law's refusal to take sides. And why did the mongrel not bark like other people's mongrels? Intensely restless, trotting up and down the balcony and then round and round the garden, rearing up against the netting, its paws shaking the dewdrops out on to the court, but never a sound out of it, or out of its masters either.

'Funny how silent they are.'

'Like as if the sound had been switched off.'

'Except you can hear P-J all right.'

Geoffrey Pagan-Jones was making the sounds the dog ought to have made, snuffling, panting, cursing, as he hacked his way back through the brambles. His round-shouldered, slippy figure came into view waving the lost ball, suffused by puppyish triumph. Then puppy-like he turned his back to us and slithered his hindquarters through the hole in the netting, the green soles of his tennis shoes dancing in the gravid air.

'Not bad for sixty-seven.'

'Can you round up sheep too?'

He chuckled his dry chuckle like the crackle of dry leaves underfoot, and his daughter Josie giggled as she did whenever he chuckled, simultaneously, not as a response or placation to her father. Sometimes, standing the other side of the net, I felt that

6

their movements too were deliberately harmonised. Pagan-Jones would hitch up his shorts, always threatening to slip down over his vanished bottom, and, as if responding to the same invisible signal, Josie would delicately settle her apple-green pants with a twitch of her pinced fingers. Her tennis outfit was uniquely all apple-green. Loose and frolicsome without being especially short, it had a kind of discarded theatricality; nymphs or fairies in an old D'Oyly Carte production might have worn something like it and complained to Wardrobe. Despite being so old-fashioned, it was as risky a garment as her father's shorts, perpetually slipping off or clinging to unpeel cool curves and let the eye wander down unhoped-for crevices. These marvellous glimpses were only temporarily interrupted by her tugging at the wayward strap or hem. As she served, with her high looping motion, a kind of perpetually aborted moonshot, the apple-green pleats flew up with the concerted enthusiasm of clapping hands at the end of an aria. The gentle, thoughtful parabola the ball then described on its way across the net seemed quite unrelated to the splendour of her action. As she played the shot, her face, small, friendly, brown-skinned like her father's, with a velvety-brown mole high on her honey-brown cheek, a moley mole not a beauty spot, wore an expression of co-operative surprise, as though she had been roped in for a pastime which was new to her but was ready to make a go of it. She had a slight squint which gave her expression a side-long sort of charm, so that when she looked at you, there seemed to be a snatched, forbidden pleasure in the look.

Tony Allenby was as bewitched by her serving as by the rest of her. Time and again, he moved gracefully enough towards the ball, but it was the grace of a trance, his feet gummed by supernatural forces to the green tarmac and the return would curl out of court with all the force of sodden thistledown.

'I'm sorry, I'm afraid my serve's just too rotten for you.'

'No, no,' he murmured, still entranced. 'It's very deceptive.'

'She *is* deceptive,' Pagan-Jones said. 'Well, she deceives me every time.'

He liked acting the simpleton, pretending not to understand

things – women, politics, art. So much of his life was spent in public shrewdness, affecting a brisk and comprehensive understanding of the situation, that playing dumb was his prime relaxation.

'You have to go straight into the creditors' meeting, mustn't hang about coffee-housing, plonk your file down on the table and launch straight in. Don't try and fuddle them with figures, give them a simple rundown – total liabilities x, total assets y, of which likely bad debts z. Then you tell them one horror story so they don't think you're a cock-eyed optimist – they tell me the chairman's just taken delivery of a new Bentley, counted six dead sheep in the paddock with my own eyes, that sort of thing – and then you give 'em a way out, a scheme with a capital S, sell this one, mothball that one, keep the core business going for six months. Doesn't matter if you have to alter the details later. What they want to know is, is there a way out. They're all wetting their knickers, and they want to believe in you.'

I believed in him, had believed in him from the moment Tony had introduced me with his shy grace to his new boss. I could see P-J slipping into the creditors' meeting in that inconspicuous amphibious way of his which made you feel he could pass into any fresh element without even pausing to catch his breath and then, quite unassumingly gathering up the strands of the meeting into his hands, so that first of all they thought here was a decent bloke and then a chap who had the figures at his fingertips and then a man who could run the business and squeeze the best out of it. He was *the* liquidator because he was himself so liquid, so fluent, so up with the current, swimming along on the back of his own luck. Even the firm's name was a tide caught and ridden. Noticed the comma, have you? Pagan comma Jones & Company. It was when I was starting up on my own, little attic in Seething Lane. Ordered the stationery from printer downstairs, stupid bugger misread the hyphen, stuck with reams of the stuff. But then when the clients started ringing up and asking am I speaking to Mr Pagan or Mr Jones, I saw the advantages of a split personality, made it look as if we had dozens of partners all with initials after their names instead of one idiot without any qualifications except

8

night-school book-keeping. Now I *have* got dozens of partners, all with qualifications like young Tony here – he's a senior wrangler from Cambridge, you know – and I just sit back and nod and sign the papers.

Yet still, Tony told me, P-J was always the first one into the meeting, sat where he could be seen and chose the exact moment to stand up and do his spiel, just when they were all getting a bit fractious and bogged down and despairing, and then he would stand up and make them feel that all could be made good again, or good enough to bring off some kind of rescue anyway. Only now his spiel included Tony (not a wrangler of any sort, a 2.2 in geography in fact) who would be brought in halfway through and stand up, sentinel beside P-J's homely roundedness, and give in his clear, light tenor the best estimate of what might be saved. Tony's voice needs a bit more describing. It had an active effect upon the room, it cleared and lightened the air so that even if you had not listened closely to the substance of what he said, you felt less heavy and fretful after he had spoken. It was a physical quality, nothing to do with the merits of what he said. Even in ordinary conversation, he was – no, not boring, certainly not wearisome – plain, unremarkable except for his plainness. But then in the creditors' meeting plainness was what they hungered for, plainness and a sense of the impending recovery of order. P-J and Tony were the angels of order, reassurances that beyond the nerve-shattering collapse and the headlong panic capitalism retained certain ultimate harmonies.

'You go in to see the miserable sods shivering in their offices. Twenty-four hours earlier, they were lords of creation. Now there they are, sitting in the middle of the buggers' muddle they've made themselves and liable to be chucked out by a common little chap like me who they wouldn't have given the time of day to last week. So you have to show a little consideration but you have to be quick too, otherwise they'll only make the buggers' muddle ten times worse. If you're going to keep them on, you've got to say so straight off. If not, you've got to escort them to the car park yourself and make sure they drive straight home.' And quick too, quick as fish leaping for the fly. 'Notice is hereby given,' P-J would chuckle, spooning the marmalade on to his cornflakes, as his eye moved swiftly down the columns of Legal Notices in *The Times* where the liquidators announced their meetings. 'Just next to the Hatches, Matches and Dispatches, you see – should be headed Deaths bracket Companies close bracket, just as sad for the poor buggers left behind.' But he did not sound sad. 'Better send Tony to that one, sod it, thought we might sneak Terrific Toys off old Corky, unsecured creditors only, what makes them think there'll be anything left on the bones for them, better to stay at home and save their bus fares. Ernst Young again, my, they are sharp this season.' And then he would look up and, serene as a sanskrit scholar, explain the difference between a creditors' liquidation and putting a company into administration or appointing an official receiver – 'kiss of death in my view, as soon as you bring in a civil servant, the assets are dead. No pep left in the business. Leave it to us practitioners in insolvency' – he stressed each syllable in practitioners with a harsh celtic relish.

'But the business is dead anyway, surely.'

'No, no, that's just the moment when you've got to keep the turbines humming. Every day you let the furnace grow colder or there's no one to milk the cows, you can be losing the creditors more money than the silly buggers who ran the business into the ground ever dreamed of losing. We're resurrection men, not undertakers.' And he gulped his thunderous black coffee with all the gusto of youth. All the time he talked business, through the half-open door when he was peeing or washing his slender manicured hands (like the hands of a young girl) or shrugging on his rusty old greatcoat or, in the evening, polishing his shoes and listening to light classical music on his old varnished walnut radiogram, Offenbach perhaps or Elgar.

'Sorry, call of nature. Only be a minute.'

And Pagan-Jones scuttled off down the tramlines towards the door in the wire netting, racquet tucked under his arm, with that same eager gait with which he approached each fresh engagement. Josie and I began to practise. The ball moved between us in a high lolloping arc. We too lolloped from side to side with slow moonstrides. Playing with Josie I was transported into another dimension. Our limbs seemed longer, our movements so languorous that I was surprised that earthlings strolling along the gravel path between the courts did not stop to watch these alien beings at play. Tony leant against the netpost and began to pluck at his racquet and sing, as he always sang, something in French, suitably autumnal to go with the dew-swollen brambles and the heavy air. What is it, I said, expecting to be none the wiser. *Quand de la fontaine*, he said, Massenet, I think. One of your grandmother's? He nodded. It would be nice, Josie said, to have a singing granny. I don't think you could have called her nice exactly, Tony said, she had a foul temper. *Quand de la fontaine* ...

The varnished lamina of maple, ash and walnut, the tight-strung championship gut, the maroon leather grip, four-and-a-quarter inches only (he too had slender hands) this cradled thing, warped and pressed and woven in a carpenter's lair of glue and woodshavings, was as firm and delicate as any Amati or Strad. As his pale-brown fingers brushed the strings, I fancied I heard behind the thin keening of sung French some faint, instrumental accompaniment, a liquid irregular andante, and only after several lines recognised the limping trickle of the groundsman's hose still playing on the dewless geranium pots by the clubhouse.

The human brain, according to Descartes, was regulated by God as a *fontainier* or turncock regulated his fountain. The thoughts gushed or didn't, giving the impression that one's soul was turning the tap on or off, but it was God (to call Nature by a polite name) who was really at the controls. The image was pleasing, neurophysiology dressed up in the costume of a seventeenth-century gardener. I liked the idea of us being turned on and off, of divine fingers giving a brisk wrench to a bright brass tap and the remorseless babbling flow being squeezed to an impotent drip and then to silence.

'He's taking an awful long time. He's probably met a friend. Shall I get Norris instead?'

'If you must, you must.'

At the end of the courts, Norris was hitting tennis balls against a peeling practice wall. His grim gaze on a spot a few inches above the white line painted on the green wall; his heavy shoulders swinging into a hundred forehands, then a hundred backhands, then a hundred forehands again; the sweatband on his low forehead pushing up his hair into a spiky tuft; Norris was all determination, not and no talent, talent didn't come into it, wasn't a relevant concept at all. When he joined us, our own little eccentricities were magnified out of all proportion. The way Josie waved her arm to the sky at the end of her backhand, as though determined to break it off at the elbow, seemed like a hysterical cry for help; my own neat little footwork a parody of fussiness; Tony's amble towards the ball an unmanly, almost camp affair.

Norris Elegant was Disposals; he drove auctioneers to accept percentages they claimed never to have accepted before; he moved with a marvellous certainty to make sense of builders' yards, spare parts depots, engineering plants, parcelling up the lots without hesitation, ringing up contacts in Aberdeen or Swansea with the news of an unrepeatable bargain in cold storage cladding or textile machinery. Geoffrey Pagan-Jones would say: 'Norris is the reason why we run the best little breaker's yard in the business.' The more he said it, in his quick confiding way, the more his dislike of Norris came across. For even he, with all his limitless self-confidence and his natural ability to like anybody he met, could not resist the feeling that it would have been indecent to pretend to like Norris. To have detected some compensating virtue in that dour persona would have been perverse, affected. Not that there weren't surprises and contradictions to be found in Norris, and well-advertised ones at that. I'm a romantic, he would say, I know you wouldn't think it to look at me, but I am. For example, I would like to die in battle, I seriously would.

'Any particular battle?'

'What do you mean? Fighting for my country, what's wrong with that?'

'I just wondered whether you had any special preferences, like Alamein or Gallipoli.'

'I wouldn't like to have died in Korea,' Tony said in that reflective way which implied that he had paused before opening his mouth even when in fact he hadn't.

'It doesn't matter what particular battle, that's not the point,' Norris said. 'It's the manner of your death.'

'In fact, you're more likely to get done in by some poor farmer whose livestock you've just flogged.'

'I like to think that we enjoy remarkably good relations with our clients.'

Almost any Sunday his robust figure could be seen pummelling the practice wall, never anybody's first choice for a partner and yet by the persistence of his presence managing to get a game before the morning was out, The alternative was, after all, Sten Svensson, the laughing Swede, a pale man in his thirties with dull eyes set close together in a baldish skull. On losing a point, he would run his hand through his few straggling strands of straw hair, and let out a curious unamused laugh, the sort of 'Ho ho' produced by a conscript Santa Claus. Although he seemed otherwise vigorous enough, his service was a notoriously feeble thing, a little hop preceding a wriggly scoop which suggested that the ball was lightly glued to the racquet and could be prised apart from it only by this means. Svensson would say, 'I'm in transport services,' often before anyone had asked him what he did for a living. 'Half-a-dozen dodgy trucks without an MoT between them,' was Pagan-Jones's gloss. All the same, Geoffrey saw some hidden charm in Sten, perhaps because Sten liked to consult him on business matters and so was sometimes preferred to Norris, whose arrival on court was always an injection of contentiousness.

'If you wouldn't mind standing a foot nearer the tramlines. I need a little more room for my second service.' He delivered this with a vindictive twist of his shoulder blades, at the same time thrusting forward his thorax like a runner diving for the tape, his whole body shaken by an orgasmic shudder as the ball left him.

'I think you'll find the ball was in.'

'Norris, it was just out.'

'I had a pretty good view from here.'

13

'It was out, I promise you.'

'I'm sorry, but ...'

No offer of a replay would appease him. In the end, we would surrender rather than walk off the court. We made a pretence of seeing these incidents as amusing and his refusal to compromise as a picturesque quirk, but he was too implacable, the threat of anger too real and damaging.

Sometimes Tony would tease him by calling the score in French – *trente-quarante, égalité* – and Norris would jerk his shoulders as though to shake off a cloud of midges. And when Tony's shots, sliced as thin as wood shavings from a plane, came towards him, he prepared to thump them back with the umbrage of a Sicilian hitman. Tony himself moved towards the ball with the unhurried pleasure of someone running into an old lover in the street. He was so quiet on his feet. In a singles game, Norris would have beaten him nine times out of ten, but then Tony rarely played singles, disliked the thought of them: the raw assertion of individual will was distasteful to him.

He was reluctant to have his name tag inserted on the Gentlemen's Ladder and, when persuaded, never issued a challenge himself but accepted invitations from more upwardly mobile players with an air of surprised gratitude – oh that would be fun, thank you – and when the gritty opponent finally struggled to an ungainly win over him, would praise the justice of the result, saying he was far too high up the ladder anyway – somehow leaving his conqueror baffled and the victory diminished. Norris Elegant's tag, by contrast, was grubby from frequent handling.

It was in the Quaich Doubles that Tony came into his own. Partners were chosen by lot and then handicapped, so that some pumped-up ace would find himself not only chained to one of the elderly ladies who made the tea but also further weighted down by having to concede fifteen points a game. Pagan-Jones revelled in these delicate adjustments. He would come in the evening before, make the draw in the bar, taking the paper slips out of his old bowler hat – wore it the day I walked into Seething Lane and never again – and then retire with his large pink gin to the office. You could see him through the fly-smeared glass of the door, old tortoise head wagging over records of past matches, then occasionally popping out again to call someone from the bar for consultations.

And Tony too would invariably be drawn to partner some sturdy matron in a long tennis dress with heavy-falling pleats. One year, he drew Iris Pagan-Jones, Geoffrey's wife, as square and slow as Tony was graceful, as peppery as he was honeyed. '*He* makes me play,' she said with a fierce toss of her head at her retreating husband. 'I don't enjoy it. He thinks it's a reward for cutting the frigging sandwiches.' She cut the sandwiches (still Shiphams fish paste, long after others had gone over to guacamole mixture and taramasalata) with fierce, resentful chops of an eroded horn-handled carving knife which might have been dug up with some Saxon hoard. Her hair, dyed not quite to the roots the colour of light tan boot polish, bounced in time to her chopping. Her squares of stale Hovis would lie unmolested on the plates she had brought, long after the delicious triangles of Marmite and lettuce and gooseberry jam and smoked salmon had all gone. And when she removed the plates, conspicuous in themselves with their slashing modernistic orange and mauve pattern amid the gentle floral plates favoured by the competition, she did so with defiance: 'That's a relief, the dogs adore them even if nobody else does.'

'Bad luck, you're lumbered with me,' she said in her grunting breathless way to Tony.

'On the contrary, I fixed the draw,' he said. And though she merely snorted in reply, he had her half-softened already. He shepherded her through the early rounds, shielding her from the full blast of younger opponents, yet without panicking her by poaching on her preserves. They were generously handicapped. Pagan-Jones would do anything not to provoke her. Yet worth more than the fifteen points a game was Tony's love of the tethered, loaded nature of the competition. Players with a fierce will to win were enraged and put off their game when some quavery lady's back-

15

hand dribbled over the net. They would start mistiming their services, bang their volleys yards over the baseline, dispute line-calls, swear at their partners. In any case, runaway success was penalised under Pagan-Jones's ingenious additional 'Quaich rules', the rule that gave a side which was five-love down a forty-point start in the next five games. But since Tony was never so bad-mannered as to allow his own side to gain such a lead, he was never subject to such penalties, and he and Iris ran out winners round after round, he serenely wondering at their luck, she snorting at it.

There used to be a photograph hanging in the clubhouse as a memento of Pagan-Jones's long captaincy: Geoffrey presenting the Quaich, a flat silver cup chased with knobbly quasi-celtic devices, and his wife's square stubby fingers receiving it with an evident reluctance as though her husband was trying to crush it against her ribs. At her side stands Tony holding a couple of racquets, looking relaxed but a little remote. It is Pagan-Jones's expression that catches the eye. His smile is not broad, nor the eye overtly twinkling, yet one cannot mistake his contentment, his delight in the visible management of circumstance. Iris's awkward stance, her flaunted absence of the geniality fitting on such occasions, and the detachment of Tony (he is standing a few inches too far away from his partner) only go to display his happiness.

It was the same kind of happiness that crackled at the corners of his dry old mouth when, still dressed in his City pinstripe, he would slip over to the club some evening in late April, put on his tennis shoes and trot round the corner of the high privet hedge to inspect the three grass courts at the end of the club grounds. He would glide his hand over the sappy green grass, the dew just beginning to silver it, to feel the nap, and then stamp his feet to test the firmness and then, if satisfied so far, call the groundsman, old Boddington, an arthritic soak who occasionally coached small children but couldn't really play, and the two of them would pat a ball to and fro for a couple of minutes, two elderly gentlemen in formal attire, except for their tennis shoes, and then if the bounce was knee-high or thereabouts Pagan-Jones would in a high tone call to Boddington, 'Play, Mr Boddington,' 'Play it is, sir,' Boddington would reply, although normally they were Geoffrey and Ted to one another, and Boddington would go in to tell his daughter Denise who helped in the office, and Denise would take the dog-eared cardboard notice which said GRASS CTS ARE OPEN from under her knitting in the Out tray and pin it up next to the bar and the season would begin and with it the summer. When it was hot, Denise would go outside with her knitting, usually a matinee jacket for one of her nieces, invariably turquoise, and sit beside Court No. 1, annoying the more sensitive players with the click of her needles and the ringing of the office telephone which she brought out with her on an extension lead.

But the tennis wasn't everything, and part of Pagan-Jones's contentment lay in his expectations of Josie and Tony. These expectations had announced themselves, quite unmistakably, almost as soon as they had come across each other, in their late teens, I think. Even then, I knew enough to see that this was a freak phenomenon, something out of its time. For there seemed so little volition about it. They were, how else can one put it, drawn together. I blush for the antique phrasing with its awful implications of fate taking a hand, twin-souledness and the rest of that noxious mush which is now not even worth parodying. Determinism is flourishing and we lap up any philosopher who undermines what is left of the poor old free will, but the one kind of determinism that is out of fashion, hideously so, is the one which was so embarrassingly at work in the case of Tony and Josie. Would their case be more convincing if we thought of it as a case and referred to them by their bare initials as in a shrink's treatise? As a matter of fact, T and J was what they were often called in the club, for the club had a mania for abbreviations and nicknames. This mania reached extreme proportions on the playsheet for the annual Pagans v. Christians charity match in which Pagan-Jones raised a Six, more properly a VI, to play a team from the congregation of the local church. For some reason the match was played in Edwardian dress. I competed once for the Christians, wearing muttonchop whiskers and ginger plus-fours (the Pagans were all dressed as Arabs). Carrying my racquet under my arm in the May sunshine, the false whiskers tickling my cheeks and the tweed tickling my legs, I endured the mockery of the Saturday morning shopping parade and wished I was somewhere else, in the freedom of some bleak, anonymous urban tenement where I knew no one and nobody knew me. Anyone, inevitably came the cry, anyone for tennis, and it was small comfort that it came from a group of Asians outside the radio and TV shop. One of them strolled to the Caribbean greengrocer's next door and from the boxes of yams and guavas and pawpaws set out on the pavement seized some shiny fruit and threw it in the air, mimicking a cannonball serve. And from the inside of the greengrocer's came a throng of laughing Jamaicans tumbling over one another in the narrow entrance between the boxes, all shouting jolly good shot and well played, sir. I lobbed a watery smile back at them, which only provoked a further explosion of parodic shout and gurgle. The entire little parade of shops had become a celebration of the Great Tennis Joke. Its mock-Tudor timbers shook, the little leaded dormer windows overhead seemed to rattle with simple pleasure.

It was at this moment that I noticed Josie across the road leaning nonchalantly in her long fawn mac, taking slurps from a can of Coke in between laughing. The way she squinted into the sun (or was it just her own natural squint) seemed somehow to share the joke between us, although I was not laughing at all.

'You are a stupid bugger, why didn't you change at the club?' Her arm in mine, her warm breath nuzzling at my ear, her long brown legs brushing against my tweed knickerbockers, and cries of game set and match from the greengrocer's as we walked up the serpentine, lilac-bosomed curves of Boscastle Avenue.

'Who's that?' I asked as she waved at a tall, skinny woman who was hurrying along the other side of the avenue in the same direction, awkwardly swinging an overnight bag as she dodged the low-branched lilacs.

'You must know her. Rhona, known as Ron. Dada's seccy. He used to take her to the opera, in English.'

18

'At the Coliseum?'

'No, no, the Carl Rosa. It really was years ago. And he took her to dog shows too. She wanted to have a labrador, but her flat was too small.'

'Late again,' the tall woman called across in a brisk, mock-challenging way.

'Late yourself.'

She laughed, a brisk, would-be gay laugh. Boscastle Avenue seemed to be full of lilac and laughter.

'This is –'

'I know who this is,' she said. 'I've seen him ... playing.'

'Not in plus-fours, you haven't.'

'I can't wait. They're ... lovely.' She threw back her head, letting the sun shine her teeth. She seemed to do this regularly after her pauses. 'Actually I'm playing with your Tony this year. I think he looks like the king, don't you?'

'King who, we haven't got a king Ron, or haven't you noticed?'

'The late king, King George, like those photos of him playing at Wimbledon, before the war.'

'He does, doesn't he? Ron's so good on likenesses.'

Rhona threw her head to the skies and further acknowledged the compliment with a strange wriggling motion while still walking extremely fast so that we were almost running to keep up with her.

'He's going to be the next chairman,' Rhona went on, 'well, senior partner, you know that, don't you, when Daddy ... goes.'

'You sure?'

'Oh yes, Daddy's determined to have him, isn't he?'

Josie pretended not to hear as she ducked under the blossom and led the three of us up the narrow gravel path along the reservoir fence, the back way into the club, half obstructed by the unpruned privet hedge which ran along the other side so thick that the plunk of tennis balls beyond sounded muffled, almost clandestine. The high green bank of the reservoir kept out the world on the other side. In retrospect when I think about the

19

club, it is the scrunching along the back path, always hurrying because we are a little late, that comes back to me most. In the spring, the cherry blossom would blow across from the gardens behind the privet hedge, and when sodden would dull our footsteps. In the autumn, conkers would gleam among the fallen leaves from the chestnut tree on the corner. It had a secluded innocence which seemed all the more precious because it only took a minute to walk through before you came out on to the tarmac of the car park and had to press yourself against the fence to give the treasurer's Rover room to turn.

But that day was not an innocent day. We were lolling against the grubby white pillars which held up the corrugated iron roof of the pavilion. And I was watching Ron, now changed into her long Edwardian tennis dress, cream-coloured with pink smocking across the bodice, a dress for a gawky child. She was standing at the edge of Court No. 2, shading her pale eyes against the uninsistent sun, herself in turn watching Geoffrey Pagan-Jones organise the next round of matches.

'She's devoted to him, isn't she?'

'Oh yes.' Josie took my arm and pulled me into the corner by the door that led to the office so that we now had our backs to the courts. She was changed now into baggy silk Turkish trousers and a gauzy purple veil wound round her head. Only her Green Flash tennis shoes betrayed the deliciously pagan effect. 'They had an Affair, can you imagine anything more corny? And Mum found out about it in the corniest possible way too, naturally. She rang Dada's hotel room in the middle of the night – he was up in Sheffield closing down some cutlery works, and Ron instinctively answered the phone, like a good secretary should. And Mum screamed at her like a fishwife while Dad went on saying they were just having a nightcap. The worst thing was Mum insisted on telling us all about it the next morning at breakfast. I hadn't finished my Shredded Wheat and all my dreams were shattered.'

We became aware, simultaneously I think, of someone behind us and turned to let the tall pale figure in the cream tennis dress with pink smocking pass between us into the office. She was carrying some sort of list, no doubt given to her by her employer and she bore it like a death sentence, her eyes almost shut and her pale lips pressed together. We moved away, awed and silenced. Throughout the day, my eye was drawn again and again – could not help being drawn – to the tall pale figure in the long skirt, running with stately grace round her backhand to drive the ball with a high swing of her racquet.

'Why didn't she leave?'

'Leave? I suppose nobody asked her to.'

'But didn't your mother . . .?'

'She just told P-J to stop the hanky-panky, and he did, well so far as I know, he did, and otherwise they went on as before.'

'Without even a labrador?'

'Without even a labrador. And she's a wonderful secretary, you mustn't forget that. I mean, that's what matters, isn't it?'

In the evening we danced on the uneven boards of the pavilion to music off the old jukebox in the corner. At the end of 'Save the Last Dance For Me' she pressed herself against me. A gesture of comradeship, I suppose, but I misinterpreted it. We walked out into the mild damp evening. Just behind the little concrete steps leading up to the secretary's office, I tried to kiss her. She slid past me without appearing to fend me off, still smiling, and then patted me on the shoulder as you pat a horse to encourage it to be obedient and I followed her back into the pavilion. Even in the gloaming, you could see the way her hips rolled beneath the Turkish trousers.

Renunciation lay heavy upon the place, happiness could be rented only for strictly limited periods, courts had to be booked, paid for in advance, and vacated on the hour. Winning was not to be too much enjoyed, nor defeat resented. As Kipling had insisted – and were not his words inscribed over the entry to the Centre Court at Wimbledon? – triumph and disaster were imposters who had to be treated just the same. This was a peculiar proposition, my old tutor said: imposters might be very different characters and the fact of having recognised them as imposters would not, in the real world, entail any obligation to treat them equally. A pretty girl who flirts with you, an ugly man who wishes to borrow money from you, a madman who tries to convince you he is Queen Victoria, may all in some sense be imposters, but you would be a disagreeable or foolish or even inhuman person if you treated them identically. Of course, Kipling, like all late-Victorian Stoics, well, like the original Stoics, come to that, or more properly the original Epicureans, got his kicks from assuming this posture of defiant indifference to the blows of fate and to her kisses too (Fate was, of course, a woman to the Greeks, several women in fact, my old tutor said, glaring at me with that high severity I used to admire so much). Thus he was not indifferent to the pleasures of indifference, and such a posture is itself an imposture, being a pretence of immunity and imperviousness which has its charms no doubt but which cannot be said to correspond to the facts of the human situation.

Sometimes, in a slow doubles match, I was overcome by a sullen loathing of the club code and I longed to hit the ball high into the bushes, or shout fuck you at Geoffrey Pagan-Jones when he fluked a drop shot, or walk off the court after breaking my racquet over my knee. Sometimes the dullness of the place was suffocating, and you looked across the courts at the quartets of white-clad players changing sides, changing ends, picking up the balls, taking their first service, then their second service, and I wondered why they weren't all choking with the mindless tedium as I was.

To all appearances, Tony Allenby never felt like that. He suffered the mischances of the game, the idiocies of his partner, the banality of the conversation afterwards with the same thoughtful good humour (the thoughtfulness made the good humour all the more impressive, so that when after a ragged match on a raw, windy March day, he said, 'That was really fun, wasn't it?' with that little pause before he said it, one suddenly felt that, despite the conditions, it had been fun or, perhaps more exactly, one wanted quite sincerely to feel so). And the gentle smile that began to play over his brown skin and his noble George-the-Sixth features, a smile that never got out of hand, began gently to brush to one side all the mistakes and irritations of the past hour.

'Do you think someone ought to go and see what's happened to Dad? He's probably got waylaid by Ted Boddington.' Tony and I started towards the gate of the court at the same time, but I was nearer and he conceded the honour, graceful as always. As I clanged the gate behind me, an unexpected foreboding hit me. My feet scrunched on the gravel, weirdly amplified. As I turned the corner at the back of court five and scurried over the car park to the clubhouse, some biblical phrase wriggled in and out of my head – what was it? – and the other disciple outran Simon Peter and came first to the sepulchre. Not that the low timber and corrugated iron shack, its green and white paint already peeling after the two-yearly lick-up by courtesy of the clubhouse volunteers, was anything like a sepulchre. Nor did Tony seem impetuous like Simon Peter.

I peered into the beer-smelling bar, my eyes adjusting slowly to the darkness. But there was only the shadowy figure of the new barman rinsing glasses. The other side of the door at the back of the bar with its flapping notices of past tournaments and rules about not bringing food into the changing room or taking towels out of it, the smell changed from beer to disinfectant and then to sweat as I came into the grubby changing room. Year in, year out, Geoffrey Pagan-Jones had resisted plans to expand and modernise this dismal nook. We don't want to turn the old place into a country club, he would say with a wag of his tortoise head. Here he was in his amphibious element, flipping stark naked from locker to shower to toilet, grabbing the protection of a towel en route, his slack, pale body glistening under the unshaded light bulbs, his long feet pale splayed starfish on the worn coconut matting.

Halfway through the hour with everyone on court, the place was empty. The blazers hung on their hooks had a sad haunted look with their shirt-tails flapping out from under them. The silence and the heavy sour smell were oppressive. The one window, above the lockers, was shut as usual.

The groan I heard from through the door to the toilets seemed

23

for a moment to be the place itself exhaling its peculiar despair. At any rate, even after tossing such a fancy aside, I was not sure that I had really heard it, had perhaps mistaken the creaking of a hinge or somebody shifting a beer crate in the car park outside.

But the second 'Oh no' was not to be mistaken, and I put my head round the door. And there, half in the cubicle, one hand leaning on the partition wall, the other half holding up his pants and shorts, the blood streaking down them, was Geoffrey Pagan-Jones.

'Shouldn't have crawled through the fence,' he muttered. 'Doctor said I shouldn't strain, but he never told me it would be like this. Oh, that new barman, frightful fellow.'

There was a terrible pallor on his face, and he was near tears. His thoughts seemed random, muddled, erratic. He went on mumbling about the barman while trying to mop the blood off his clothes. I took a towel at random from a peg and clumsily swaddled him like a baby, while he muttered apologies. 'I'll get you a drink,' I said, feeling that he needed a few minutes to – what was the phrase? – adjust his dress and I was more hindrance than help in the narrow space between the cubicle and the wall. 'Thank you, thank you,' he said, with a pathetic mimicry of the habitual fluency of his gratitude, and I escaped back into the bar. The barman was a raw-boned boy with red cheeks and great red knuckles. He insisted on introducing himself: 'John Edward Davies the name is, sir' – a trace of Welsh in the voice but only a trace – 'Started this morning. Is that gent all right, sir, did you see him in the changing room, white as a sheet he went and made a dash for it, was it something I said, but I only told him my name. Is he all right, sir?' His repetitions and his sirs made me more nervous still. I knocked back a whisky and took one out for Pagan-Jones, but by the time I got there, he'd scuttled out to his car, and I found him sitting in the front passenger seat, white and scared and I went to fetch Josie to drive him home.

As Tony and Josie came round the corner, I saw John Edward Davies appear at the rickety green door of the clubhouse. He leant against the door frame looking at us with a vacant stare. He could have offered to help, collect Pagan-Jones's kit, but he leant there, gawping. Instead it was Tony who went to get the kit and skipped up the steps at the side which led to the changing room. Pagan-Jones's distress was obvious, to the rest of us agonising, but John Edward Davies seemed quite unmoved, as though he had qualified for exemption from human sympathy as a member of some slave race who, being denied civil rights, could not be expected to feel like us. With the irritation of panic, I tried to think of some order to bark at him and could think of nothing and would have been silenced anyway by the terrible gaze that Pagan-Jones was sending back through the closed car window.

'I think we'd better go straight to the hospital,' Tony said, breaking this staring competition between ghosts.

'Oh no, Tony, home first, home. Poor Norris, he won't get his set in. He hates an unfinished set, does Norris.' A trace of life came back to Pagan-Jones as he saw Norris Elegant waving and mouthing his concern, eyebrows flapping like rooks alighting. But Pagan-Jones kept the window closed and contented himself with a royal wave as Josie reversed the car, squirting the gravel into the dusty bushes in her haste.

I turned away from the car and caught the stony eye of the barman, only it was no longer stony, there was a glint in it and a twitch to the red raw lips as though he had held in his laughter long enough and was about to burst. Then he too turned away.

The return home was only a fleeting one. They operated on him two days later and removed the growth – the size of a tennis ball, they said, which tickled the patient (could it be mounted and gilded and presented as a trophy?) – and they rigged him up with a bag, but he was not the man he was, or said he wasn't.

He came back to the club mostly to watch Tony and Josie play. He would sit out on the shabby veranda leaning alertly on an old walking stick or with a blue-and-grey rug over his knees if the usual wind was sidling in and out of the veranda pillars.

'Not bad,' he would murmur, 'not bad,' referring, I thought, not so much to the quality of the play as to the rightness of their coupling. To me too they were a golden couple. When their honey-brown arms were outstretched side by side on the rickety green tin table where we had drinks outside after the game, they seemed limbs of a superior race, quite unlike my dry and flaky forearms. Their faces, Tony's particularly, were bright but still as a summer afternoon, not expressive. Their limbs spoke for them, seemed to express affection, mockery, impatience more than their lips and eyes did. They seemed inseparable, not geographically, for she was training as an anaesthetist up in Manchester, but made to be laminated together, their harmless grace too perfectly suited to be wasted on anyone else. The exact degree of their affection was indecipherable – that was part of its charm. When he put his arm round her waist, it was done so quickly, so lightly that nothing could be made of it. Had they – even that simplest of questions was one which my mind felt no inclination to go for, although in normal circumstances my mind is anything but pure and has only to catch a glimpse in a changing room to imagine churning buttocks and animal groans. Their engagement was so fine, so pleasantly mysterious, that I found it impossible to imagine them falling out of love and going through the clumsy business of disengagement.

Once or twice on my way home, I went and called on the Pagan-Joneses in their cream roughcast nineteen-thirties house lurking in its girdle of rhododendrons, with its steep gables and leaded windows. Pagan-Jones would open the door with a trace of his old expectancy, as though he had been waiting for me in the hall most of the afternoon. In his own house, there was something stagier about his carry-on. He seemed to be putting it on a bit to highlight the laggard nature of his wife's welcome. There was a century's wait before she brought in mugs of tea and plonked them down on a low table intricately inlaid with different kinds of wood, faintly recalling the handles of our tennis racquets. The lip of the mug tasted of washing-up liquid. Her domestic arrangements were desolate. She was at odds with the house, could be heard hissing and clucking at its imperfections.

This kitchen, she would say with indignation. Or, I don't know what I'm supposed to do with a hall like this. She left things around the house: in the high-roofed hall, stepladder with feather duster balanced on the top step; screwdriver and dud bulb beside the unmended lamp, broken tiles and a spilling packet of tile cement in the bathroom. These were not symptoms of neglect – the house was tidy, the loose covers fresh – but rather tableaux of protest against the burden she was expected to make light of. Pagan-Jones skipped round these obstacles as though they were not there. He treated his wife with a careless jocularity as though she was not permanently close to boiling point, brushing aside her exasperated, 'When are you going to get that man to do the roof?' with, 'Now have you seen these? Rather fun, don't you think?'

The black-and-white bills with their heavy-scripted old print looked stark against the blowsy floral wallpaper which rioted through the Pagan-Jones's ground floor:

To be sold by Auction by Mr Swerve upon the order of the receiver on June 4, 1827 at half-past ten o'clock at the Golden Lion, Ipswich.

BLACKSMITH'S STOCK IN TRADE

The Furniture
which comprises one fourpost bedstead, three good featherbed and bolsters, Excellent mahogany Counting House Desk with Secretary, small wainscoat ditto, fine elm Flour Hutch, 4 Port Tubs, 4 Copper Boilers and numerous culinary requisites.

The Stock in Trade
And shop fixtures consist of Two Pair Smith's Bellows, Three Anvils, Three Vice, Two Stone Water Troughs, Pair Sheaths as fixed, Mandrell, Hot New Rods and Hooping, about Forty Dozen New Horse Shoes, Ten New Scythes fixed for use, Press and Sway Drilling Machines, about two tons of NEW BAR IRON, Quantity of old ditto etc etc ...

In the yard is a most substantial and useful Trade Cast, 2 Ladders,
Bee House with contents and various useful articles.

Then, seeing the visitor's face droop, Pagan-Jones would murmur, 'Chap went bust, you see. Had to sell the lot. Sad, awfully sad.'

'You don't really think it's sad,' his wife said. 'You think it's fun, you just said sad.'

'I'd like to have made a bid for the Bee House though.' Pagan-Jones gave that easy chuckle that slithered round the accusation and rounded it up like a difficult sheep. But then he too was rounded up now, brought home to roost, irretrievably landed.

'We ought,' he said, 'to have a ruby wedding party.'

'There's no ought about it. Who would we ask? We don't know anyone worth asking.'

'We could have it at the club.'

'And let all those freeloaders drink the place dry at our expense. Anyway, a party at a tennis club – what a ghastly suburban idea.'

'Well, we happen to live in the suburbs.'

'There's no need to boast about it. What a bunch of pricks.' The sudden saltiness of her language was unnerving, like the speech of a foreigner who does not grasp the force of the words.

'Iris! She was brought up in a naval family, you know.'

'For God's sake, Geoff.'

'I'm sorry, dear.'

'And don't try to placate me, either. You'd better have a go at what's left of those sandwiches. There's nothing for supper.'

Nothing, he mused, half plaintively, half reflectively as though this was some interesting news about the nature of the universe.

'We should never have left Enfield,' she said. 'We had a lovely house, late Georgian with a Victorian wing. It even had its own tennis court – for *him*.'

'Now that *was* suburban.'

'No it wasn't. From the garden you could see across to Forty Park. He was one of the last High Sheriffs of Middlesex, you know.' She cackled at the thought of it. 'Always tarted up in some uniform he was then, High Sheriff, Prime Warden of the Livery, you name it, he was poncing around in it.'

'We had a magpie trap in the garden,' P-J went on, unmoved. 'You used to love that magpie trap, didn't you, dear? Used to come into breakfast every morning carrying a couple of dead magpies with a great big grin on your face.'

'Shut up.'

'Extraordinary contraption, just a wire cage with a flap, really, plus your decoy magpie, of course – Montgomery, after Montgomery Clift, Iris's favourite.'

'Shut up.' She left the room with a slam of the door that rattled the windows.

He chuckled but the chuckle had lost its old confidence, came out more sad than wry. Stripped of the bounce that had made him so attractive, his teasing displayed a streak of meanness. Time passed slower in his company than it used to, because it was passing slower for him too. And when I asked him about business, he spoke of it with a hint of detachment. 'Of course, I'm just a figure-head now,' not expecting me to believe it, but provoking suspicion that there was something in it all the same. 'The young bullocks are running the herd. I just munch the grass and nuzzle the more nubile heifers now and then. Pull those curtains to, would you, dear boy, I don't much care for these dripping twilights.'

As I drew the heavy lime-green brocade curtains, it seemed like taking part in some ritual of decline and departure, its rubrics themselves so seldom rehearsed that they were in danger of being forgotten. When I left, he barely raised his hand from the arm of the chair which, being upholstered in the same lime-green brocade, seemed part of the ritual too. And I felt sad too. His decline into old age seemed to mirror the end of my own youth which, inconspicuous, not to say beige, as it had been, insisted on a kind of farewell. As I trudged home from a dull relentless singles match with Norris, the club too seemed part of what had to be described as my past. I wanted no more of that creosoted shack with its green corrugated-iron roof and wobbly white veranda pillars like some benighted sharecropper's hutch in the Deep

South, or the smell of creosote and sweat in the changing room, or the bindweed rambling the court netting, the blossom bosoming out over the fencing on the narrow path and the strangulated cries of 'Sorry' floating through the privet and honeysuckle hedges. Without the vibrant presidency of Pagan-Jones, these sights and sounds had lost their savour. The place seemed forlorn and petty, a charmless survival of things that were not worth the keeping.

But farewells are seldom so neatly trimmed and so I found myself, nearly a year later, after I had returned from a long tour of America, summoned to play at the club, but by Tony which was a surprise as he was not in the habit of issuing the invitations, being like me, merely a player in the Pagan-Jones circus.

'Singles?' I said, with an edge of surprise as though he had invited me to take part in some indecency.

'Why not? It's been a long time.'

He was there waiting for me. He looked different, thinner perhaps, tenser certainly, with the drawn face of a spectator peering down the road for the runners to come in sight.

He tossed the racquet with an impatient twirl of his wrist. M, I called, but it landed with the gilt W uppermost, and he took the service, moving to his position with the righteous strut of someone with a disagreeable task to be disposed of. His service usually dabbed the red clay without hostile intent. Today it bit and swung like an angry woman tossing her hair. I could make nothing of it. Disconcerted by his brusque approach, my own service refused to settle into any rhythm; the ball seemed reluctant to find my racquet in the air, screwing off the rim more than once; my second service, reduced to a decorous pat, was easily cut away. By the time I had roused myself, I was four-love down. 'So much for the first set.' In the second set he continued to be remorseless, with no echo of his habitual court grace, hitting the ball harder, watching the seams on it, winning points that he would never normally have run for, but losing some too, by trying a little too hard for the angles. He beat me again, with a kind of rough emphasis that was quite unlike him.

'I felt as if I was playing against Norris,' I said afterwards.

'Oh, you won't be doing that much now. So you'll have to put up with me instead.'

'Why not?'

'He'll be far too busy. Just time for an early-morning singles with the pro and then off to the office in the chauffeur-driven car. He starts as chairman next week.'

'No,' I said. 'But I thought you –'

'It was meant to be sewn up, wasn't it? I certainly thought it was.' As he told me the story, I may have missed some of the details, mesmerised as I was by the sudden sharp, sardonic tone of his voice which had a thin quality to it, like that of some early musical instrument, long forgotten but now painstakingly restored and arresting our attention by the strange purity of its tone. Pagan-Jones had summoned Tony into his office the previous week, told him he was desperately sorry, he'd never disliked doing anything more than this, and if he had had *any* say in the matter, the outcome would have been entirely different, but there it was, the board had made up its mind and he was just a broken-down old passenger these days, and they had decided that Norris Elegant should succeed him as Chairman (he, Pagan-Jones, would be gently kicked upstairs to be President of the company) and they would very much like it if Tony would agree to succeed Norris (ah, the odd formality of the corporate announcement) as head of Disposals, an assignment now to be unarguably beefed up by the acquisition of a small South Essex auctioneers, Swerve & Stott, a fine old concern, just now standing in need of a modest injection of capital and expertise, an injection, in short, of Tony. The premises lay hard by the north-eastern quadrant of the North Circular Road, a fine location.

'Jesus,' I said.

'Yeah, that's what I thought.'

'So what did you say?'

'I said yes. What else could I say?'

'What does Josie think?'

'Josie? Oh I don't expect she's very interested.' He too sounded uninterested. I might have been asking him about the reactions of

31

a cousin in Australia.

'You mean you don't know?'

'I haven't seen her since June. That's when we split.'

'Split? I can't imagine it.' In fact, I was so taken aback that I plunged on brainlessly, saying how I had thought that they were made for each other, I had been expecting to hear that they were married, or at least engaged by now, how sad it all was, and so on – none of which I had meant to say and instantly wished unsaid. But he seemed somehow flattered by my effusion, or relaxed by it. And he smiled, with a touch of his old grace, and said how nice it was of me to say all that, which only encouraged me to ask how the split had happened.

'We couldn't, that's all.'

'How do you mean?'

'We just couldn't do it.'

'Couldn't do what?'

'Oh not that, not that at all. *That* was fantastic.' After the earlier welcome, I now felt my intrusion was being properly resented and I withdrew to a dignified distance and said that I didn't mean to be nosy.

'Don't worry, forget it. I need to talk about it, I think. I'm probably too uptight,' he said, looking anything but, now fully loose-limbed again in fact. 'She felt the same, you know, felt we weren't getting any closer, we were just gliding past each other, or not past, alongside like boats carried by the current.'

This image, so unlike him in its vividness but not in its accuracy (for there was always a certain accuracy about what he said, when he ventured to be definite) captivated me. I instantly thought (and the image came back to me in dreams for several nights afterwards – which shows how in love with them I was, in love with the idea of them as a couple) of two skiffs on some meandering English river with the two rowers resting on their oars and glancing and smiling at each other, now and then interlacing their brown hands and then again breaking off to duck under the willows or set their boats back on course with a couple of easy strokes.

32

'Sounds lovely to me. Much better than crashing into each other the whole time.'

'Perhaps. Josie wanted a bit more, well, contact, I suppose you could say. To be honest, I didn't mind so much. I mean, I minded about her, but I thought what we already had was wonderful.'

'So you mean it was really she who broke it off.'

'Well, it wasn't like a break in fact, more of a controlled drift.'

'Towards the weir?'

'Towards the bank. She just tied the boat up and walked off.'

'Without so much as a goodbye.'

'No, no, there was a kiss and a wave. It was a friendly parting.' But he sounded unconvinced, as though he thought the friendliness had been mostly on his side. For even when he had been talking in warm terms about the nature of their love, his voice had kept the thin and alien tone, and the hurt had sounded through.

'You'll come and see me at Trotter's Corner, won't you. Just get on the North Circular and keep driving in the general direction of the North Sea.'

This melancholy meeting had an odd effect on me. Till now my thoughts of Tony and Josie had been romantically, relentlessly pure. No erotic shot had slipped even into the late-night showing of my unconscious. But now, overnight and every night, my dreams were filled with images of couplings. Their long brown limbs slithered and sucked against each other, bracing and relaxing with an angry rhythm. The soft velvet mole on her cheek brushed lightly against his thigh, and then again, and again. A low moan and then a sharper gasp, from which of them I could not be sure − and now, suddenly somehow indistinct but entwined within their terribly distinct thrashing bodies, a third person, whose identity soon became unmistakably, even in the numb twilight of the dream, that of the dreamer himself. Was he with them, part of a threesome, or some sort of observer, on a different plane but somehow superimposed by accident? Or was he perhaps only a reflection of the dreamer in the viewfinder? Then the third person began, clumsily at first but with growing vigour, to take part. At which moment the censor who normally invigilates these sessions must have returned to the controls and released me. I woke with a start of relief and decided to wear the red tie with blue spots.

But the sadness of their separation hung about me for days, cold and dank like the fogs of my childhood. And that, I see now, was a sign of my not quite spent youth. The hard shell of middle age had not yet encrusted my expectations. I still imagined that something which was fine was thereby likelier to last, rather like the medieval proof that God must exist because his existing was so much nobler than his not existing. As detailed above, I found it difficult even in my dreams to conceive that a love which looked so desirable from outside could be so willingly relinquished by the lovers.

The concrete on the underpass was sweating dark streaks as it swallowed the wind and the rain from the East. The orange-yellow and crimson lights on the garage forecourts brightened the chill murk of the morning. Beyond, low grey hills implied Essex. Off the North Circular, an old highroad, traffic-clogged, led to some unidentifiable suburb sliced by the dual carriageway. A boarded-up pub, the Jolly Highwayman, had gipsy caravans in its car park. Behind the car park there was a field with the mist still breathing through the thistles and a couple of shaggy ponies cropping the grey ectoplasmic skeins. On the other side of the car park, concrete panels fenced off the storage area of Swerve & Stott, established 1812, wearing its antiquity unhappily that dismal morning. The office was a shabby pebbledash bungalow with a portakabin next to it. Beyond, a great rickety hangar sheltered the stock, a mountain of desolation.

'Welcome to Trotter's Corner,' said Tony. 'This section here's the pasteurising equipment. Lots of dairies going under just now. Interest rates went up, milk price didn't, phut.' We stared at the gleaming silver tubes and the pale-green control units standing disconnected on the dirty pallets that protected them from the mud and the cinders. 'We've got some new boilers coming in tomorrow,' he said to a couple of gloomy men in sheepskin coats, who I thought were inspecting the pasteurising pipes but then I heard one say to the other, 'So I said to him, Listen mate, don't you fuck me around, or I'll shaft you so fucking hard you'll think you're a fucking kebab.' His companion nodded and went on staring at the tubes, then after some thought said, 'He's a cunt, that one.'

The other one turned to Tony and said, 'You got any cheese vats?'

'Not here, they're not worth moving. But there's a couple on site out Bishop Stortford way.'

'No fucking vats,' the man said to his companion.

'You've seen the boilers?' Tony asked brightly.

'We don't want no sodding boilers,' the man said, and the two of them trudged off across the cinders, tossing a dull cheers mate back at us through the fog.

'They don't look much like farmers.'

'They aren't, they're equipment brokers, middlemen, they – oh God.'

A huge man in a long brown milkman's coat and black wellingtons was striding across the wasteland towards us. Tony grabbed my elbow and scurried me over to the bungalow, pulling at its flimsy door which wouldn't open, then banged on the window, gesturing to a moonfaced man in an anorak who was sitting by the fire reading the *Mirror*.

The moonfaced man, huge too, six foot four of him and seventeen stone or thereabouts, heaved his body through the flimsy door and lumbered at a good rate towards the pasteurising machinery, but already the other giant was hacking away at the machinery with a long-handled axe which he must have been sheltering under his brown coat, carving long slashes through the thin metal of the control panels, now and then splintering the glass of the dials. When he turned to the pipes, all he got was dents and hollow clangs, so he went off down the alley between the machinery deeper into the hangar. He had a peculiar light leaping stride, like a heavy man playing ring a ring o' roses with some small children.

'He's been here before,' said Tony. 'Used to farm three hundred

35

acres out towards Royston. The bank closed him down last
month. His wife tried to get him sectioned, but when he goes to
hospital, butter wouldn't melt. Squaddie, can't you –'

'I'm not going near him in that state, Mr A. He's got to blow
himself out first.'

The crashing went on, then a rumbling clatter with a bang in
the middle of it, and a human cry of pain and rage. We slunk in
single file down the alley.

Here in the foggy depths of the hangar the machinery was
partly shrouded by great sheets of dirty polythene, rising towards
the girders of the roof which seemed far-off and skeletal in the
invading mist. It was even colder here. Our breath sent pale white
puffs into the gelid air.

We found the man sprawled against a large blue machine, the
torn sheets of polythene flapping in a tangle of murdered metal.
One huge metal drum was still loosely hanging on its axle above
us; another had rolled behind the man in the brown coat but not
before it had caught him a nasty whack on the side of the head.
Blood was pouring down his neck and round the collar in a thick
neat line so he looked as if he had been decapitated.

'It's a reel charger,' Tony said. 'Incredibly expensive. We had
some Dutch people coming to look at it yesterday.'

The man stared at us. His eyes rolled and bulged like the eyes
of a diseased rabbit.

'Fuck off,' he said weakly.

'I'll get an ambulance,' Tony said. 'Squaddie, you better stay
here.'

Squaddie had taken the axe, and had shouldered it. In the misty
half-light of the alley he looked as stern as a messenger of death
or some other unpleasantness.

The man in the brown coat looked tired now. His face had
gone soft, and I was afraid in my English way that he was going
to cry, but he just looked at me.

'They got you too, have they? Or are you one of the vultures?'

'No, I've just come to see a friend.'

'You won't find no friends here. This is a fucking graveyard, mate. They bury people alive here.'

'I'm sorry about ...'

'Eighty thousand quid. A rotten bloody eighty thousand quid and they halved the value of my stock and called the fucking loan. I hadn't missed a payment, not one, and they closed me down.'

'It must be –'

'You don't know nothing about it, so why don't you keep your fucking trap shut.'

'Now then,' Squaddie said. 'That's enough from you, laddie. You've had your rest and now you're going walkies.'

The man in the brown coat got up quite amiably, as though suddenly hearing someone speak his own language, and was marched off down the alley towards the bungalow. Squaddie still shouldered the axe with one hand and held the man in a half-nelson with the other. The mist seemed thicker now, although it was nearing midday and the wahwah of the ambulance sounded with a profound and piercing melancholy.

'He's the worst. But we get others trying to buy back their kit or muck up the auction or just unable to keep away, taking a masochistic satisfaction in seeing their stuff go up the spout.'

'I'd have thought they'd never want to see it again.'

'The printers and the machine tool boys don't mostly, but the farmers are different. They get attached.'

Tony sat on the rickety revolving chair scrunching a string of amber worry beads, and worried was what he looked, or not so much worried as blanched by sorrow.

'Well, they cocked it up, didn't they? That's the bottom line. If you don't have to pay the price for cocking it up, this place'll get like bloody Russia. Halfway there already, if you ask me. Stott's the name. Roger Stott. I got left behind with the office furniture when they flogged the family firm.' Roger Stott had a gurgling sort of relish at the back of his voice which contrasted nicely with his sallow face and awkward lopsided gait. And he had a running auctioneer's way of talking so that each time he came into the room to look for something there seemed scarcely any interruption from his last appearance several minutes earlier. 'If you start feeling sorry for them, you're in the wrong business. Our job is simply to shift the stock on to someone who can make better use of it. You don't help anyone by feeling sorry. That Norris, he's got the right idea. I can't say he's my type exactly, but he knows where it's at.' Roger Stott began warming his bony shanks at the fire with a grin on his thin lips which was designed to provoke but somehow didn't. 'Of course, I'm only a hired hand now, part of the mighty Pagan empire, just a satrap, that's what they called them in the Persian empire. I like ancient history, gives you a bit of perspective on things. Just when you think everything in the garden's lovely, that's when you've got to watch out, because the barbarians are at the gates and next thing you know their hot breath will be down your necks and you're just another satrap making sure the emperor's shit gets shovelled.'

'A well-paid satrap,' Tony said.

'Oh, a comfortable satrap, very comfortable, I don't deny, but a satrap none the less,' and with another skinned smile he was gone again.

'Do you ever sing now?' I can't think why I asked the question. It seemed calculated to deepen Tony's gloom, but he answered with a brightness as though he had been bursting to talk about the subject.

'Yes, I do, much more in fact than I used to. There's a choir just out in the country, first village you come to but we come from a radius of twenty miles or more, and we sing once a week, everything you can think of. John Edward Davies, you remember the barman from the club, the one who Geoffrey couldn't stand, he got me into it, he's a professional singer, more than I am.

'*Quand de la fontaine* ...

'*La bergère* ...' His voice seemed richer now, had lost the thinness which had been so haunting. He sounded more accomplished. Or perhaps it was the acoustics of the long low office which sent the sound chasing round the bare walls, fluttering the girlie calendar and the sheaves of regulations for fire drill and health and safety.

'If you can bear to hang on for half an hour, you might catch

Josie.'

'Josie? But I thought you'd ...'

'She comes and helps with the books here twice a week, to earn a few bob, while she's looking for her first anaesthetist's job. Oh shit.'

'What?'

'Look.' He gestured to the window. A great anguished face filled the smeary pane. His bulbous nose was pressed against the mud-spattered glass. His face had a thick bandage around it.

'He must have escaped from the ambulance.'

By the time we had rushed outside, he had smashed two of the windows with a chunk of breeze block. He paused and turned his swollen swathed countenance in our direction. His lips too were bleeding and swollen, and he spoke with difficulty, in a sluggish sedated way.

'I know your name.'

'Well, Mr Wall.'

'I know your name. And you know mine. So this ain't the end of it.' The ambulance was bumping over the cinder puddles, and he took off at a heavy trot towards the field at the back. Through the yellowing mist, I could see the ponies grazing amid the thistle and ragwort stalks. The ambulance men got to him just as he reached the fence, and grabbed his legs as he was about to clamber over it. For a second, I could see his arms raised high in defiance or perhaps simply like a man about to jump and then the ambulance men had him down on the ground. They had difficulty in lugging him across to the ambulance, because of his weight not because he resisted. As he stumbled up the steps through the open doors, he turned again and bellowed in a voice more mournful than menacing:

'I know your name.'

'You should have got the police,' Roger Stott said in his low calm voice. 'Those cruddy ambulance men are as much use as a fart in a thunderstorm.'

'Well, he is ill, he'll finish up in hospital either way.'

'Yeah, but we want him locked up properly. We want to prefer criminal charges. That's the only way. It's no good trying to dodge trouble.' He spoke with the inner peace of one who liked walking straight up to trouble and spitting in its face.

'I expect you're right. I just didn't think of it at the time. He was bleeding so much.'

'I'm paid to think of things at the time. I'll get on to Inspector Fitt.'

As Stott walked off, Tony said he was not sure he could take much more of this. Well, I said, there was no law forcing him to stay. No, but there were obligations, he felt he ought to show he could make a go of what was, after all, the sharp end of the business.

'Not everyone has to work at the coalface.'

'No, but if you're sent to the coalface, you can't just chicken out.'

How pale he looked in the sulphurous fog, a ghost in this wasteland. Around us, I felt immense stretches of nothing, arterial roads dragging through scattered settlements to end at nothing places, long shingle beaches scoured by the east wind, a few empty huts on the foreshore. This place wasn't the face of anything, it was the ultimate back side.

'You don't need to stay here,' I said.

'There's Josie.' And his voice was so flat that I thought he meant she was an item to be considered, not that he was simply stating she had arrived, which she had, her brown cheeks reddened by the cold outside. With her big floppy chestnut boots, great leather jacket, and red and gold mittens, she looked like an ad for the delights of winter. Compared to Tony, she had a rosy, busy glow and gave me a kiss so full it seemed indecent on these loveless premises. She brought, oh everything – life, feeling, a sense of the absurd – to the long low bungalow-room with its scuffed carpet-squares and grubby furniture from the surplus stores. Both of us watched her with bemused fascination as she warmed the room up, took off her jacket and mittens, put the kettle on and drew up a chair. At the same time, Stott put his head round the door with the gleam of battle in his dark eyes and said the Inspector wanted

40

him and Tony to go down to the station to make a statement.

'So,' said Josie, suddenly going cold on me when we were alone.

'So.'

'What do you think?'

'About?'

'All this. Do you think it's right for him?'

'No, of course I don't,' I said.

'I feel responsible, you know, I really do.'

'You, why?'

'Because, oh, well it's all a bit complicated.' She paused and then went on, 'I suppose I do need to tell someone. Well, not need exactly, but if I don't, I think it's going to drive me mad. I mean, I have told a girlfriend, two in fact, but they didn't see anything much wrong with it and perhaps a man would see it differently.'

'Tell me then, if you want to.'

'Well, Tony probably told you that we called it off, by mutual agreement, that we both decided it wouldn't work. That's what we agreed to say, anyway, but it isn't what happened. What happened was that I chucked him.'

'Yes, he more or less said.'

'Oh, did he? Well, it's hard to explain really. Something about us being too much alike, it being too perfect, too easy, do you know what I mean? I expect you thought we were made for each other. Everyone did.'

'Me too.'

'Well, I don't think people are made for each other. Perhaps they should be, but they aren't . The best you can hope for – what you ought to hope for, really – is that you react to each other, or make each other react, you know chemistry, striking sparks, that kind of thing. Well, Tony and I weren't striking any sparks. He was too perfect really, too perfect for me anyway.'

'A bit boring?'

'Oh, a bit boring too, but that was all part of his being perfect. But anyway, the point was, Dada absolutely worshipped the

41

ground he trod on and if he knew I'd ditched him he'd never forgive me and he can be a real bastard, Dada, when he's not forgiving people. So we thought it would make life easier if I just said we'd split by mutual consent because we could see it just wasn't going to work, you know that sort of bullshit. So I trotted along into Dada's crappy study with all those china dogs and said my lines looking as demure as anything. And of course, he got completely the wrong end of the stick because what I had forgotten because I'm so amazingly modest is that Dada also worships the ground I tread on, worships it a lot more because of the father-daughter thing, and so he immediately jumped to the conclusion that it was Tony who'd given me the push, and so all hell broke loose.'

'What sort of hell?'

'Well, he immediately ruled Tony out of the race to succeed him as chairman and looked around for a Siberia to exile him to. Well, they didn't happen to have a Siberia in the empire at the time because everyone operates out of that matey little office in Finsbury Circus, so old Pagan-Jones goes and buys a Siberia specially, would you believe? And as soon as he's got it, for a song actually – that Stott person isn't nearly as sharp as he thinks he is – he dumps Tony right in it when the poor love's got no more idea of being an auctioneer than my woolly rabbit.'

'But P-J keeps on saying he's out of things since his operation, that he's completely powerless, a doddering old figurehead and so on.'

'And you believed *that*? Well, you are innocent, sweet, but incredibly innocent.' (And here it should be recorded that she stroked my cheek lightly.) 'The old snake uses everything and everyone and he certainly milked that cancer dry – ugh, what a horrible phrase. As soon as he came out of hospital, he was practising doddering, it gave him a wonderful cover for doing things he hadn't got around to doing beforehand and one of the things was promoting Norris Elegant to Supreme Master of the Universe and shunting poor old Tony to outer darkness or Trotter's Corner, whichever was the further, as a punishment for having trifled with his daughter's affections, though in fact he never trifled with anything in his life, least of all me.'

'You mean, he's really been controlling the firm all along.'

'Well, perhaps not when he was actually under the anaesthetic, but otherwise yes. In fact, I expect he gets his own way more often now that he can concentrate on the bits he really wants to control because he's an invalid and can't be bothered with routine chores.'

'So all that moaning about his total impotence . . .'

'Lies, all lies,' she said, her eyes sparkling despite herself at the thought of my having been so totally duped.

'Well, where do we go from here?'

'Well,' she said, 'you could always go and call on Dad and appeal to his better nature and say, you know, that you quite appreciate him giving Tony this chance to open up this new business and so on but, quite honestly, you've been down here and can see that he hasn't a clue and wouldn't it be better to put him back to doing what he's really qualified for and fantastically good at which is good old traditional liquidating.'

'From what you say, it doesn't sound very likely to melt his stony heart.'

'Perhaps it won't, but somebody ought to tell him – he ought to be given the chance to do the right thing. I mean, he sometimes does actually do the right thing, usually by accident I admit, but still every little helps.'

'A bad business, a very bad business,' Pagan-Jones muttered, only muttering in order to stifle the chuckle which would otherwise have broken out. 'They do take it hard, some of these chaps. Farmers are always the worst.'

'Surely they all resent it, don't they?'

'Lord no, for half of them liquidation comes as a blessed relief, I'm the liberator. With one bound they are free, everything written off, a new life begins. Some of them are actually angling for it, you know. That Sten Svensson, he's been on at me for ages, couldn't I persuade Barclays to apply for a liquidation order, use my good offices, etcetera. He's a crafty bugger, you don't think of Swedes as devious, but he's dead devious that one. I know for a fact that he's sold all his lorries at knockdown prices to this leasing company which he controls and is leasing them back at market rates, so all the profit's flowing into the leasing company and his old firm's piling up all the debt. Let the old firm go bust and he waltzes off with the cream. You wouldn't think it to look at him with that silly dribbling service of his. About time he took some tennis lessons, he can afford them all right. What were you saying?' He was lost in admiration of Svensson's ingenuity.

'I just don't think Tony's really the man for that particular slot, you know.'

'What makes you think so? What could he have done about that madman, what could anyone have done?'

'No, I meant generally. I don't think he's cut out to be an auctioneer.'

'Didn't say he was, did I? Stott knocks down the lots, that's what we pay him for. Tony is a managing director. He knows perfectly well what an M.D.'s meant to do, or he ought to by now.'

'All the same, I don't think you're making the best of him out there.'

'Think I ought to have him back here, do you? Well, you've got another think coming. He's no good that boy, no use at all. Won't have him in my office. I could see from the start he wasn't up to it.'

'I thought you rather liked him.'

'Liked is different. I didn't dislike him at all. Always glad to see him at the club but you can't expect me to go on liking a chap who treats my daughter like that.'

'You don't think it was a bit mutual?'

'Look here, I can see you don't know the half of it. Your friend Mr A. Allenby may look like butter wouldn't melt in his mouth but you can't expect me to think much of a young man who knocks my daughter about and then ditches her.'

'Knocks her about? Are you sure?'

'You think my daughter would lie to me about something like

44

that?'

'She didn't say anything about it to me.'

'Of course she wouldn't. She's got her pride, hasn't she? And anyway, she's too much of a lady. Don't hear that word much nowadays, do you, not much call for it I suppose.' He muttered 'lady' to himself again, not without satisfaction. The lines on his tortoise face criss-crossed and set into stern ill humour. I abandoned the subject and said goodbye as quickly as was decent, too distressed to bother hiding my feelings. Presumably he just wanted to build up a damning case against Tony and threw in the nastiest slander he could think of. I could not believe Josie would ever have said anything like that. Even after splitting up, she seemed unable to keep away from him, and whatever else it might have lost, their relationship seemed to have kept its delicacy.

A slumbrous calm possessed the premises of Swerve & Stott. Outside on the car park nothing moved. The ruts and puddles in the crushed cinders winked at the pale winter sun. Just under the shelter of the hangar, a Coventry Climax was edging the forklift in a leisurely, almost flirtatious way under a blue control unit. The office was quiet as a senior common room. Roger Stott was reading a paperback translation of Ovid's *Metamorphoses*. He sat at his desk, sharp and upright. He might have been interviewing the book for a position with the firm.

'What're you reading Rodge?' Josie asked.

'Story of Danae and the shower of gold.'

'I like the idea of that, just lying there, the lazy cow, and being screwed by this great golden shower.'

'Yes, but remember what happens, silly moo gets knocked up.'

'Not her fault though. How could you take precautions with a shower of gold?'

'You could keep the window shut. The point is her father, he's trying to protect himself because he's been told by the oracle his grandson will be the death of him. So he locks her up in this tower of brass so she remains intacta. Doesn't do a blind bit of good, in swans his nibs and has his Olympian way with her.

45

Result – Perseus. Now he locks both of them up in a box, chucks it in the ocean. And *that* doesn't do any good either, because an honest fisherman – and that's something I'd like to see – rescues them and looks after them. And the baby grows up to slay Medusa, rescues Andromeda, marries her, presents the Gorgon's head to Athena etcetera etcetera, oh and just by way of an encore accidentally kills his father with a discus. All of which goes to show, if you see a shower of gold coming in the window, hand it in at your nearest police station.'

'Oh I don't know Rodge, she had quite a life after all.'

'Well, if you fancy bobbing about in a watertight box in a Force Ten gale and spending half your life with a poxy old fisherman ...'

She laughed and threw herself back in the creaky wooden swivel chair, her chestnut boots sprawled across the dingy desk with the nonchalance of a principal boy. But I was thinking of her lying on her bed on a warm night, the sheet thrown back to catch the breeze through the open window, the old striped viyella nightie rucked up and her sleeping head nestled into the pillow, and then in the distance somewhere up above a strange clinking whirr, far away at first and then coming closer, a rushing whoosh and then a gold blur passing over her brown skin ...

'I like the idea of it all being fated though,' Josie said dreamily. 'I wish I had a destiny, one you couldn't do anything to alter, however hard you tried.'

'You have, my dear, didn't anyone tell you? Free will lost out. It's all written down in the genetic code, so you might as well stop worrying. That's what you trendy-wendies out there don't seem to have taken on board.'

'Out where, Rodge?' Josie asked with a languorous yawn.

'Hampstead, Kensington, Chelsea, you know as well as I do.'

'I think I'm probably a trendy-wendy, Rodge.'

'Of course you are.'

'All right then, how can you tell?'

'Those pantomime boots – and that goofy look.'

The gas fire puttered a gentle accompaniment to this banter. On my first visit the office had seemed such an outpost, a place where you could hear the winds of outer space howling. Now it felt like a refuge which was all the safer because nobody would have thought of looking for you there.

'Where's Tony?'

'He's looking at some stuff on site, out Dagenham way. Small components firm, got caught by the cutback at Fords. I don't envy him,' Stott said. 'They're a rough lot down there. They'd have your balls for garters.'

'You mean guts for garters.'

'Down there it'd be your balls.' He returned to Ovid, still laughing an evil laugh.

'Look, I wonder if we could have a word in ...'

'Don't mind me,' Stott said, 'my ears are sealed.'

'No, they aren't, they're flapping,' Josie said. 'Let's go outside.'

Out in the thin mild air, she turned to me with only lukewarm expectancy.

'Well, I spoke to P-J and as you said, he wouldn't budge, wouldn't have Tony back in his office, refused to believe that you had anything to do with the break-up, blamed him entirely, and then also – well, I suppose you ought to know what he's going around saying – he also said you'd told him that Tony knocked you about, hit you, in fact.'

'That, of course, is complete nonsense. I just can't think how he got that idea into his head. He is evil sometimes, really evil.'

It was strange to see her soft plummy lips and her lovely brown skin set tungsten-hard, strange but touching in its unfittingness, like a dripping surrealist watch. For a moment, I felt almost privileged to assist at this family quarrel, it seemed so high and strong. The sense of privilege only went up a further notch when she said, almost under her breath, in the preoccupied mutter of a marksman who is getting his victim settled in the crosshairs of his sights, 'Well, he can go fuck himself. And you'd better bugger off too. I've got to get on with the accounts, the auditors are coming tomorrow.' She dismissed me in a choking voice which had lost all its earlier friendliness. And after she had gone back inside, I stood there for a moment absorbing the shock waves which broke over me with all the greater force because the source they came from was still partly, no mostly, hidden. For all my trotting to and fro, I knew so little of what fuelled these quarrels. Pagan-Jones clearly felt just as strongly, was equally obsessed by his own set of grievances. Yet old men were licensed, even expected to be envenomed by resentment. Josie's resentment, met out here in this blank March day, made me falter at the knees, at other parts too no doubt.

'Boadicea camped here, you know, just behind the garage.' Collected, more or less, I was turning to go, only to find Roger Stott at my side, walking in step with me like a police escort.

'Really,' I said.

'So we think,' he said. 'Just before she was finally defeated by Suetonius Paulinus.'

'Ah,' I said.

'She must have been a wonderful woman. A widow, of course. They're the ones you've got to watch out for, widows.'

'Yes.'

'That Allenby, he won't last, you know. Not here. Hasn't got the stomach for it.'

'No.'

'In this game you need a bit of chutzpah. Jewish for cheek that is.'

'Yes, I know. Pagan-Jones was saying the same thing.'

'Was he now? He's an artful old bugger. Not Jewish, though, is he, sounds more Welsh. Can't think why he sent Allenby over here. There isn't enough work for him to do. And he's costing us twenty grand near enough, with the car and the pension contributions.'

'Well, you know how Roman emperors used to send their rivals out to distant postings.'

'Ahh.' Stott's whole person was suffused with satisfaction. Perhaps because he held himself so stiffly, any emotion seemed to register all over him. 'The satrap syndrome. But he didn't send *her* out, did he?'

'No, she came of her own accord, I think.'

'Used to have a thing together, didn't they? Used to be ... engaged.' He might have been about to reveal their joint participation in some sexual deviation so vile as to be virtually unknown to decent people.

'Yes, more or less.'

'Well, then, why'd she follow him up here? Plenty of girls round here could do the books well enough, if you keep an eye on them.'

I gazed into the lifting fog, blinking at the gauzy sun, and tried to think of an acceptable answer and in thinking surprised myself into realising that I was not quite sure what the truth was.

'I bet you she's still sweet on him. Gave him the push and then saw she's made a grievous mistake. So she's trying to get him back without having to go down on her bended knees.'

To my annoyance, I found this sounded plausible.

'Question is, though –' Stott pursued his speculations with a remorseless delight in butting in where he was fairly confident of not being wanted. 'Question is –' He had a way of slowing down when he sensed that his audience was beginning to resent him – 'why did she give him the push in the first place? There must be some explanation which isn't the obvious one, i.e. that she got fed up with him, because he's not the sort of chap you get fed up with. He's very *easy*, I don't mean just nice because nice blokes can get up your nose, but he's easy. I can appreciate that because I'm not an easy chap. I tend to rub people up the wrong way. Have you noticed that at all, people usually notice that quite soon after they've met me.'

I said nothing and he went on: 'Perhaps she just didn't fancy being married to an auctioneer selling bankrupt stock out on the North Circular. Oh, have you met my husband, he flogs pipes and whatsits out at a little place just north of Walthamstow, no, you wouldn't have heard of it, my dear. So she decided to go back to Daddy and Mummy. But in which case, why's she come out here then? I tell you why, it's pity, that's what it is, compassion for the unfortunate. Two bowls of soup please, miss, if you can spare them.'

49

'Well,' I said, stung at last. 'No.'

'No?'

'No, I don't think it was quite like that.'

'Why wasn't it?'

'Because, well, because they split up before Tony knew he wasn't going to be chairman and so before he came down here, not that it matters much really.'

'Oh but it does, there I must beg to differ. That throws a different light on the business, a quite different light.'

I began to walk towards my car, somewhat briskly, but he stayed beside me with his odd dogged lope which made it look as though his shoes were sticking to the muddy cinders.

'That brings me back to the number I first thought of. You remember, Theory A first variation: she's still in love with him but she wants to see him prove himself. And out here is the proving ground, the place where he's got to do the business. Well that's a pity, isn't it, because I don't think he's going to make it. I think she's in for a disappointment.'

'Oh do you?'

'Yes I do. It might surprise you but I'm a pretty accurate judge of character, I can usually tell who's got it and who hasn't. When everyone else is still seeing sunshine radiating from some fellow's arse, I've already filled in my card and handed it to the ref. It's a kind of instinct, really. On the other hand, though, she might like the smell of failure. A lot of women do, you know, they find it sexy. So she could be just hanging around waiting to see him fail really big. Funny thing is, if you've been surrounded by success all your life, you can get quite a taste for failure. I can see you don't believe me. Beats me too, but there it is, it's a fact.'

Through the misty air, we could just hear the telephone ringing in the bungalow. Josie had gone home, so we crunched back over the cinders. It was Tony.

'Look, could you help, I'm stuck, they've slashed my tyres. What's your car, a white Cortina, and the registration number? Turn right after Gate No. 4 in the body plant and you'll see the sign half a mile down the road, the door will swing open just long

50

enough to let you in, oh bugger I think they're listening in, good-bye.'

We drove what Roger Stott said was the back way down empty minor roads where the houses were eerily unkempt, with tall cabbage stalks and broken-down sheds in their gardens, past mysterious installations behind concrete fencing posts and locked gates, these too with an air of neglect, the gates not meeting properly in the middle, secured by rusty chains, the security hut shut up or full of blown litter, and then at country crossroads sitting in fields of dew-drenched kale a Courage pub in sullen brick and to one side a car park vast and empty, the concrete of its hard standing cracked and crumbling. We passed through a scrubby wood, the hawthorns grey with mud and blinded by torn and sodden cement bags and as we came out the other side, we saw, all at once, the long low sheds of the car plant stretching away down the road and beyond them the sky lightening towards the river.

Stott counted the gates as we crawled past, but there was no need. Even from the main road, we could see the crowd outside our destination. Stott locked the doors. I saw a smile on his thin lips as he lunged to get at the passenger door behind me. There was no smile on mine. The noise came first, a hoarse angry bellow, a wretched dispossessed sound. Then, as we turned into the gates, they rushed at us, but it was a clumsy jostling rush, and we had time enough to nose through the gates and Tony and Squaddie and another man had time enough to close them behind us.

'We'd better go inside for a bit so we can take them by surprise when we come out,' Tony said. 'Park over there behind the shed and turn round first because you'll need to come out with the foot hard down and frighten them back.'

'Do you do this sort of thing often?'

'Never done it before, but I may take it up professionally. I enjoy it.'

He scarcely needed to say so. It was all done with the brisk pleasure of a sword dance. Inside the shed, Squaddie was brewing coffee on a primus stove under the light of a bare bulb strung a few feet above us. 'They cut the electricity off, we had to bring

51

our own generator.' We sat on packing cases in the cold darkness amid the abandoned lathes and motionless conveyor belts.

'They were switching over to German imports up the road even before the bank called the loan. It's primitive this kit, apparently, they hadn't a hope. I don't know what we'll do, there's no chance of selling the stuff on site with that shower outside and it'd cost a bomb to shift it up to Trotter's. We'll probably have to wait and flog it as a single lot when it's all rusted to buggery.'

Outside, the bellowing was just audible. Thinned by the distance and the fog, it sounded still more anguished and lost. Yet I could not help enjoying the bitterness of the coffee, and I gulped in the mist with the relief of a winded runner.

'Well, time to go over the top, chaps.'

We were led out through a side door. Tony hushed us and motioned us to open the car doors quietly, while Squaddie and the other man, a dark ghost in a donkey jacket, went for the gates. 'Don't wait for the gates to open, just go flat out as if they already were.'

This advice was against nature, and I did not properly follow it, so that we were still moving too slowly as the gates swung open. They came for us with a roar of urgent terrifying rage, hammering on the roof, squashing their red and rheumy faces against the glass, and then as we slipped them, they turned away and made for the gap between the gates.

'Oh fuck, they're inside, we better stop at the pub and phone the police.'

'Why', I said, aping a calm which I was nowhere close to feeling, 'didn't you think of that before?'

'Because, dear boy,' Tony was relaxed, seigneurial, lolling in the back seat, 'because they might stick us for the expense of guarding private premises.'

'Surely not when they're out in the road.'

'Well, they aren't out in the road now, are they?' He laughed with such abandon that I could not manage to point out that if they weren't it was only because he had not got the police first. I had never seen him so exultant.

'Aren't you going back with the police?'

'No, I'm afraid Squaddie will have to do that. I've got a sale to take over in Notting Hill. You couldn't ...? You are kind. I'm sorry to treat you as a chauffeur, but it's that sort of a day.'

An unfamiliar voluptuousness seemed to suffuse him when he was bending me to his will. I had not known him so wilful and, to my surprise, the role he thrust upon me stirred little or no resentment (besides, Notting Hill was not much out of my way).

'Where are we going?'

'The Beaudesert Hotel.'

'Sounds grand.'

'Not a bit, it's one of those godawful cheap hotels round the back of Paddington. The sort of place the council dumps problem families on.'

In the long street of tall stucco buildings the Beaudesert sign was hard to spot. It was on the corner, beyond Devonshire and Bedford and Norfolk but otherwise indistinguishable in this ducal forest except that the paint was peeling off the drainpipes and rubbish had silted up under the portico. The hall was cold and damp and the crimson brocade wallpaper was coming away from the cornice. The lots for sale were piled up under temporary arc lights which cast a cold eye on the toppling pisas of white plates, the battered laundry baskets now full of roughly ironed sheets and tablecloths, the giant tea and coffee urns sullen and no longer burnished. Somewhere under the dusty Turkish carpet, a seesawing floorboard made the trays of cutlery chink when someone trod on it. The potential bidders wandered about with their hats and coats on – especially hats: serious purchasers of bankrupt stock went on wearing hats, queer dark green trilbys, rakish tweed Rex Harrisons, even berets. Tony stripped off his jacket as well as his overcoat. He was wearing a grey waistcoat – 'Can't take an auction in a coat, if you're hoping to warm up the punters.

'Well, here goes.' Tony hopped up onto the step of his battered wooden rostrum and greeted the punters with a subdued good morning. They gathered round him with a sluggish, almost resentful air as though they had gathered in this dusty gloom for some quite different purpose.

'Good morning, ladies and gents, we have a superb selection of hotel fittings and equipment for you this morning, some first-class Irish linen, good quality Sheffield plate and some very fine mahogany and oak hotel furniture, all the lots are of the standard you would expect from a West End hotel.' His tone was quite flat and sapless. When he came to the adjectives, his voice went dim as though passing through a tunnel. Dispiriting honesty steamed up from every sentence, its tang as damping as the fog outside. While he tried to stir the assembly into some show of life, my idle hand flipped through the pile of yellowing bed linen at my side. It was marked in red thread Commercial Hotel, Hastings, at least the first two sheets were. The third had a brownish stain across the corner, through which The Chequers, Ramsgate, was just legible.

Ah if those sheets could talk, if all this wandering bedlinen could whisper of the bodies that had tossed and sobbed and sweated into them, of all the clutching and twisting and, too, of all the hours of still and happy sleep, the last inalienable relief – the mind, worn out and a little unhinged by the morning's work, romped pleasurably through these well-trodden thoughts, only now and then recalled to reality by the voice of the auctioneer, half muffled by the thick damp air (every time someone came in through the clanking revolving doors, another wedge of fog from the street spread over us).

'I don't think I need tell you ladies and gentlemen that in this auction there are no reserves. Everything must go, as the man said.' Under the cold white light of the arc lamp, Tony looked as dead as marble. He looked more like some piece of late-Victorian statuary than a live auctioneer. All the exuberance of the dash through the gates had gone from him. 'Now then ladies and gentlemen, we're all busy people. The sooner we're done, the sooner we can all go home, and have a cup of tea or – yes, you sir, thank you sir, seventeen pounds, and eighteen and nineteen, you won't find better linen outside Mayfair.' This improbable claim killed the bidding, and I fled.

It was quite soon afterwards, twenty minutes or so, that I heard on the car radio that one of the pickets had been injured, quite badly, crushed in the closing gates, according to one account, hit by a blunt instrument, according to another. At all events he was in hospital and Tony was in trouble.

And that was the last I heard of him until I ran into Tim Oates, the Captain, who always knew where everyone was and what they were doing and feeling and lost no time in telling you. His most remarkable gift amounting to second sight was to keep you posted about friends of yours he had never met.

'Yes, it's so far East, if you exit left you come out in Finland. The wind in the wings'll freeze your balls off. Even Puck has to wear thermal underwear.'

'They do Shakespeare then?'

'Oh, it's proper old style rep – the bard, Dame Agatha, Noël, the lot – and of course these musicals, or musicales, with real vocalistes. No, no more Chardonnay for me thank you, I love it but tum simply can't take the acid. And your friend, he sings?'

'Like a lark.'

'Oh lucky thing.'

Against a vast and shimmering sky, the long tawny bank of shingle was broken by the winding creek, now at low tide a broad stretch of mud with clumps of samphire and sea lavender, blue and hazy mauve. What was left of the creek curled round the foundations of the Sinden Theatre, sucking and slapping like a tramp who can't get to sleep. Above the tarred weatherboarding, a bent and rusty weathercock kept erratic account of the wind. In the glass foyer which had been tacked on at the front, some unexcluded draught made the posters flap. 'Yes, it's a converted barn, maltings apparently, but someone forgot to tell the rats about the conversion. Don't pause too long for effect, or the audience will hear the patter of their tiny feet, Wendy says, don't you, Wendy?'

The small woman in the heavy sack-coloured knit shook her arms to shiver the cold out of them. 'Just so long as the audience outnumber the rats, that's all I ask.' She talked out of the right side of her mouth and had tugged her elfin face in that direction. The cigarette helped the dragging effect, so too did the East wind probably. She seemed at the mercy of the elements. Her voice had an elongated nasal cadence, at once helpless and ironic.

'Oh you're his *friend*, aren't you? You need a friend out here. You used to play –' and here a pause for wonder was registered – 'tennis together, didn't you?'

'Yes.'

'Bit windy here for that sort of thing.' She stared at the bent and quivering sea grass on the bank outside.

'I'm only down for the show.'

'Oh well, *enjoy*. Pity you didn't come next month. We're attempting Rattigan. On second thoughts, you're better off with this production. And Tony sings like an angel, don't you darling?' She gave him a medium-strength squeeze which he accepted with grace.

'If you're Wendy, Tim Oates sends his love, I ran into him the other day. We had a drink together.'

'The Captain? Thank God he's given up acting. He was a menace to the furniture. The A.S.M. used to keep a special stock of sticking plaster for him. When he played the Ghost, after he'd fallen off the battlements, he looked like a walking road accident. I was Ophelia, and oh baby look at me now. But you'll enjoy *Up Lazarus!* It's a great show. Lots of catchy numbers.'

'Why'd you choose Lazarus?'

'Well, it's a terrific story, rising from the dead and all that. And then there are the women. You don't often get good women's parts in the Bible.'

'Women?'

'His sisters, Mary and Martha. I'm playing Martha, cumbered about much serving, remember?'

> 'Sweep and sheen
> polish and clean
> wish we had
> a washing-machine.'

Her singing voice startled me. It burst from her small body with

56

melodious power. She sketched a rudimentary dance shuffle as she sang.

'And then you see, it has a fantastic ending with Lazarus being taken up to heaven while the bloated plutocrat goes down a playground shute to the other place.'

'I didn't know that was the same Lazarus.'

'Oh come *on*. You think this is *history*? Listen, they don't even know if the Mary who's Martha's sister is Mary Magdalen or not. And they don't know either if Mary Magdalen was the same as the tart with the heart of gold who washed our Lord's feet with her hair. After all, they can't even agree whether she poured the ointment on his feet or his head. I mean you'd notice that difference, wouldn't you, if you were there?'

Tony listened to her with an eager happy concentration. He seemed to be laughing before she had said anything funny, but not to endear himself, just out of delight at himself being there in the dusty foyer with its walls of tarred planks and flapping posters and the glass doors letting in the gale every time somebody came in to book a ticket. Best thing that ever happened to me was how he had described the sack from Pagan, Jones & Co. (the union had withdrawn the allegations of assault as soon as Geoffrey had promised to dismiss those responsible, a promise he showed no reluctance in keeping).

What was more surprising still was his indifference to the fate of the picket who turned out to be concussed and to have a broken arm but not to be dead. Tony registered this distinction but not strongly.

'Well, of course, I'm glad he didn't snuff it. I didn't fancy being up on a charge of manslaughter. But you can't expect me to feel too sorry for him. He was about the worst of the lot, threatened me with a bloody great tyre-lever. I mean, you don't develop a huge amount of human sympathy for someone who's been calling you a bleeding Tory Fucker for the past three hours. As it happens, I voted Liberal last time and Labour the time before. In any case, he ought to be satisfied with getting me kicked out.'

He spoke without resentment, his voice gentle and void of rancour. At the top of the spiral stairs, a rawboned lad in jeans and a blue poloneck leant over the spindly railing and tapped his watch in Tony's direction.

'Christ, is that the time? Sorry, I've got to go and have one last run through with Simon the Leper,' jerking his thumb at John Edward Davies who clattered down the spiral and slapped me on the back with considerable warmth.

'Simon the Leper?'

'He was the Pagan-Jones of Bethany, according to the script anyway, the leading Pharisee as he entertained Jesus, and the disciples, and Lazarus, of course.

> 'Come on down to Simon's house
> He's a leper white as snow
> But when you've got time on
> Your hands, Simon's
> New house is the place to go.'

The limping jingle was somehow jaunty and mournful at the same time, reminded you of other tunes like it, but not strongly enough to be at all attractive.

'Are you coming?'

'No, I don't think I need to just yet,' Wendy said. 'You two boys just warble away together, get something going, then I'll do your positions later.' She watched them go through the black door into the auditorium with a wry, nigh maternal fondness.

'Strange, isn't it,' she said to me. 'You wouldn't think that lad's father had been hanged – or perhaps you would.'

'Hanged?' The words had slipped out of the side of her mouth so furtively that I was not sure I had heard right.

'Yes, his dad killed a man, in an off-licence. During a robbery. I don't expect he was a very good thief. Hit him with a bottle. Last man to be hanged in the county, or the country – I can't remember which Tony said. You must ask him. Hanged, can you believe it?'

'And he's ...'

'Playing Simon the Leper. Good strong leper's bass. Your friend is Lazarus naturally, true *Heldentenor*. If we can get someone to come over from Aldeburgh, he might get taken up aloft in this world too. Only trouble is, he can't act for toffee. Freezes as soon as he comes on stage. So I tell him to make a virtue of it and just stand there and sing his little heart out. Then he begins to relax.'

'That's funny. In ordinary life, he always seems so relaxed, too much sometimes.'

'It always works like that. It's the twitchy little people like me who can do the business on stage. When I'm auditioning, I can usually tell before they start doing their piece. The ones with a really awkward social manner are the ones to watch. Fancy a walk? I'll show you the North Sea.'

She took my arm as we clambered over the high leg-sapping bank of tawny brown and grey pebbles. The rasping cascading noise of our feet blotted out the dull slap of the tide. Wendy's arm locked hard in mine. I felt pulled along as we came down on to the sand and stopped to inspect the pigeon-breasted sky, our bodies braced against the burrowing wind.

'. . . about his parents?'

'What, whose, oh Tony's, well, nothing really. I only got to know him through playing tennis.'

'Englishmen.'

'Aren't you . . .'

'Of course I'm bloody English. That's how I know, because I've suffered.'

'Suffered how?'

'You know, reticence, inability to express the faintest glimmer of emotion, inability to express anything at all, in fact. That's what makes them such great actors. There's a marvellous sense of letting something out, almost unconsciously, whereas those foreign show-offs have shown it all off a million times already. Doesn't make it any easier to live with them, though.'

'Are you married?'

'Of course I'm not bloody married. Was I ever, yes for five months, it was a race between us to discover who'd made the biggest mistake and I won, quite easily I like to think. So you

59

don't know anything about Tony's background?'

'Not a thing.'

She said nothing but smiled to herself and left me. I walked at a brisk pace back towards the little low town at the end of the shingle with the red gables of my hotel pointing into the prevailing wind.

The marram grass in the low dunes whipped my thin trouser-legs. Perched above the road, the low bungalows looked out to sea. The light was going. The sun sank quietly behind the bungalows, slipping away without a proper farewell, a guest who didn't think much of the party. It was odd to see the sun going down over the land. The glass of the bungalow windows was suddenly black, although it was no more than twilight yet. I missed the bravura of the western sunset, a performance which contained the promise of repetition, otherwise known as tomorrow. This eastern tramonto was desolate and final, like the moment when you recognise with a shudder that the person you love is dead, irremediably dead, and that memories are small comfort.

Looking for the switch to turn on the bedside light, I happened upon the dark red Gideon bible and thumbed through to find the Lazarus story. Only St John had it, and in some detail. Martha's character was clearly indicated; she was the one who, when Jesus told the weeping Jews to roll away the stone, objected, 'Lord, by this time he stinketh: for he hath been dead four days.' On the other hand, only St Luke had the story about her being cumbered about much serving and being ticked off for complaining that her sister wasn't pulling her weight. Curious to have two stories so mutually illustrative of character and so closely linked and no evangelist telling both of them, particularly when all four had some version of the washing story: in Matthew, the scene was in Simon the Leper's house in Bethany and a woman had an alabaster box of very precious ointment and poured it on Jesus's head and the disciples complained about the waste, and Judas Iscariot immediately went off to negotiate the betrayal with the Chief Priest. Mark also had Jesus in Simon the Leper's house in Bethany and there came a woman having an alabaster box of 'spikenard very precious' and she too poured it over his head. Again Judas went straight off to the Chief Priest to start the betrayal. In Luke, Jesus was in the house of an unnamed Pharisee and the woman, still unnamed, was a sinner and this time anointed his feet, but the purpose of the story is forgiveness, not to rebuke the disciples for quibbling about the expense. Judas is nowhere in sight, and the betrayal does not get under way for another fifteen chapters. In fact, Luke's version is much more independent than the fourth gospel's. John, after having devoted the whole of the previous chapter to the raising of Lazarus, tells us that it was Mary who took a pound of ointment of spikenard, very costly, anointed Jesus's feet with it and wiped the feet with her hair and the house was filled with the odour. Then in the next verse, the spikenard still filling his nostrils, Judas asked why this ointment was not sold for three hundred pence and given to the poor, asking not because he cared for the poor but because he was the team's bagman and accustomed to pilfer from the kitty.

How curious it all was, if one was to believe John and his was only an intenser version of Matthew and Mark. The whole tragedy set in motion because of the terrible expensive fragrance of the nard (a perennial herb found in Nepal whose roots contain a highly aromatic oil which may be rubbed up with fat into an ointment, according to the dictionary of plants of the Bible at the back of the Gideon) and the woman, perhaps a sinner, perhaps not, possibly Martha's sister, possibly not, but passionate, impulsive, sloppy – were her movements of adoration so wild that she poured it over both his head and his feet or that some spilled from one to the other without her intending it? And this sloppiness, this extravagant passion was the last straw for Judas, the tightarsed thief of poorboxes, chosen by some lapse in management selection technique to be treasurer to the party, perhaps because of his grinding meanness.

And then I noticed another thing: it is only St John, the novelist of the four, who tells us that Judas is the son of Simon. The same Simon who is throwing the dinner, the generous leprous host? That makes sense, much better sense in fact than if his

61

complaint about the spikenard is taken in isolation. Judas, the son of the house, comes in tired and dusty (they have been virtually on the run out in the wilderness ever since the raising of Lazarus has put the wind up the chief priests and Pharisees) and what does he find – a huge great banquet being prepared to celebrate the raising, with Lazarus and Jesus as joint guests of honour. No expense spared, Martha and Mary having more or less taken over the place, his inheritance being thrown away on a crackpot prophet whom he has begun to fall out of love with (perhaps he is already dreaming of leaving the disciples and settling down to farm Simon's land now that the old leper has become so frail). And then the spikenard ... all through the prolonged negotiation with the chief priest, the smell of the nard must have been still in his nostrils, as sharply apprehended as Martha had anticipated the smell of Lazarus's corpse. Would he have betrayed Jesus if there had been no spikenard, would Lazarus have been raised – and the chief priests and Pharisees so fatally alarmed – if Jesus had not loved Mary and Martha? Luke didn't make the link and as a result he had no concrete motive to offer for betrayal: 'Then entered Satan into Judas surnamed Iscariot' – any hack thriller writer could have improved on that. No, the spikenard was the key. What a peculiar story, its oddity drew me gently into sleep as a sad East Anglian dusk made up for my blinds not being drawn.

I woke an hour or more later than I had meant and had to hurry along the promenade back to the theatre. They were well launched as I edged along the row of tip-up wooden seats which tipped up with a clap as each person rose to let me past. It was a bad moment to come in. The stage was so dark my eyes took several minutes to focus on the little group of figures kneeling at the left. Then a voice, conversational, low, ingratiating: 'Well, Father, I know you're always listening. But there were all those people standing by and I had to say something, just to let them know who I was and who sent me. I don't need to tell you that, do I?'

Silence. The place seemed very cold. My neighbour's peppermint breath seemed to freeze in my nostrils. Then somewhere at the back of the stage, there was a faint silvery glimmer. One of the kneeling figures got to its feet and yelled, 'OK, Lazarus, come on out.'

And Tony Allenby came forth, swaddled tight from head to toe in strips of sheet with another strip wound round his head, leaving only the barest slit for eyes and nostrils.

'Right, let's go, take off the bandages.'

I was deeply moved, the Chicago cop accent Jesus had suddenly adopted seemed quite apt. The lights gradually went up and the women began to unwind the bandages, moving slowly round Lazarus in a stately dance. First his shoulders, then his midriff became visible; he was covered in a white chalky substance and still seemed marvellously dead. Then the women began to sing in a low buzzy way to a tune which sounded just like the other snatches I had heard from Tony and Wendy, reminiscent but also unmemorable, a limping jig of a tune:

'Up Lazarus
You're one of us
This is your lucky day
You're really on your way
So welcome back
You're right on track ...'

The singing grew louder, and one by one the women darted forward to embrace the chalky figure. By now my neighbour with the peppermint breath was sobbing. I recognised the short figure of the third woman to come forward. She gave Lazarus a specially fierce hug, and then came to the front of the stage and cupped her hands to her mouth to make a tiny megaphone. 'Lazarus is raised,' Wendy bellowed in that surprisingly strong contralto, 'Lights!' The auditorium was a blaze of light. 'Now,' she said 'give thanks that Lazarus is risen, hug your neighbour, EMBRACE THE FUTURE!' The women on the stage jumped down into the auditorium and began mercilessly hugging the people in the front row. Lazarus stood alone on stage, basked in white radiance. My neighbour with the peppermint breath, a bald man with a small moustache, first turned to his left to kiss what looked like his wife and then with no semblance of hesitation enfolded me and followed it up with a moist peppermint peck on my cheek. It was at this touching moment that a large man in a long brown coat shambled on to the stage. At first I assumed that he must represent the peasantry of Bethany come to gawp at the miracle and was not at all surprised when he approached the motionless white figure of Lazarus and enveloped Tony in a bear hug. It took me a moment or two to realise that he was not embracing Tony but attacking him, butting him in the solar plexus, and then throwing wild punches at his chalky head. The two of them skidded across the stage together, Tony beginning feebly to retaliate while the man in the brown coat began to shout you fucking cunt, you destroy a man's life and then think you can go prancing about on the stage thinking you're fucking Laurence Olivier, well, you've got another fucking think coming. By now, two men had appeared from the wings and were clawing at his brown coat without much success. But Martha and Mary clambered back up on to the stage and threw themselves at his legs with such passion that he only staggered another half-step before crashing to the ground. Once he was down, the stagehands had no trouble in dragging him off like a slaughtered bullock. Curtain.

We shuffled out into the foyer. 'I didn't quite get that last bit,' the bald man said.

As soon as I had shaken myself free of the crowd, I ran out through the glass doors to go round to the stage door. In the distance, I could already hear the wail of police sirens. Had the man in the brown coat been trying to fight his way on to the stage for some time before he finally burst through the wings to gatecrash the Raising? Looking down the road as I hurried round to the back of the theatre, I saw a menacing black hulk reared against the huge East Anglian sky. It was a second or two before I recognised it as the bucket and back hoe of a JCB blocking the road. Mr Wall was making full use of his legal right to retain the tools of his trade while in a bankrupt condition. The police sirens closed in and were reinforced by angry hooting. A searchlight came on, revealing the empty driver's cabin. Doors slammed and a voice started squawking through a megaphone but could not be heard as they had not yet turned off the sirens.

'... talk to us John ...' a mutinous siren began wailing again '... your wife ... your problems, discuss ...'

I advanced timidly in the role of helpful citizen, only to find myself rudely collared and my arms wrenched out of their sockets and pulled behind my back. 'Now then, John.'

'I'm not John,' I said.

'Well, whose is this JCB then, John?'

'He's in the theatre, over there,' I said.

'All right, John.'

'I'm not John.' In my rage and panic, a dim puzzlement was also surfacing. Why me? And then in the cold glare of the searchlight, the insistent brownness of my coat, its mongrel gingeriness, an ill-starred snip at the sales, clarified the wits I had been terrified out of.

'Although it is true I am wearing a brown coat, I am not the person you are seeking.'

The touch of pedantry about the syntax convinced them.

'Sorry, sir. It was a pardonable misunderstanding.'

'He's over there in the theatre.'

'We know that, sir. So if you'll excuse us, we'd better be getting along.' They broke into a trot, having managed to convey that it was I who was detaining them. Was there a course at police college on never putting yourself in the wrong? If so, it must have been the best-attended course, and not just by policemen either.

I did not feel like hurrying back to see Wall being led away with gyves upon his wrist. Benjamin Britten could write an opera about it with Tony as Wall and whoever was playing Judas cast as the area manager of Barclays Bank.

I wandered over on to the low dunes of the foreshore. The wind had dropped but the shore-grass still whipped at my legs through the thin trousers. The sight and sound of the sea at night certainly brought the note of eternal sadness in. It was a note I had heard before, limitless, discouraging, the night before older men died, two at least in my own presence, my friend Joe's

Uncle Peter collapsed from a heart attack during an argument about Italian words for macaroon, my distant cousin who had laboured under the same name as the hero of *Kidnapped* and had killed himself in a seaside boarding house. Both had reached the end of the line, reached the station where there were no further connections to be made. These melancholy thoughts were not directed at Mr Wall, who was simply a Pursuer. It was an accident that *Up Lazarus!* was in repertory here and not in some inland spa at Droitwich, say, or Harrogate. No, it was Tony who seemed to be running out of space.

As I climbed back on to the little road, they were loading Mr Wall into the police van and a policeman hopped up into the cabin of the JCB and was backing it into a layby. By the time I was back in the theatre, they were back in the seats and the curtain was going up on the banquet in the house of Simon the Leper. This was a merry, bustling scene: pewter goblets being lifted to bearded throats, red wine trickling through the grizzle, lips smacked, napkins brandished. The scene was dominated by Martha played by Wendy in Mistress Overdone style, handwiping, perspiring, thrusting pewter plates over the heads of carousing disciples with an abundance of Lord bless us and keep your hands to yourself young man, while Mary sat dreamily at Our Lord's feet playing with her waistlength ringlets. Our Lord kept his back to the audience throughout the play – just as well with his acne, Wendy had glossed – an ingenious device, but one which required careful manoeuvring if conversations with Him were not to take on the aspect of a football scrum viewed from behind. Still, the clatter of goblets and the swish of madder and ochre robes made a brave show, and when Wendy advanced to front of stage to deliver 'Wish we had a washing-machine' – at least the second-best number in the show – Act Two looked like keeping up the brio maintained throughout Act One, up to and including Mr Wall's surprise guest appearance. All the elements were there – a beautiful Magdalen who poured the oil over the head and feet of the back-view Saviour with movements that were both delicate and passionate, a Saviour with a lovely speaking voice, light but with a memorable authority, and a ratlike resentful Judas so instantly dislikeable that the mystery of his election to the Twelve, let alone his appointment as Hon. Treasurer, seemed odd. Yet as the play continued, a certain unmistakable unease crept over the audience. Something was wrong, or rather it was obvious what was wrong, namely Lazarus himself, and the obviousness made the wrongness ten times worse. It was not that he did what he did badly, though he did. He did not, after all, have very much to do. Lazarus could well be excused for taking things quietly; after being dead for four days, a short convalescence was in order. He might also be expected to retain a certain pallor for a time, much as a tan may linger after a holiday in Florida. Yet nobody could have intended him to sit so white and wooden at the feast. He was meant to have stopped being a ghost. Some evidence of flesh and blood was to be expected. Nor should his voice have been quite so sepulchral, well, it shouldn't have been sepulchral at all. When he called, 'More wine, sister Martha,' it sounded like a death rattle. And when she retorted, 'Wait your turn, Laz, I've only got one pair of hands,' her exasperation sounded heartfelt. I realised that the advantage the first act had over the second was that Lazarus had been dead throughout it.

One thing Tony's woodenness could not distract us from was Mary Magdalen letting down her hair. It had been loosely coiled till now and she shook it free with a convulsive wag of her head, almost as though she was having a fit, and it tumbled down in a great chestnut torrent. She took the alabaster box – more like a small urn, in fact – and began to shake it over Jesus's long white feet, again with frantic movements. And this sight too was a touching one, reminding me of watching my father in bare feet wearing his biblical dressing gown when he walked out on to the crumbling terrace to sniff the first wallflowers of the year. Mary began to rub the feet with her hair and suddenly the sweet moment was gone and we were watching a clip from a commercial for some beauty product.

Mary turned out to be nothing remarkable to look at without her wig on, beaky-faced and pale but hearty and welcoming.

'What do you use for the spikenard?'

'Sunflower oil, we get it in gallon drums from the Cash 'n' Carry. Costs a bomb, all the same. It's great for the skin actually. Jesus'll have a real peachblossom complexion by the end of the run.'

Of the two, I noted with surprise, Martha was the more seductive offstage, at the first-night party (which was held on stage). She had thrown an old shawl round her shoulders, the one she had worn at the Raising, and her eyes glittered in her stage make-up. She and Lazarus were strolling round arm-in-arm with glasses in their hand, Lazarus still chalky and half-naked. I had not realised how thin he was. Death and the maiden.

'Well?'

'You were wonderful,' I said.

'No I wasn't,' Tony said. 'I can sing but I can't act.'

'Oh darling, where would we all be if we knew our limitations? You must learn the first rule of acting: fool yourself.'

'Wendy's doing her best, but I'm a slow learner. It's the movement I find so difficult.'

'Oh darling, lighten up. We're celebrating, remember?'

And Tony too celebrated as the singsong and the dancing got under way, and Mary Magdalen and Judas started kissing each other all over and the fat old Chief Priest did his Stubby Kaye impression of 'Sit Down You're Rocking the Boat'. The rest of the cast took up the chorus, waving their hands and bending their knees in unison to a dark empty auditorium. They really were a ship's company, vagabond on the dark sea, cut off from the land and its lubbers. Out of place, I crept away to my hotel, the last image on my retina being Lazarus, chalky, laughing, hand-jiving with a Martha by now squiffy, stumbling but unquenched.

The east made up for its dusks with its dawns. The golden gleams pierced my hung-over eyelids and pressed the start button on my headache. For a few moments I lay still to see if there was any chance of the doze turning pleasant, but the ache demanded attention. The air coming in through the unclosed, uncloseable sash window was too bitter chill for an attempt at the sea. I stumbled down the backstairs, guided by the ever-growing smell of chlorine to the hotel pool in the basement. It was a dank stretch of water, forty feet long at best, surrounded by changing cubicles with the paint peeling off the doors. Beyond, some white plastic beach furniture and a potted plant made up the lounge area which looked as if nobody had done much lounging in it since it was opened.

To my surprise, the pool was not empty. A woman with long dark hair was striking up and down it with a brisk backstroke. As her arm hit the water behind her, her oval face seemed pure and still amid the splashing. She came to the end of the pool, stopped swimming and hoicked herself up on the edge with her elbow.

'Hi!'

'I didn't recognise you,' I said, and I had not, she looked so strong and firm in her swimsuit.

'Well, come on in then.'

As I changed, Wendy shouted through the cubicle door news of how the party had ended: Mary Magdalen and Judas had had it off literally on stage, poor old Victor the Chief Priest had passed out and had to be carried back to his digs, and she herself had been too pissed to remember a thing, only she had the impression it had all ended rather nicely.

'Nicely?' I enquired, lowering myself into the chlorine froth she had whipped up.

'Oh, *you* know.'

'Ah.'

I swam grimly up and down, our outstretched fingertips clashed as we passed in the dank narrows. The noise of our voices clanged around the distressed cream ceiling and banged off the peeling doors. Each time I passed her, I took to clenching my fists to avoid the clash, but we were both tiring and rolling out of a straight line so her fingertips hit my fist and my heels struck out at hers. Now she was doing a sleek crawl and her round bottom bobbed out of the water and filled my aching head with distant twangs of desire.

'I didn't know swimming was meant to be a contact sport.'

'We weren't exactly synchronised, were we?'

'He's a bit stiff, your friend, but I like him, especially when he's stiff. Oh dear, we don't say that sort of thing, do we?' She grinned and threw the skimpy blue towel around her and shook her long dark hair.

'You could have played Mary Magdalen without the wig.'

'Martha's a better part, ducky, she gets all the sympathy. I mean the audience are really on Judas's side, aren't they? They think what an exhibitionist cow and the money could have gone to Oxfam. I wonder why Tony's like that.'

'Like what?'

'Like he is.'

'How do you mean?'

'Why does he . . . hold himself back?'

'It's a sort of politeness, I think.'

'But it isn't really polite is it, not in that context, would you say?'

'I don't . . . oh, I see.'

'The French call it caresse, but I call it standoffish, don't you? I like people to be happy, and he isn't, not really.'

She put her head on one side and looked like a wounded bird again, and older too. The envy I had felt for Tony ebbed, but quietly, like the thin frill of water that has outreached the tide and mostly soaks away into the sand.

Out on the shingle after breakfast, John Edward Davies was throwing pebbles into a calm sea.

'Great show, didn't you think?'

'Terrific.'

'No you didn't. You thought it was shit. Everyone thinks it was shit. Because it is shit.'

'As a matter of fact, I was actually rather moved when Lazarus was raised, I thought that was a moving moment.'

'Don't be so bloody patronising.'

'Oh, all right then. Don't you like being in the show?'

'I like singing.'

'So does Tony. Funny, both of you fetching up on the stage

70

together.'

'There's no coincidence about it at all. We are both victims of the same man. Jones had us both out. I knew he would.'

'What do you mean?'

'Don't you know about my father then? That's the first thing anyone ever says about me, I'm under no illusion about that.'

'Well, I had heard –'

'There, you see.'

'But I only heard yesterday –' although I don't know why that should have made it better – 'and anyway, I don't see why Geoffrey should have it in for you because of your father. I mean it's nothing to do with him, is it?'

'Then you don't know the whole story. I suppose you wouldn't.'

'You'd better tell it me.'

'Oh, I don't mind telling it. In fact, telling it is part of my mission in life, in a manner of speaking, or so it seems to me.' His way of talking swung between apology and defiance, or was both at the same time, and yet for all its Welsh warmth was peculiarly impersonal too, as though he was being interviewed for a this-is-your-life show. And his raw, brooding figure, legs braced on the tawny bank of shingle, was clearly staged. I had come upon him moodily chucking pebbles into a calm sea because that was what one came upon people moodily doing.

'My mam was convinced that my dad was innocent. Can't think why, he'd knocked *her* about enough and he'd got a record of violence, but anyway it gave her something to think about, see, so she had all these cuttings from the local paper as well as the nationals, covering everything, arrest, trial, right up to the execution.'

'What had he done?'

'Hit the manager of an off-licence over the head with a bottle. He was trying to do the till at the time, the man, I mean, not my da, though he probably was too, he never could resist the sight of an open till. The man had a thin skull, but that was no defence. Squalid little crime, really. But then he was a squalid little man, my father. He wasn't good enough to hang really.'

71

'But …'

'Anyway, in the local paper it gave the names of all those who attended the execution of John Edward Davies – same name as me, you see, I was born posthumous, he was only twenty-three, and my mother named me after him as a bit of defiance, about the only defiant thing she ever did in her pathetic life, I should think. She died a couple of years ago, and it's really for her sake I'm doing all this.'

'All what?'

He grinned, a raw wolfish grin. 'Got you interested now, have I? I like to get people interested. I haven't been properly educated, so getting people interested is about the best I can do. Well, so you see, I've got the list of all those who were there: the governor, the padre, the doctor, and so on. And I haunt them.'

'Haunt them?'

'Haunt them, but not just a five-minute now-you-see-me-now-you-don't act. I establish myself in their vicinity.'

'How do you mean?'

'The doctor was easy. He was the GP who did the next-door town, so I put myself on his patients' list. He was quite a good doctor in fact, and I had a lot of trouble with my feet at that time, verrucas, in-growing toenails twice, and so I was always in and out of his surgery. Next patient. What's your name? John Edward Davies. Went white as a sheet. He couldn't ask, of course, didn't need to ask because I look so like my father.'

'And the padre I suppose you …'

'That was more difficult, because the nosy bugger spent most of his time in jail, but I found that he stood in for a pal of his in a parish out Northampton way. So I went along, sat in the front row every Sunday for six months, and stared. I can do a good stare.' He opened his dark green eyes wide under his arched eyebrows and stared at me. Even out on the shingle, on a clear morning, I found myself shuddering. 'And so in the end he had to ask my name, although he already knew what the answer would be. I thought he was going to be sick. Strange what the sight of one human being can do to another. I wished my mother had been alive so I could have brought her along too. She was pretty well broken up at the end, but he would still have recognised her as the pregnant woman he did his God-moves-in-a-mysterious-way act to.'

'What about the governor?'

'That was easy. He was retired, of course, by then, and getting a bit doddery, so he needed a part-time gardener. He didn't like the sight of me peering through the rhododendrons any better than the rest of them, but he couldn't get rid of me because he was one of those trendy liberal governors who believes in giving the unfortunate a chance. So I did him over good and proper, and after six months he was a walking wreck, which only left Jonesy.'

'Pagan-Jones? How –'

'He was High Sheriff and as you may or may not know the High Sheriff has to attend every hanging, to see fair play in the Queen's name. So there he was, having wriggled his way up the ladder and crawled and greased to the entire Establishment, and what do you know, first bloody thing he has to do is attend a hanging. The trouble was, he was more difficult to get at, and short of starting a business and deliberately going bankrupt I couldn't think of a way to make contact with him professionally. I was beginning to despair, because he was the last stage in the mission, the climax really, and I just couldn't get at him. And then one day I was hanging about outside his front gate, doing my pre-liminary reconnaissance and I saw him walking off down that lit-tle path to the tennis club with his racquets under his arm, and I instantly saw how to crack it. The previous barman had left the week before. It was a piece of cake.'

'And did he recognise you straight off?'

'The name came first. He was away at the time of my appoint-ment, on holiday, and they took me on without consulting him because they needed someone straight away. So when he comes in and the secretary introduces me, and this is our new barman, John Edward Davies, he couldn't really look at me, flinched at the mention of my name.'

'Are you sure you're not imagining some of this? I've never

thought of him as a flincher.'

'Oh they all flinch when I give them the staring treatment.' Again, he fixed his sea-green eyes and his arched brows on me and, although we must have been talking for ten minutes, familiarity did not rub off the strangeness of him and he still managed to chill me.

'I see what you mean.'

'It's not just the guilt, see, it's what I might do to them, how I might take my revenge. They don't realise that that is my revenge. I hate violence, couldn't hurt a fly to save my life.'

As he was talking, my knees began to tremble under me. The night before, the early swim, standing on the unstable shingle – well, there were plenty of reasons for the weakness which spread up through me. But the relentless driving-on of John Edward Davies had something to do with it. He was so rawly insistent on pursuing his quarries and pursuing the story too, battering away at me in that voice which had lost most of its Welshness but not the harsh richness. Suddenly the mild gleam of the morning, the sea horizon a milky yellow, the land horizon a sleepy jumble of red roofs, the stillness of the huge sky – the whole amiable scene seemed heavy and sinister and I wanted to be off on the next train. My heart beat like a piledriver all the way up to Liverpool Street and it was only when the train squeaked to a halt in those great grimy halls that calm returned.

On the overhead walkway, sniffing the diesel fumes with grateful delight, I bumped into Josie.

'You've just come up, have you? I expect it's your train I'm trying to catch back down again.'

'Are you going to see the show? I liked it really, parts of it were very touching, I mean you had to endure some corny stuff –'

'No, no,' she said, impatient, flushed, hitching her bag over her shoulder. 'Or rather, I mean, yes, of course, but not just that. I got this, it's like in an Agatha Christie, isn't it, I can't think who ...'

The postcard she pulled out of her bag was an aerial view of the Great Eastern Hotel at sunset. On the back, a laborious hand: *Dear Miss Jones, I think you ought to know that your boyfriend is betray-*

74

ing you.

'It's so peculiar, isn't it – the Miss Jones and the betraying. It might have been written in the nineteen-thirties.'

'In a way I think it was,' I said. 'Anyway he's out of date, about Tony being your boyfriend, isn't he?'

'Oh no, *you're* out of date. I must run.'

She ran off along the walkway with that well-remembered loping stride, as though she had a small obstacle about nine inches high to clear at every other step. Some novelist says somewhere that there is no pleasure in life so great as meeting a woman who is eager to see you. Equally, there is no minute desolation quite so piercing as saying goodbye to a woman who is eager to be off to see someone else (there are far deeper griefs, of course, but nothing which applies such a sharp and stylish pinprick to the self-balloon). And Josie like Tony moved with such high and natural elan that, without being egotistical, she could seem quite unconcerned by people she was not fractionally in love with. She did not rub it in, even unconsciously, but there was no doubting that she was beyond one's reach, belonged to a different, unknowable species, one whose grace and suppleness demanded admiration, but only as you admire the gleam and twirl of goldfish in a pond.

The next I heard was from Captain Oates, who seemed to have become an intimate of the little circle on the strength of a recent visit to the Sinden Theatre.

'You have to take your hat off to Wendy. I mean she's practically a hunchback, certainly a dwarf, and she pulls all the talent for miles around. It does help to be the directrice, I agree, but even so. I mean, hardly has she explored the delights of your friend, and what delights, seldom in my young life have I seen someone so irresistibly beddable, anyway, in no time at all she casts him aside – admittedly mostly because his girlfriend would insist on coming down, not the way to further the stage career of one's beloved, I could have told her that – and she instantly takes up with a bit of Welsh rough, sacks your friend and promotes Taffy to sing Lazarus.'

'But he's a bass,' I said weakly.

'Transpose, my dear, transpose. The music's such crap the part could be sung by a baby hyena and nobody would notice the difference. At this rate, she'll have gone through the entire cast before they finish the run, which must be soonish because she tells me they're starting rehearsals for *The Deep Blue Sea*, and she's playing Hester with Taffy in the Kenneth More part. Not exactly how I would have cast it. I know Hester's supposed to be older, but she is meant to have been a beauty and Taffy doesn't sound exactly like one of the Few. Anyway, as far as Wendy is concerned, he's one of the Many. Oh dear, I don't know what makes me like this in the mornings. But do go down and look up the poor lovebirds. At least Wendy carrying on like that enabled them to get back together. All the same, I expect they're awfully bedraggled. People usually are in a post-Wendy condition. One needs to convalesce.' This was startling. If Oates was to be believed, not merely had they come together, but it seemed somehow that Wendy's erotic caprices had been responsible for the reunion. Far from Tony's straying having finalised the split and confirmed the disenchantment, the old passion had resurged stronger than ever. They were using their edges now, Oates said. Edges? I queried. Like in skiing, he said, the more you use your edges the quicker you get down the mountain. Is that a good idea, I asked.

They were living at the end of a row of brick cottages on the outskirts of Colchester. On the dusty verge in front of the cottage was a road sign saying 'Britain's oldest recorded town'. There was an Essex prudence in this claim, as though the town lived in fear of a challenge from some unrecorded bootleg city of unbeatable antiquity.

'It's furnished, as you see. The husband died, and the wife went to live with her daughter, to recover.' Josie waved her arm at the china ornaments on the mantelpiece and the lace antimacassars on the settee and the old-fashioned bakelite radio on top of the chest of drawers. 'It's a period piece.'

'My period.'

'Mine too. We're cosy here. We're recovering too, I suppose.

76

Tony's working in the local Social Security Office now, doing the Supp Ben. You need a refuge after a day with your clients. *Clients!'*

We walked out into the garden, down the concrete path between the rows of runner beans. The leaves on the stunted hawthorn hedge at the bottom were curled and brown. The wind rattled the beansticks and whistled through the barbed-wire fence beyond, a thin clandestine sound as though to summon a partner in crime. There was nothing to see on the far side of the hedge and the wire, the ground was too flat.

'I'm surprised you didn't leave East Anglia.'

'So am I really, but we were flaked out and didn't have any better place to go, or any money to go with.'

'But –'

'I'm disinherited, for the moment, as long as I stay with Tony, Dada says. Perhaps whoever took me off would have got the same treatment. He suffers from creative dissatisfaction, you know, that's his real trouble. That's what makes him such a brilliant liquidator, he's always looking for a bettter solution. He's fed up with Norris Elegant already.'

'Who isn't?' I peered over the barbed wire at the dull undulations of plough, the pale straws of the stubble still undigested by the clay soil. A few gulls pecked at the crumbly ridges, then flapped, took off, cried a surly cry and settled on another ridge with an air of expecting little better. We had been bred, uniquely perhaps, to admire restlessness, the explorer always forging on to the next valley beyond the next horizon, or paddling up the last creek, the scientist well into old age setting himself new theories to test. High minds were supposed to be insatiable, but what about low minds? Didn't we think the less of them too when they retreated into contentment and calm? Yet it was an uncomfortable life, being on the receiving end. Restlessness, however brilliant, was better admired from a distance.

Behind us, a homecoming halloo from the kitchen door. Tony Allenby stood in the doorway in a fawn raincoat carrying an old briefcase. He looked ready to drop.

'Yes, since you don't ask,' he said, ' it has been a nightmare day.

77

The customers can't get the hang of the new regs for the clothing and bedding allowance and nor can I. They think they're being cheated and I expect they're right. It's the first three months in Supp Ben are the worst apparently. Pensions are said to be a doddle.' As we sat down to tea, I smelled the sour smell of the office on him, a dull stale odour which seemed more vegetable than human, like gone cabbage. 'Still,' he said, putting the scalding tea to his lips, 'I like to think this is one job I can't get the push from, unless I make a pass at the branch manager and she's a bit above my weight, about two stone I should think, and has to shave twice as often as I do.' He let the resentment dribble out of him, seemed in fact to be watching the dribbling from above as though this dim destiny was happening to someone else. Querulousness never managed to stick to him. And then a kind of irritating reasonableness began to seep out of him. He felt obliged to give full credit to the people in the Ministry who had made the rules so flexible to take account of the ever-changing circumstances of their clients: 'So if someone gets the boot halfway through the week, there are these emergency payments which can tide him over without infringing the basic principle of the waiting period . . .'

'You don't have to crawl to us.'

'No, seriously, it is rather ingenious. I mean, of course, there ought to be more resources, but the system . . .'

'I can hardly wait to start claiming,' Josie said. 'More tea, Gus.' Somewhere in the cottage the wind was rattling a door and a draught from the cheerless evening outside was nibbling at my ankles. The telephone rang, an old-fashioned flustered ringing, and Tony took it under his chin while continuing quite easily to eat his toast and peanut butter. The client's squawk shivered the cheap china on the table.

'Can't it wait till Monday?' The woman at the other end told him why it couldn't in her thin, up-and-down keening voice. Mrs Thorpe's common-law husband, Tony explained afterwards, strictly speaking ex-husband because he had moved out and only visited her when he was drunk, had come back the night before, beaten her up and then vomited all over the curtains. Didn't she mean carpet? Yes, he had asked her that too, but curtains was what she meant, because he had ripped them down claiming they were his property because he had paid for them, which he hadn't she said, and then tripped up in them, fallen down, hit his head and gone to sleep. So she had left him because she hadn't the strength to throw him out and of course he had been sick all over them, the curtains, lucky he hadn't choked on it or not so lucky in fact and the cleaning bill was £25 and wasn't she entitled to a special allowance.

'And is she?'

'Yes.'

'Good.'

'Yes, it is good. It is a good system really, you see.'

'So we're going to spend the rest of our life here deciding whether to pay for vomit to be cleaned off people's curtains. Doesn't that sound nice? I'd better make another pot.' Josie stared with her slight squint into the dark brown teapot. The squint which once gave her face a charming obliquity, now made her look uncertain, even suspicious.

The two of them seemed blanched and withered, and yet at the same time I envied them. They had somehow escaped from ease and were, there was no other word for it, living. Their fingertips were feeling the cold edge of the ledge they were hanging on to. Tony's job was good and drab and noble and her marrying him (that had happened two months earlier, they told me) that was noble too. They had parted and endured solitude and betrayal and come together again. They had seized the moment, and though they would not have dreamed of saying so, I had not. That was why, for the first time since I had known them, I longed to be away from them, not to be forced to compare the slack sag of my life with the intensity of theirs.

Under the bare light of the shadeless bulb in the hall her face seemed darkened somehow. Around the velvety mole on her cheek there was a browner shadow, barely visible under the powder I noticed she had put on, which was not like her. No, it could not be a bruise I told myself, and looked away and kissed her goodbye on the other cheek.

The heating had broken down on the train back and the cold set my teeth on edge. I could not help thinking about the brown shadow on her face. I felt I ought not to, and yet somehow it seemed like a secret between the three of us, a secret which brought me closer to them. But that was an unhealthy fancy and so I diverted my thoughts to sun-kissed scenes and scents, especially scents. Had Tony's sour smell come from his cheap suit with its thin brown stripe running through the dull grey polyester or from his nylon shirt not being dripped and dried often enough? How handy it would have been if Josie had been able to break open an alabaster box of spikenard and distract our senses.

What, I wondered, would its fragrance have been like? Was it strong or subtle, heavy and animal or light and flowery? There was a chemist on the platform at Liverpool Street. He seemed puzzled, and a little insulted, and recommended me to a herbalist in Covent Garden where a confident young man in an Indian tunic looked blank but persuaded me to buy a reprint of Culpeper's Herbal instead. The great herbalist, an unpleasant vindictive character according to his enemies, had plenty to say about spikenard: 'Naturally an Indian plant, of a heating, drying faculty. It is good to provoke urine and ease pains of the stone in the reins and kidneys. It helps loathings, swellings, or gnawings in the stomach ... The oil is good to warm cold places, and to digest crude and raw humours; it works powerfully on old cold griefs of the head and brain ... Two or three spoonfuls thereof being taken help passions of the heart.' How could we have got along without it? To help loathings, to warm cold places, to work powerfully on old cold griefs, to say nothing of digesting crude and raw humours and helping passions of the heart – what more could anyone want?

And yet Culpeper said nothing about its smell, failed even to give the brief description of the plant's appearance that he gave with most other plants. Perhaps he had never seen or used spikenard and was operating entirely on hearsay when listing its effects (although there was among the illustrations a smudgy picture of an unremarkable plant with a red and yellow flower). An obsession took hold of me, an obsession that was as powerful as it was pointless; it seemed essential, urgent even, that I should smell this oil which had set off a chain of such terrible events, which, at a stretch, could even be described as the fragrance that had shaken the old world and made the one we were sitting in the ruins of.

I looked at other herbals, ancient and modern, and read of further claims for the powers, ranging from the everyday to the semi-miraculous, attributed to spikenard – further adding to my impression that the average herbalist throughout the ages had survived by saying the first thing that came into his head or anything that would impress his patients and cheer them up – but nowhere could I find any coherent or exact description of its odour, that odour that had filled the house of Simon the Leper and lingered so balefully in the nostrils of Judas. I wrote to a mail order company in Hampshire which boasted of being able to supply esoteric and hard-to-get herbs, but their catalogue was a pitiful flimsy thing and had no mention of spikenard; another nursery in Lincolnshire was no more help, although the proprietor who included a picture of herself in dungarees on the cover of the catalogue wished me luck in my thrilling quest. Some friends who were off on an Awayday break to Istanbul promised to enquire in the Spice Market, and with that hope for the moment I let the chase rest, dreaming only now and then of a wizened figure in a fez weighing out a few drops of the priceless liquid into some cunningly wrought phial of oriental design.

It was when I was mournfully chewing lunch at *Frag* magazine that the thought came to me. That satirical organ, an impish legend in its day, still kept up a shabby front in a dusty alley off the Tottenham Court Road between the audio and video shops. Its young tearaways were grey and middle-aged now, weathered by drink and divorce but not by despair, even if the reserves of irrepressibility were running a little low. There they all were round the long table, Moonman, Willie Sturgis and their court, all still

81

eating the same bangers and mash, still making much the same jokes with the same whoops and jeers in that same dim light filtered through the gloomy windows and breaking on the same blank streets – but no, I am thinking of them as they were when I last visited them three or four years ago, and this was ten years earlier when they were still greenish and their tweed jackets still had matching buttons on them.

There had been some talk about the Middle East, a titbit connecting illegal arms sales to a British politician (the politician had to be British for the scandal to count, there were no global pretensions about Moonman), and someone had said this man was into drugs too, and suddenly my memory hit the buzzer – a deplorable phrase, Moonman would have said – and I turned to Clapp, the melon-faced owner of the shop below (from which the magazine rented the two upper floors), and enquired, 'Clapp, do you still keep herbs with all that junk downstairs?'

'What, cocky?' He was already a little deaf and it was difficult to hear amid the shouts and jeers. In any case, Clapp was engaged in ladling out the mashed potato, dumping the glutinous white paste on each plate with a disdainful splat.

'Herbs, Clapp, do you still keep them?'

'All the elixirs of life, cocky, I keep them all – books, toys, erotica of all descriptions, inexpensive wine-making equipment, and, of course, natural remedies.' He looked at me through his huge spectacles with that fierce aggrieved look which sometimes raised a laugh, an uneasy one, from newcomers to the table.

'Spikenard, Clapp, do you ever have oil of spikenard?'

'Spikenard, darling, what do you take me for? You'll be asking if I've got tarragon or a little bit of mint next. Of course, I've got fucking spikenard. How much do you want? A gallon? Enough to have a bath in?'

'Just a sample.'

'All right, come on downstairs when I've finished with the mashed.'

And so he led me down the stairs, past the magazine office where a couple of pretty Fionas were already at their typewriters, down to the dark and stuffy room on the ground floor with the cluster of flyblown mauve plastic grapes on top of the dusty tubes of the wine-making equipment and the case of wooden children's toys, the blocky simulacra of unwooden things like trains, elephants and hedgehogs.

'Here we are then, let's have a butchers in Aladdin's cave.' Clapp ferreted around in the jars and bottles on the shelves at the back. Finding nothing, he turned to the side and drew back a grubby black velvet curtain, so grubby in fact that I had not noticed it before, and behind, on another shelf of taller jars and bottles, his plump hairy fist closed round the brass handle of an ornate glass jug with a hinged brass lid. He found from somewhere a small medicine bottle and wiped it with a dirty rag, then carefully poured from the jug into the bottle.

'Spikenard,' he said. 'That'll set you back thirty bob in old money.'

The oil was thick and heavy, a deep golden colour, deeper and heavier than extra virgin olive oil. And its odour filled the room.

It was a rank, oppressive, sweet-and-harsh smell, a smell which seemed to exult in its power, which wanted to crush the world as uncompromisingly and irredeemably as the roots of the nard had been crushed. What did it smell of? Honey and rum, like hair oil in old-fashioned barbers, but only to start with, then the harshness came to the fore and it was as metallic and viscous as four-stroke engine oil, but then beneath the machinery smell, the smell of grimy gun barrels still smoking and motorbike fumes on a summer's day, there were vegetable smells, rotting and yet flourishing, the amiable savour of parsnips and the weasel potency of asparagus urine and the darker insinuations of broad beans, and then coming fast behind were animal smells, lurking prowling pacing the cage, the smell of armpits and old men's bedrooms and club lavatories and menstrual moments and catteries and kennels too, because the animal smells were not reliably or consistently human – or was part of this part of the odour the smell of Clapp's shop and, come to that, of Clapp? – but then in turn beyond these thick noxious excretions and secretions there were fragrances: the fragrances of upland valleys in spring, so faint, so delicate, jonquils and violets and, later on, lilac blowsy-bouncing from breeze-blown boughs, inclining the observer to excesses of alliteration, and early roses, not the modern cultivars, but the swooning little paper-yellow flowers of pimpinellifolia and the fresh clean scent of the early damask roses. And it was these roses, in southern England the roses of mid-May, that stayed after the marshy stinks had faded. But I had only to pinch my nostrils to begin the whole chain all over again with the hair oil, and I found that I could not get through to the roses without passing through the stinks.

'That's a belter, that one. Some of the punters swear by it. Niffs like a nun's crotch if you ask me. Says so in the Bible too, St John chapter twelve, verse three.'

'Yes, I know,' I said.

'You know it all, darling. One pound fifty pee.'

All the way home, the perfume of the spikenard lounged in my nostrils and I started thinking about the brown shadow on Josie's face again and about how even your friends never told you every-thing, let alone the truth.

Ago

'To you it must just look like a wasteland ...'

'No, no, it doesn't at all.'

'There are no English lawns, no hedges.'

'It looks wonderful.'

'That is perhaps the sunset. But at night it is freezing. Caves are the only shelter. And there is nothing to eat except ...'

'Locusts and wild honey.'

'You Protestants know your Bible. But you do not take it as literally as my countrymen did, in the fourth century anyway. Then those mountaintops were full of monks, there were flocks of them, like goats.'

The mountains were turning to a grey violet in the quick-setting sun. He flung an arm in their direction. His oaten-creamy cassock sleeve fell away and she could see his muscled hairy arm up to the elbow and beyond. His fine eagle's features looked a little heavy in the fading of the day. She began to feel chilly and wished she had not thought the Shetland shawl too old-maidish to bring along with her to Father Halabi's – did one call it a rectory or a clergy house or what? Maronites, she knew, were Catholics of a sort, although different, but then she realised she did not know the word for the dwelling of a Catholic priest either. She took another sip of the strong sweet coffee from the little cup on the three-legged brass tray-table and turned to look again at the view, lubricating the coffee grounds on their way by rolling her tongue around her mouth. Father Halabi was murmuring now, she could hardly make out what he was saying (her hearing had been impaired since a childhood mastoid infection).

'The servants are asleep, the doors are shut, the muleteer rings his bells through empty streets –' his voice grew louder and took on a sarcastic tone – 'And we are snoring or scratching our heads, or lying on our beds meditating on endless deceits. But they –' fiercer, more passionate, almost too loud now – 'they on the mountainside, they gaze already upon the things of the Kingdom, they hold converse with groves and mountains and springs, their work is Adam's work in paradise. You have heard of St John Chrysostom, John Golden Mouth?'

'Oh yes, we say a prayer of his in our church: Almighty God who dost promise that when two or three are gathered together in thy Name.'

'That is a suitable prayer for Protestants. I am sorry, I did not mean to be rude. He is a hero of mine, he was the greatest preacher of his age, his spirituality, his intensity, his eloquence – there was no one like him. But I cannot agree with his views on marriage.'

'He was against it?' Beatha enquired.

'He believed that the world was fully populated already.'

'But surely –'

'Oh, like St Paul, he believed that it was at least better to marry than to burn. The wild beast had to be tamed somehow. But virginity was better still, a great deal better.'

'And does your Church still believe that?'

'Some do, some don't. Come to the edge of the roof, Beatha – that is short for Beatrice, is it not?' He took her arm as she scrambled to her feet. Pins and needles were fizzing down the backs of her legs. They must have been sitting on the cushions for longer than she had realised. Time did not pass so quickly with Dr and Mrs McFadzean in the dim dark dining room at the Mission, and the little cakes Father Halabi had given her were so delicately flavoured, scented even, compared with the McFadzean Dundee cake. And Father Halabi, as he took her arm to lead her across the dusty flat roof to the white parapet, was he himself not faintly perfumed too, but not effeminately so, his fragrance was manly, herbal. The McFadzeans both smelled of toothpaste.

'I am Michel,' Father Halabi said, 'after the archangel.'

'Actually, Beatha's short for Elizabeth.'

'Ah, the mother of John the Baptist.'

'I don't think I'm very maternal,' and she felt herself blushing and was grateful for the twilight. People with freckles shouldn't blush, her mother said, and her mother with her pale ivory face was usually right about that kind of thing, just as she was right about people with frizzy hair being foolish to go out in the rain (although the dry air here was no help to frizzy hair either). Even at her worst hours at the McFadzeans – hours of tedium and homesickness – the last thing Beatha hoped for was to see her mother coming in through the heavy wooden door that led in from the narrow Street of the Tailors.

'There, aren't you glad you came?' Within the last five minutes, the mountains had turned to a plum purple and the gleam of the setting sun was heroic and golden. 'I could not let you leave our church without showing you a Maronite sunset.'

Her hesitations in coming had been personal rather than religious. The McFadzeans had encouraged her to accept the invitation. Being sensible people, they had reluctantly realised that they were unlikely to convert many Moslems. Their only success in that line after eight years had been Mohammed, now George, the odd-job boy at the Mission, who was an orphan with no family to speak of and whose reasons for converting were largely practical, since he received extra wages for cleaning the chapel. The only hope, and a fair enough hope, was to draw converts from other Christian churches. Friendly contacts with the Maronites, the Orthodox and half a dozen other churches were all worth taking up. 'It's a long way to come to convert a Papist,' said Dr McFadzean, 'but the Good Lord loves a detour.' Dr McFadzean had a turn of phrase. Beatha preferred him to his wife who had a harping way with a topic that wrung the life out of it. Yet Mrs McFadzean too had been eager that Beatha should go and take mint tea or, as it turned out, coffee with Father Halabi. It was only Beatha herself who felt that, even though the nineteenth century was over and women would soon be getting the vote back home (she had a lazy confidence in the inevitability of progress and took little interest in the struggle), she felt that it was not quite right here for an unaccompanied woman to pay a call of this sort. Christian Arabs were, after all, Arabs, but then she told herself not to be so silly (or so pringle, as her mother's family put it in their intolerable private language). Paying a call on one Maronite priest did not transform her into Lady Hester Stanhope. She was not shy exactly, but proud of being backward in coming forward.

Still, Father Halabi – Michel – was easy to talk to. He did not pluck at your sleeve like the Arabs in the street. Everything about him was casual, like an Englishman, except his English, which was stiff and needed practice.

'It is a treat for me to hear an English voice.'

'But you've known the McFadzeans for some time, haven't you, and the Andersons?'

'Presbyterian Scottish is not the same. It is too guttural, too much like Arabic, or Syriac. You have been to one of our services?'

'Not yet, I'm afraid.'

'I love our Syriac because it is so ancient, but I sometimes think I would prefer ...'

'A modern language?'

'I am a modern man, whether I like it or not.' An old woman shuffled in with an oil lamp. She turned up the wick and in its flaring blue-edged light he looked anything but modern.

'And why are you working in a Scottish Mission?'

'My mother was Scottish. I'm C. of E., of course, but it doesn't matter, we all rub along together.'

'You're lucky. We have not yet learnt to rub along. You know there were three hundred Christians massacred in this city only ten years ago, the women raped, the houses burnt.'

'Yes, it must have been terrible.'

'It might have been more terrible. The entire Christian population might have been wiped out. I think Mary Magdalen probably saved them.'

'Mary Magdalen?'

'When in doubt – and we are very often in doubt – we pray to Mary Magdalen. She had saved us many times before, in 1401, in 1273 –' He flung out a string of dates, too many for her to take in. 'Unfortunately, she does not always save all of us.'

'But why her?'

'You must know the story.'

'About her being a prostitute and repenting and wiping Jesus's feet.'

'Yes, that story. But there is a second instalment, our story, which is that after the Crucifixion she was so distressed that she wandered out into the desert, hardly conscious, not knowing what she was doing, and she was picked up by a camel train of rich merchants who naturally assumed, seeing her wandering about with her clothes loosened and her abandoned air, that she still was what she had originally been and treated her as such, passing her from merchant to merchant, and then when they reached their destination throwing her out into the street without a sou, and so, *bien sûr*, she did in fact become a prostitute again, she had very little alternative, so she went on until quite old and then she became sick and she dragged herself out into the desert to die and she went up into the hills and fell asleep under an olive tree. And when she woke up she prayed to Jesus and Jesus appeared to her and told her that that day she would be with Him in paradise and then he wiped, no washed – which is better?'

'Either is quite right,' Beatha said.

'Washed *her* feet with the precious ointment, the pot of spikenard – you remember from the Bible – and then she died. And they built a church on the site over her tomb, the Church of the Second Repentance. And every ten years, on her feast day they open the tomb and the fragrant oil is still seeping – you say seeping – from her feet as fresh as two thousand years ago. It is a charming miracle, don't you think?'

'Why do you look so sad about it?'

'Do I? I did not intend to. Perhaps because it is my responsibility.'

'The miracle?'

'We are responsible for the shrine. It is on my family's land, the other side of the mountains. I will take you there. It is very pretty, fertile country, not like here. There are vines, and olives and figs. It is beyond that round peak there, to the right.'

As he pointed to the velvety dark outline of the mountains, he seemed suddenly sunk in gloom. The more he described his ancestral paradise, the lower his spirits. She asked him whether he had brothers and sisters. He had an elder brother, a younger brother, three sisters and a widowed mother. All the sisters wanted to go to the American Mission College. He had been there and had been unhappy, he had made no friends.

'I can't imagine you making no friends,' she said, and blushed again and hoped that the oil lamp had blanched the blushing. But his eyes were not on her, and there was no flirting in his glum self-absorption.

'I suppose it was a shock to the system. We were not a sophisticated family like many of the Maronites. We were like country squires, very provincial.'

'Well, you certainly aren't provincial now.' Why was she being so pert? She could not understand herself. It must be something to do with his downcast eyes. She wanted to lift him, to cheer him up.

'You don't think so? I am just a façade.' And he looked up and smiled, a surprising chubby smile. He had stopped looking alarmingly handsome. The eagle look had gone from his face and, if he looked like any animal at all, it was now some amiable rodent, a chipmunk perhaps, or a vole. She had not noticed his front teeth before, they were rather long and very white.

'Oh, we all put up façades, don't we?' she said by way of comfort.

'You too? I don't believe it. I am sure you are solid all through.'

She thought that this sentiment might have been better put, but she had to admit that this was how she felt or –

'Yes, but more like a sponge, really. Everything soaks straight through and squeezes straight out again.'

'Sponges are beautiful objects. Our local sponges are famous, you know. The boys dive for them off the coast.'

'I'm an inland sponge then, I can't swim very well.'

'Nor can I.' And he laughed, but she didn't believe him. He bore no resemblance to the sort of man who couldn't swim, a class of person identifiable at a glance.

In bed that night, curled up on the little folding iron bedstead which Mrs McFadzean took with her when they went travelling to see the sights of the Holy Land (like the man sick of the palsy, Dr McFadzean jested, my wife takes up her bed and walks), Beatha thumbed through Murray's *Guide to Syria and Palestine*, but she could find no mention of the Church of the Second Repentance. Nor could she find the name of the Halabi village anywhere on the thick clothbacked contour map at the back. Had it all been a tease, or a dream, or both at once? The section on Inhabitants was not encouraging: 'An Arab always tells you that his house is yours, that he loves you with all his heart, would defend you with his life &c &c. This all sounds very pretty, but it will be just as well not to rely too much on it.' Michel had not been so fulsome, but some of the things he had said could be classified at least as &c &c, and perhaps she had been a little too credulous, or no, not credulous but friendly. And the guidebook (admittedly it was an old guidebook but not that old) was decidedly positive on this point: 'Any approach to undue familiarity should be immediately checked; the permission of such familiarity will be attributed by the Arab to weakness of character.' Mr Murray's recipe for dealing with dragomen and indeed all classes of Arab was 'unvarying courtesy, accompanied by an unvarying firmness' – was it proper for a guidebook to underline like that, it sounded so gushing. She wondered whether Mr Murray himself was the author of the guidebook – there was no other author mentioned on the title page. She had walked past Mr Murray's premises in Albemarle Street once, with her mother, and her mother had pointed out the brass plate and told her that 'my Murray' had been Byron's publisher, at which Beatha had remarked only that he must be getting very old, which for some reason annoyed her mother who was devoted to Byron's memory. Beatha had been properly educated, at a school for the daughters of indigent clergymen in Hertfordshire, and had been instructed to overlook the shortcomings of Byron's character and concentrate on the shortcomings of his verse.

It was cold in the attic room at the McFadzeans, and Beatha found herself shivering under the threadbare blankets which were striped like the blankets the horses wore in cold weather on the downs at home. The windowpane rattled in the light breeze, and the dogs barked in a desultory conversation across the city.

She could not sleep, but for the first time in the month she had been there she knew she was happy and hugged herself in her pretty sky-blue flannel nightdress. She felt even more excited than the first time she had walked (rather faster than everyone else) along the gently winding vaulted passages of the bazaar past the open stalls of the silversmiths hammering away on their dirty hobs and the carpenters carving their pieces of walnut and inlaying them with silver and mother-of-pearl for the wedding chests, and the shoemakers, some of them only small boys, stitching at the soft yellow slippers and the gondola-shaped red overshoes, and the heaps of spices in the spice market, red and yellow and a mysterious pale turquoise, and the fruit from the fertile valleys – the oranges and peaches and grapes and apricots and figs and prickly pears. Even after several visits, though, she was still nervous in the bazaar, afraid of betraying that lack of self-confidence which she did not need the guidebook to tell her how much the Arabs despised. When Mrs McFadzean sent her out to buy fruit for the Mission, she bargained in a listless, resentful fashion that annoyed the fruit-sellers, partly because she did not wish to seem like a gushing tourist. But it was only now that she felt she was beginning to travel properly and to be able to look back on her previous life from a distance.

She got to sleep by counting the dreary scenes she had escaped:

the crocodile to matins at St Margaret's Bushey, the family prayers in the holidays (reciting the Lord's Prayer with cook's bottom three inches from her nose), the family promenade along the Pine Walk up to the top pond after lunch on Sunday. It was odd that there she was in a mission, seeing that at home so much tedium was attached to religion, but then she had really come out here to relieve suffering rather than to spread the Gospel and it seemed suffering was only to be relieved by respectable persons if accompanied by a dose of religious instruction. Unfortunately, she soon discovered that the McFadzeans were not much interested in physical suffering, although Mrs McFadzean was a qualified nurse. Dr McFadzean (he was a doctor of divinity, not a real doctor) took particular delight in drawing her attention to medical complaints that they could do absolutely nothing about. You'll find, he said, quite a few cases of Aleppo Button in these parts. It starts as a wee red pimple, you won't notice it for a week or two, then it increases to the size of a sixpence, and for the next two or three months discharges a certain quantity of moisture, then forms a scab which falls off and leaves an indelible mark, nothing to be done about it, nothing at all, he concluded on a note of triumph. Dogs and cats get it too, he added, it is to be found the whole length of the valley of the Euphrates, up to and including Baghdad.

'In this air,' he said, fussing round her as she was packing for the trip the following Monday, 'the medicine chest is a mere honorary appendage, you can throw pills and potions to the winds. I would suggest only this little mixture of rhubarb and magnesia in case of diarrhoea. I have added a few drops of laudanum to allay the discomfort, although my wife does not approve. But of course prevention is better than cure, and a sensible diet is half the battle. So I have packed this wee hamper for you: some preserved meats, biscuits in air-tight tin cases, a few packets of macaroni and vermicelli, and two tins of Indian tea, the tea in the country is execrable. Since the water must always be boiled, in any case, one might as well refresh oneself with a good sergeant-major's brew.'

'Thank you very much,' she said as his plump white hands

packed the dismal items back into the battered wicker hamper. 'But will I need all that if I'm staying with the Halabis?'

'In the Levant, one should always travel prepared. You could perhaps make a present to your hosts of one or two of these articles, but the rest will keep and we shall be glad of them back at the Mission.' He closed the hamper with a triumphant snap and stood up with a satisfied grin on his face as though he had just finished eating a huge meal.

Outside in the narrow street, Michel was waiting with the horses. He stood between the two animals in his brown habit, motionless like the horses, only his brown eyes flickering. Beatha could hardly prevent herself from saying how like the horses he looked but she knew that wouldn't do and merely opened by remarking how punctual he was.

'You expect *us* to be late.'

'No, no, I didn't mean that.'

'I'm sure you didn't, but plenty of you do, the Americans even more than the English. An Arab can always startle an American by arriving exactly on time.'

'The virtue of punctuality is somewhat exaggerated,' Dr McFadzean opined. 'But perhaps I am of that opinion only because it is a virtue I don't possess' – which was true. Beatha had noticed his dazzling gift for lateness amounting almost to genius and all the more conspicuous in a character which otherwise incorporated most of the puritan virtues, or perhaps only appeared to. Once or twice, Beatha had come upon him daydreaming in his armchair or standing at the doorway staring vacantly up the street. When he realised that she had seen him, he would start into purposeful activity, picking up some devotional book or striding up the street in a businesslike fashion. But glazing over was what his pale watery eyes did best behind those thick glasses.

'You should come too, you and Mrs McFadzean,' Father Halabi said.

'Alas, we have work to do,' Dr McFadzean said with a mendacious melancholy.

'Another time perhaps.'

'Another time. May I wish you godspeed.'

He turned to go, and for the first time Beatha looked seriously at her horse, a broad-beamed low sort of animal, gingery roanish in colour with a sour look in its eyes. But it was the saddle that unnerved her, a grubby boxlike contraption with a cracked leather seat and pommels that were little more than wooden pegs with flannel wrapped round them, quite unlike the delicate curved pigskin pommels of her mother's side-saddle with their inside pads of doeskin so soft you could fancy you had a living animal between your knees.

'There,' said Michel, 'ladies saddle, *selle de dame.*' And, muttering a prayer to herself, she leant over the saddle and grasped the far edge of it and put her left foot into the crude square stirrup and sprang into the seat first time, to her gratified surprise, without the usual knocking of her hip, leant back, hooked her right knee over the pommel, adjusted her big-brimmed straw hat and sat proud, sniffing the smell of baking bread and dried dung and the cold air of the desert morning.

George alias Mohammed, acting chaperon, came skittering up the cobbles on his scabby old donkey and the party set off briskly to make the best of the morning with the cries of roosters rising above the barking of dogs and the occasional foghorn blast of a fractious camel. They rode out through the old Saracen gate, past the ruins of some ancient aqueduct. The smell of cooking smoke and dried dung gave way to the thinner fragrance of thyme and rosemary. Great blocks of masonry lay tumbled around in the thorn trees. Here and there a few white chalky stones had been borrowed to make a miserable low enclosure for livestock, but these compounds too had fallen into decay. Their track ran through a small marsh, half-dried up now, but with pale blue tiny irises and red and white anemones and miniature yellow tulips with red stripes not yet properly open, just like in her mother's spring border at home, only here natural and free-flowering in the tufts of grey-green marsh grass rising out of the mosaic of cracked mud.

'Just like the ones we have in the garden at home.'

'They came from here originally, those tulips.'

'Yes, I know.'

'The fathers of the Western church hated flowers. St Jerome and St Ambrose forbid flowers to be put on the tombs.'

'Forbade.'

'Of course, forbade. But here in the East we always love flowers. Your paradise is only the Persian word for a garden.'

Beyond the marsh, a huge white sarcophagus with figures, mostly effaced, carved on its sides lay cracked open with the trunk of an olive tree growing through it. Further in the olive grove, there were smaller tombs in the same white stone, all cracked open.

'Looting, massacres, earthquakes, wars, malaria. This is all that is left of the Garden of Eden.' He rode close at her side, but never so close that their legs touched. She noticed with relief that he seemed no more at his ease on a horse than she did. She wondered, though, whether the inside of his thighs were beginning to ache as badly as hers were just above the knee.

'I am not a horseman,' he said, answering her unspoken thoughts. 'My brother rides all day, he is the farmer. I am more sedentary.'

But jogging along on his sleepy bay horse with his feet sticking out of the dusty stirrups he looked easy enough. They turned off the main track to the right, uphill through a forest of thin, broken-branched pines. The horses' hoofs fell silent on the carpet of ancient pine needles, and the sun began to feel hot when it came through the trees. She took her straw hat off and tied her long paisley cotton scarf so that it covered the back of her neck and then she put her hat back on again. The ache spread further up her thighs and began to beat dully around her sitting-bone – or that was the name Captain Thwaite had used, perhaps the proper anatomical term was too improper. Riding astride couldn't be more uncomfortable than this, and if it was indelicate for women was it not also inconvenient for men? Where, after all, could they put their – such thoughts often came to her, she realised, when

96

she rode, which was not often.

'Arab women are allowed to ride astride, aren't they?'

'Yes, of course, it's easier, more logical. A leg either side of the horse helps you to stay on. See there, the hermit caves.' He pointed to an irregular row of black oval holes in the white lime-stone cliffs above them. 'They were let up and down by ladders, and then the ladders were taken away to remove the temptation.'

'The temptation to return to the city?'

'Yes, they were city dwellers, often of good family. On Sundays and festivals their relations would come out to see them and bring a picnic. And religious young men would come to discuss holy things with them. So they were not always alone. But they could see the lights of the city below them, perhaps could even hear the sounds of the revels.'

'That probably made them feel even more holy.'

'I'm not so sure. Some of the hermits had been wild young men themselves. The Bishop of Ephesus used to dance with naked girls on his shoulders. They appreciated pleasure, so they knew what they were abandoning.'

'Do you know what you are abandoning?'

'Oh, I'm not a hermit. Anyway in our church priests can marry and have children until they become bishops and even then some of the bishops are quite slow to put their wives away.'

'How nice. If my husband was a bishop, I hope he'd be slow.'

'He wouldn't dream of putting you away.'

'I expect he would. He'd probably become a bishop just to have an excuse.' She craned her neck to look through the trees at the caves high in the cliff face, but her horse began to munch the grass on the roadside and she had to pull at the worn old rein to get his head up. Beyond the trees the track twisted through a rocky pass with falls of dazzling white scree poured across the road like giant's sugar. The sun was high and hot and the jagged peaks just above them were black against the fierce midday light. They stopped at a muddy little pond to let the horses drink, and Beatha found that she was short of breath and her heart was bobbing against her ribs.

'You need a rest and so do I,' Michel said. They sat side by side on a long slab of stone. Michel pulled out of his robe a little white book with a gold cross on it and began reading out of it, muttering the words to himself. She was startled. Her urbane companion had suddenly turned into a priest, no, worse than that, into a primitive priest, one who moved his lips as he read.

'Oh, I'm sorry,' he said. 'It's become an automatic habit. We were taught it at the *séminaire*.'

'Seminary,' she said severely. 'It's perfectly all right.'

'We always move our lips when we read, you know, to absorb. We think silent reading is superficial. It is quite a modern invention, you know.'

'Is it?' she said, unsure whether he was joking.

'So we read rather slowly. I'm sure you have read many more books than I have.'

'I'm sure I haven't. We don't have all that many books in our house and practically no new ones.'

'You think only new books are worth reading?'

'No, it's just that the old books are all, well, inherited, in beautiful leather bindings, but you wouldn't actually want to read most of them.'

'Ah, a gentleman's library.'

'Just a library,' Beatha said. The beginnings of a headache were grouping behind her right eye, but her heart had stopped palpitating, and she preferred it when they set off again. For a quarter of an hour – it seemed longer – they rode deep in the shadow of the jagged peaks, the shadow interrupted only now and then by a furtive ray of the sun beyond the pass. The sudden chill depressed her. What was she doing here, with this strange Arab with long teeth dressed as a priest? It was all a charade and a sinister one too – or not a charade exactly, there might be some awful purpose behind it, not an ambush by brigands, that she had been led to believe was an ordinary hazard of travel, but something less material, more subtly desolating. Desolate in the desert, she repeated to herself, and shifted her aching bones in the saddle. Something on the tip of her nose began to itch. The beginnings of an outbreak of Aleppo Button? But it was only a persistent horsefly. She brushed it away and kicked her horse to make it scramble up the path, which had become steep and narrow. Desolate in the defile in the desert, she muttered.

Then she could see the sun splashing the path ahead, and the jagged peaks which had seemed so dark and terrible became dear little dinosaur's teeth glittering pink and gold and white in the dazzling noonlight. And the sinister figure ahead of her turned round in his saddle with the chubby grin of a schoolboy.

'Look, we have come through, that was the water's head.'

'Watershed,' she could not help saying.

'You should be a geography teacher.'

'I was quite good at geography.'

'Well down there, you see our chief geographical glory: the cedars.'

She squinted into the sun but could see only a few dark specks on the bare mountain slopes below.

'They are not as large as the famous cedars above Kadisha. So many have been cut down.'

Beatha had already heard this from the McFadzeans. If I may adopt the words of Ezekiel it is not only the Lord who breaketh the cedars of Lebanon, our Moslem friends have been hard at work too, Dr McFadzean had jested. She was prepared to be disappointed. Yet she was still saddened as they rode through the little patch of stunted and broken trees. Their lower branches had been lopped off for firewood. And between the trees there were black rings where the fires had been. Only one or two of the trees had achieved the majestic height and girth of the cedar on the lawn at home with the criss-cross wooden seat built round it, where they had tea and cucumber sandwiches in the shade when it was hot. As a girl, she used to lie on her back and look up at the great feathery branches spreading over her so huge and delicate. And from her bedroom window she would look down on the same feathery frosty blue-green branches and dream of lying on them and being gently swung about in the light south-westerly breeze. She was glad when they came out on to the bare mountainside and began trotting downhill towards the beginnings of the terraces of vines and mulberries and the rich green valley beneath where there were white buildings blinking in the sun and tall full-bosomed cypresses and trees with bright yellow-green leaves fanning out in the shape of parasols. Soon she could make out some fubsy (another of her mother's family epithets) little white domes sitting in a grove of silvery olives.

'There, the Church of the Second Repentance,' Michel said. No, after all, there was nothing sinister about the experience. On the contrary, this was a sort of heaven, and as Michel's little round mother and his three plump sisters crowded round her in the courtyard, and she slipped her leg over the wooden pommel and slid limply to the ground, she felt giddy weak and in paradise.

The water from the brass ewer was cold and delicious on her face and neck. The coffee was hot and sweet, and she took the little cakes of nut and honey as often as she was offered them and the little confections of mint and yogurt too. They could speak to her only in French, a rather hard guttural sort of French not like her drawly diphthongy English French, but she thought their conversation enchanting. Their long white teeth flashed welcome and encouragement at her.

'*Vous chantez?*'

'*Chantez?*'

'*Nous aimons bien les chansons françaises.*'

'*Ah oui.*'

'*Les chansons françaises sont beaucoup mieux que les chansons arabes. Venez, venez.*' And they pulled her into the long dark sitting room where there was, to her amazement, a grand piano and all around it some heavy furniture which might have come straight from Mr Maple's shop in the Tottenham Court Road: a big sofa with French scrolls and curlicues on the arms and the back and high-backed armchairs to match, and a canterbury filled with sheets of music just as they had at home.

'*Tout ça vient de Paris,*' the sisters said with pride. '*Et le piano est vraiment allemand, de Berline, tout à fait nouveau.*' So it was, black and gleaming and huge, with Blüthner and Co, Berlin, in old gothic

100

script, and in a trance she sat down at it, her legs as weak as over-cooked vermicelli, and the sisters began thrusting pieces of music into the rack.

'*Vous aimez Debussy? Très moderne, mais charmant. Jouez, jouez.*'

And Beatha, who was a poor sight-reader, launched into the piece with Michel's sisters crowding around her, their full dark hair brushing against her damp sandy frizz. And they sang with a harsh twang which suited the music (at any rate, it was not like the way they sang Debussy at the Wigmore Hall, when she and her mother went up for the Tuesday matinee concerts). Pausing for breath, while the sisters' hands fought to turn the page, she saw Michel at the side of the piano. He had changed into loose cotton trousers and a white shirt.

'Debussy is too complicated for me. I like a simple love song. You know *Manon*?'

He began to sing, unaccompanied, while the sisters scrabbled in the canterbury to find the music.

'Ah! Fuyez, douce image à mon âme trop chère,
Respectez un repos cruellement gagné . . .'

Beatha found she could no longer sit upright on the piano stool. Her spine began to droop, and she thought of her mother saying oh Beatha no banana backs in this house, if you please. And then the feeling melted from her legs too and she knew in the splitting of a second that what she was about to do could only be described as swooning, and, what was worse, swooning not in the privacy of her room or after eating something that disagreed with her but swooning while a priest was singing a love song, not to her per-haps, but not away from her either. And what a priest, no pale curate with an adam's apple bigger than his chin (a wishbone, in family parlance), but a scion of the most mysterious and ancient of churches, the guardian of a deplorable miracle, one who con-ducted the mass in the very language that Our Lord actually spoke, or so she thought, the precise details were hazy in her mind, but then everything in her mind was hazy. And it was not as if he sang especially well, either. The harshness which in his sisters was teased and tamed by a girlish tremolo came through strong and straight, it was nearly a bark – yet perhaps even so, a liquid sort of bark, a bark that dogs might howl at the moon. Not musical, though, anything but. Even in her hazy state, she noted that now and then he was a little flat. Well, perhaps that was better. If he had sung like a nightingale, she was sure she would keel over immediately, instead of just keeping her balance on the little hard piano stool. Yet even as she was beginning to be proud of not toppling, she toppled slow and limp into the round brown arms of Michel's sisters. That was bad enough, terrible in fact, but worse still was when Michel pushed between the girls, with a rough anxiety, and took her in his arms, clasping his arms round under her bosom, to be precise, and dragged her to the Maple's sofa, where she lay paper white and palpitating with only a sickening lurching feeling of shame preventing her from losing consciousness. But lose consciousness she did, for two or three minutes anyway, and the last thing she remembered was the sound of her father's voice in the next room saying to her mother, 'Beatha a missionary? You know I don't care for practical jokes, Winnie.' Or no, that was not quite the last thing. The last thing was Michel's worried brown eyes and his long white teeth just butting over his lower lip (she had not noticed they did that). He looked like a rat in trouble, a kindly rat.

Afterwards, when she had washed and taken off her riding clothes and rested and floated off without effort into the sweetest sleep ever slept, the incident was gone over and ground down into the minutest particulars, the apologies repeated sometimes singly, sometimes in chorus, the words *très, très fatiguée* and *regrette beaucoup, beaucoup* coming back again and again. The arrival of Michel's elder brother, Antoine, and his wife, a thin neat woman with heavy eyebrows, only provoked a reprise with the brother rebuking them all for their thoughtlessness and regretting that he had ever bought *ce sacré piano*. He was shorter and stockier, a coarser version of his brother, his French more uncertain, his manner more uneasy. The *politesses* required by the occasion were a strain on them, and the relief when he was called away again to the farm so obvious as to cancel out the *politesses*.

'My brother doesn't like society,' Michel said. He was walking her across to the Church of the Second Repentance.

'Well, I don't care for it much either.'

'I don't mean high society, I mean the society of people. He is a *solitaire*. If he had a religious vocation, he would be a hermit. My younger brother you would like, he is away in the city, making money, we hope. Ah, the mass has already started.'

'Aren't you conducting it?'

He looked at her, surprised. 'No, no, of course not. I am not yet a full priest.'

'So I shouldn't call you Father?'

'Certainly not. Anyway, you haven't.'

'I don't like calling people by their names. But I thought of you as *mon père*.'

'I take that as a compliment to my serious behaviour.'

The church had an ugly modern façade with gothicky arrow slits which made it look like a dirty comb. From the paved court-yard in front of it, she could not see the sweet old domes, those creamy chubby comforting eggtops glimpsed as they were com-ing down the hill. Instead, there was a modern spire, graceless,with a broken-off unfinished look to it. Inside, the low chanting grew louder and she quickened her step.

'You do not need to hurry, it is not like an English service.'

He led her through the low pointed arch, so low she had to duck and felt like Alice after taking the growth mixture. Inside, the dark air was laden with incense and the drowsy chanting of the dozen umbrous shapes in the dusty aisle. Michel ushered her to a couple of rickety rush-seated chairs on the far side next to a large plain tomb of crumbling white stone. He pointed at it: the tomb of St Mary Magdalen. Really? she said with a shiver. Don't be alarmed, he said, it won't leak. At first she thought she hadn't heard properly – his chair was scraping on the uneven paving stones – and then she was annoyed, feeling a Protestant revulsion against this easy intimacy with the miraculous. I was just shiver-ing because of the cold, she said. I'm sorry, he said, I didn't mean

103

to shock you – I'm sure you did, she muttered back. No, no, I promise, he said and then fell to praying.

She sat rigid on the rickety little chair, a model of Anglican deportment now. The chanting came only dimly to her ears, an undulating murmur, sometimes reverent, even grovelling, and then rising to a sharper, shrill questioning as though coming gradually to an awareness of disappointment, a sense of covenants unkept, and then dying again to a sad resignation. What is it like, this Syriac mass? she could hear her father ask (he always wanted to know what things were like). Is it a beautiful language? But she no longer could tell the difference between beautiful and ugly, at least not here. In England one could always tell. What a pretty house, her father would exclaim as the dogcart rattled down the back lanes, and her mother would say that the so-and-sos had just moved in or moved out of it. But here, ugly seemed just as good as beautiful, there was no dividing line, and the voice of the priest, which was as sharp as a knife on the grindstone of the old Irishman in the green apron who used to come out from Guildford once a month, was also harmonious and soothing.

It was right in the middle of this tangled musing that she became aware that he had touched her hand with his. It was certainly not a clasp, somewhere midway between a stroke and a pat, a reassuring contact, the kind you might give to a fretful horse or an elderly relation who was worried about missing a train. But there was affection in it too, she thought, a comradely sort of affection perhaps. And then she admitted to herself, which she had not admitted at the time, how glad she had been to hear that he was not yet a full priest, although even if he had been, she was glad too that the Eastern churches took a more sensible view of celibacy, not quite like the C. of E. perhaps, but sensible.

Through the incense-throttled gloom she could just see the priest performing what she now knew enough to recognise as the Elevation of the Host (as part of her undercover missionary work, she had attended all sorts of masses, Greek, Roman, Nestorian, although this was her first Maronite), and in that moment of humble soaring, that wonderful bridge between the human and

104

the divine, what she heard was the voice of her mother saying they were holding hands and you know I can't stand goony people – it was a voice of mock despair rather than dislike and Beatha could not remember who her mother had been talking about, the Whittingstalls possibly, for they had been married only last summer, but even in the mockery there lay a generation or two of learning not to show one's feelings by word and particularly not by gesture. There was something serious there to revolt against and in the dusty dark of the Church of the Second Repentance Beatha revolted. Deliberately, after another thirty seconds or so, to avoid any possibility of its being an accidental prolonging of his gesture, she responded with a warm but tentative dabble of her fingers upon his, the little glancing, flickering touch she used to test the temperature of bathwater. And he smiled at her and it is not too much to say that from this moment their fate was sealed.

She certainly did not shrink from using the word fate to herself. Their paths had, well, I would rather not use such phrases, but their paths had crossed. That the crossing had been confirmed by the interlacing of hands on holy ground, the holiest imaginable, seemed to her an occasion for joy rather than embarrassment. Where better, after all, for he soon confided to her that he was quite a frequent attender at Protestant services in the city. He had in fact seen her at Dr McFadzean's, but it was not surprising if she had not seen him because he sat at the back and wore Western clothes.

'But why do you go?'

'I like the simplicity, the directness of the approach to God. In our Eastern churches we are too encrusted with ritual.' She did not at that moment – although she did so later – confide that the encrustations were what she liked best. This submitting oneself to the ceremonial mediation of the Church seemed to her more genuinely humble than Dr McFadzean's extravagant self-abasement before his Maker. 'The mumbling, the parrot-like repetitions, there is no feeling in them.' His long vole's teeth flashed with feeling. The silvered olives brushed by the mountain breeze seemed to quiver with it. Feeling was everywhere, glistening on her own damp pale skin, winking on the creamy eggtop domes below them. She could have stayed there for ever, not to prolong that moment – such visitations of happiness could only be brief – but to live in the hope of the moment's being repeated. The Church of the Second Repentance – she had become enchanted by the phrase, chanted it to herself. There surely lay the greatness of the faith they both shared, in its eternally recurring possibility of being saved. Round and round it would come, again and again, it was never too late.

She borrowed a long dark dress from the tallest of the sisters, Anna, and a scarf to go with it. Anna showed her how to wrap it round, and she put on the sandals they all wore and slopped happily round the courtyard with its delicate little wooden arches. Sometimes it seemed like a dusty old farmyard you might see in France or Italy. Then at other times when the sunlight was on the crumbly plaster and the painted wooden pillars, it was more like an Eastern palace.

'We have changed places.' Michel was wearing loose cotton trousers and a tweed Norfolk jacket and a silk scarf plumped out at his throat like the one Teddy Whittingstall wore when he came to play tennis, or sticky as they still called it (her mother had been a pioneer of the game, had once partnered Major Wingfield in a mixed doubles on the lawns at Roehampton). Michel always looked smaller when he wore European dress and she felt like saying she wished he wouldn't but knew it would be impertinent even now that they were such friends. They were exactly the same height, five foot seven inches. Madame Halabi and the three sisters were much smaller. When they sat together on the sofa chattering and laughing, they bundled as close together as kittens. And kittens was how she thought of them until she realised quite soon that they were better educated than she was and also were unashamed of showing it. Anna was studying *Phèdre* for her baccalaureat at the French College, and they talked about the play as though it was happening in the next-door village and Racine was a jumped-up local schoolteacher.

'*Il ne connaît pas les femmes, ce M. Racine.*'

'*Il n'avait pas de femme lui-même.*'

'*Mais tout de même, il savait écrire.*'

'*Oui bien sûr, mais écrire ... pfui ...*' Madame Halabi held up her surprisingly dainty fingers in a gesture of disdain for the writer's life. She was proud of her fingers, and her daughters liked to flatter her.

'*Elle a des fines attaches, tellement élégantes. Regardez ses pieds,*' and the smallest daughter, Mimi, the middle one, would remove her mother's sandals and show off the delicate toes. '*On dirait une Botticelli, n'est-ce pas?*' Madame Halabi clucked her delight as she groped, with no great haste, for the little gold sandals under the Maple's sofa. She had views on literature; she preferred Lamartine to Victor Hugo (*il parle trop fort*), but French poets were dry and feeble compared with Arab poetry, which she could quote at some length. And Beatha found this, too, entrancing, the clucking and warbling of this birdsong, harsh and liquid at the same time, interrupted by snatches of uncertain French, as Madame Halabi tried to keep her abreast:

'*Et maintenant le poète dit que son amant est comme un perdreau –*'

'*Comme un ... ?*'

'*Oui, parce que ...*'

With Michel the conversation was more political and historical, about the Arabs and the protecting powers, their mutual misunderstandings, the Arab resentment, the condescension of the French and the British, the unnerving intrusion of the Germans (on the undesirability of *that* they could all agree). She was used to such talk. The McFadzeans and their visitors, Arab and European alike, talked of little else, sometimes hesitantly and tactfully, rather too often with a dogmatic lack of sensitivity that made her wince. But at least they seemed to agree that sooner or later the Arabs would be dragged into the modern world. One mourned the passing of the old world, the camels and the minarets, of course one did (though not the passing of the harem and the more primitive parts of Islamic law), but progress was progress. Michel's view was different, although she did not immediately grasp how it was different.

'Of course,' she started off feeling her way, 'it's sad, I love it here, I can't bear to think of it changing.'

'There's no of course about it. Whenever an English person says of course, I smell a rat.'

'Well it *is* sad.'

'No, it is not. First of all, because there is no sign that the Arab will change at all.'

'But the railways and so on . . .' she began, and then faded.

'Oh, the railway comes, but the Arab simply gets on it and gets off it without changing his mind one iota. And the same with any other modern invention. Most of them aren't modern anyway. Banks, for example. The Babylonians were sophisticated bankers when you were running around naked in the forests.'

'You sound like an old colonial. You can't change Johnny Turk.'

'Your old colonials were extremely wise. They had spent a whole life living with these peculiar tribes. They knew them *au fond*.'

'Nonsense, they're ridiculous people, hopelessly bigoted. When they come home to retire, they are figures of fun. They talk in such clichés.'

'I didn't say they knew anything about their own country. But us they know.'

She looked in amazement at his neat small figure in his tweed jacket. His irritation made him look dark and severe. But she was irritated too.

'I thought most young Arabs were really eager to learn European ways.'

'I am, but I am not most young Arabs. They are only interested in steam engines and phonographs.'

'What's wrong with that?'

'What's wrong is that you will think they have all become like little Englishmen just because they have become *enragé* for your mechanical toys. That is what will make conflict. That is the tragedy, not that they – we will change but that we won't. It's as foolish as being sentimental about camels. There's nothing poignant about camels. They're vicious beasts.'

108

It was her last day, he had promised to take her for a last walk, but he seemed to have forgotten. All afternoon he was in a foul temper, stamping about the far side of the courtyard with short schoolmasterly steps. As the sun began to dip below the hill, she was going up to him to issue a tart reminder, when his elder brother came in dusty and tired and Michel took him by the arm as though arresting a criminal. Antoine shook off Michel's grip and barked back at him with fierce bull-like movements of his head. She could not hear what he was saying, and then they both began to talk much quieter so that she could not even hear the sound of their voices. Then Antoine led his brother into the little dark room behind the sitting room, an office full of papers, which she had scarcely glanced into. Now, sitting out under the pillars, she could hear the sound of their voices again but not what they were saying. In the whole week she had been there, she had not heard the brothers exchange more than half-a-dozen words. Michel had talked twice as much to George alias Mohammed, who was making himself useful on the farm and came in each evening with his donkey's paniers laden with brushwood and a big smile on his raw lips.

The argument or negotiation, for as the talk went on into the twilight the tone of it sounded more reasonable as though details of some grand arrangement were being worked out, cast the whole house into silence. The sisters seemed awed. Madame Halabi, usually darting about with swift little tittups of her Botticelli feet, was nowhere to be seen. *Elle a mal à la tête*, Anna said, but then added a *peut-être* which suggested this was a guess. Beatha wished she herself was somewhere else. She was out of place not because the scene was alien to her. On the contrary, she thought she recognised all too well the tremble in the air. The little vibrations of anxiety and disappointment recalled the night her brother had told his parents he wasn't going into hop-broking but was joining the army, or the moment after lunch on a steamy July day when her sister had announced that she was going to marry, not as expected Teddy Whittingstall but his younger brother Ronnie, who had a harelip and was considered odd (Teddy was rumoured to drink but at least you knew where you were with him).

And she herself was agitated, *nerveux* as Michel's sisters put it, for, indelibly English though she was, she had never troubled to hide annoyance. Beatha, her mother would say, I wish you'd learn to bottle. She was scornful of women who never let their feelings show because their places depended on it: governesses, parlour-maids, shopgirls. This scorn, Beatha persuaded herself, was not snobbish, because she sincerely hoped that in the same position she would not kowtow. And so, although she owed the Halabis so much, she did tell Mimi that it was *agaçant* that Michel should spend her last day talking business when he had promised to take her up the hill for one final look across that enchanted valley. The blossom was over and the vines were bright grapy green and the trees along the shingly river below were a bushy silvery meander and here she was waiting all day while they argued.

Then the two brothers came out on to the loggia where Beatha was sitting with the girls in the dusty wicker chairs.

'*Où est maman?*'

'*Dans sa chambre.*'

'*Vas chercher.*' And Mimi rose with mock servility to carry out Antoine's order. Madame Halabi appeared in no time, as though she had been waiting just inside the green door at the end of the loggia rather than in her room at the end of the long flagged bed-room passage. She had been crying, damp sootblack smudges under her eyes.

'*Enfin, maman,*' Michel began. He spoke nervously, close to a gabble, beginning almost every sentence with an *enfin*, it seemed. The speech sounded prepared, yet none the less agonised for that. *Maman* knew, they all knew what he had been thinking about for a long time. He was sorry he had distressed them by subjecting them to such a long agony. Perhaps it would have been better if he had just come home one day and said, *Enfin maman, je deviens protestant*.

Ah, so *that* was it and she could see them all looking at her. Was it just to see how she would take the news which they had all been dreading for months? Or did they blame her for this terrible conversion – no, they couldn't, it had been a long time brewing, *enfin* he said and *enfin* must mean months rather than days, long before he had met her. But yes they could, certainly they could, because if she hadn't come along it might have been only a passing fad, like wearing tweed jackets and silk paisley cravats, something he would grow out of and return a wise and seasoned priest to his own people. She wished, desperately wished that Michel had chosen to talk in Arabic and not in French so that they could all understand. She, after all, did not need to understand, did not wish to understand. Michel's religious views were nothing to her, they – and then she remembered with a terrible lurch in her stomach, as though George alias Mohammed's donkey had kicked her, that this was what she was here for, this was her secret mission, so secret she managed to conceal it from herself most of the time. She had made a convert.

Her entire body trembled with terror as she grasped that there was no way out of the responsibility. The more she said it was nothing absolutely nothing to do with her, the more Dr McFadzean would murmur in that peculiar way in which he ladled out compliments as though he was paying them to himself, You're too modest, lassie, you don't know your own powers of persuasion. She could imagine the gossip in the tiny Protestant community of the region. A Maronite priest snatched from the bosom of his family – and after only a week!

Useless to say what she really felt, which was that if anyone going to convert she thought it should have been her because for the first time in her life she had met the true spirit of what ought to have been her faith, if she had possessed one in any heartwhole sense. But she did not know how to say such a thing in English, let alone in French, and so what she said with a full awful consciousness of it's being inadequate, feeble and English was, '*Je suis désolée.*'

'*Désolée.*' Madame Halabi inflicted a ferocious sonority upon the word, transforming Beatha's weak and cowering adjective into a majestic ejaculation brimming with tragic scorn. It was the same tone in which she read Racinian alexandrines aloud to them, the same too as the melancholy '*Vide!*' she uttered after she peered into the empty couscous bowl, but here elevated to an even higher ledge of Parnassus (the Parnassiens were her favourite modern poets, but they were not accorded the same grand sonority).

Beatha sat with head bowed while Madame Halabi, slowly at first but gathering speed, began the accusations which she knew would be heaped on her. At that moment, she wished that Madame Halabi had known how to bottle. Silent rancour, however bitter, would have been preferable to this terrible avalanche. First of all, she had been a guest, a cherished guest, perhaps she had not been long enough among Arabs to know how seriously they took the obligations of hosts and guests, almost as seriously as they took the ancient traditions of their faith. It might seem odd to the all-conquering English, but they were proud of speaking the tongue of *notre seigneur*.

'*Maman, maman,*' the daughters wailed, but to no avail. *Malgré son norfolk*, Michel was an innocent. In spite of his perfect English, he was a naif, he knew nothing of the world. Perhaps Beatha was not to blame, she had simply spoken to him with the freedom of an English miss. *Sans doute* he had misunderstood her. As for Beatha herself, she was not a beauty, she looked fit for the convent, but Michel knew little of women. For him she represented the allure of the strange.

'*Maman,* shut up.'

'*Ah, il me faut* shut up, *quel affreux mots, jamais mère n'a entendu de tels reproches de la part de son propre fils.*' The daughters were sobbing now and so was Beatha, although with one reserved part of her mind she could not help admiring Madame Halabi's tirade, while longing for it to be over.

'*Je dois partir, maintenant, madame,*' she said between sobs.

'*Oui, oui, bien sûr, mademoiselle, il vous faut partir tout de suite avant que vous nous apportez encore des malheurs funestes.*'

Michel rushed forward and shook his mother by the shoulders, then spoke to her savagely in Arabic. The two of them shouted at

112

the same time for what seemed like hours. Finally, Madame Halabi agreed to be led away to her room by her daughters.

'We'll leave in the morning,' he said. He was still shaking with rage.

'You don't need to come. I'm sure George will look after me.'

'Of course I'm coming. If I didn't escort you, it would look as if you were to blame. *Maman* must learn that I make my own decisions for myself. I would have become a Protestant if I had never met you.'

'I know that, of course,' Beatha said, although not without a flicker of disappointment.

'But I would be grateful, very grateful, if you would help me through the next few months. They will not be easy.'

'I will do everything I can, but you must realise I don't really know much about religion, I mean about theology and so on.'

'It's not theological advice I need, I've had plenty of that already. No, it's just friendship pure and simple.'

'Oh you've got *that*,' she exclaimed.

'Well, then I am happy, and I hope you are too. Don't worry about her –' the sound of sobbing grew louder beyond the green door – 'she'll reconcile herself. She is not as bigoted as she pretends, she is not even very devout. But she loves a grand scene.'

'She did seem genuinely upset.'

'What is genuinely? Her heart is genuinely broken, tomorrow it will be genuinely repaired.'

It was a cold grey morning when they left. Only the girls came out to say goodbye. Madame Halabi kept to her room. The brother and sister-in-law were not to be seen either. The warmth of the girls' hugs brought Beatha very close to tears again (never, she thought, had she cried so much in a single week and decided never to cry so much in future if she could help it).

They plodded up the track to the way over the mountains. The only cheerful member of the party was George alias Mohammed who had enjoyed his life on the farm but was now looking forward to the city again. Beatha felt too washed out to break into Michel's gloomy brooding. Then the horse stumbled crossing a dry shingly ford and gave her a nasty jolt which provoked her into questioning him.

'Why, would you mind me asking, why did your brother mind so much? Is he very religious or is it something to do with family honour?'

'Not everything in the Arab world is a matter of honour, and in any case he isn't especially religious, although he is rather conventional. No, the trouble is that Antoine is lazy.'

'But he seems to be working all the time.'

'Exactly. And he doesn't want to have to do any extra work. He expected me to ... look after the shrine.'

'But there is the abbot and those three sweet old monks.'

'There are other duties.'

'What other duties?'

'You ask too many questions.'

'Oh, there's a secret?'

'Use your imagination, if you have any.'

She was jolted. He had never been rude before. On the other hand, answering back came easily to her.

'Didn't you know, English girls don't have any imagination. They have to be told everything because they are so dense.'

'All right then. I shall please your hard little Protestant heart by confirming your worst suspicions. We have, as I told you, the hereditary responsibility for looking after the shrine. And that responsibility includes the duty to look after the ceremony of the miracle because it is said – without any historical evidence – that one of our ancestors was a witness of the first time the miracle occurred. It is a task that is passed on to one member of each generation and my father passed it on to me just before he died because he saw I was so pious.'

'He'd be turning in his grave now, I suppose.'

'I don't think so. He was a cynical man, but he believed in tradition, or rather it amused him.'

'So what do you ...'

'Every ten years, on St Mary Magdalen's feast day, there is a great high mass celebrated with the bishop present, and at the end

114

of the mass, the bishop proceeds to the tomb and takes out the little stone plug at the far end of the tomb where the saint's feet
would be and out comes a little trickle of spikenard oil, and then
a little more, and the whole church is filled with the fragrance and
the bishop gathers up all the oil in a silver basin and he blesses the
sick and the injured, dipping his finger in the oil and making the
sign of the Cross on their foreheads or on their feet, naturally the
miracle is especially efficacious for ailments of the feet. It is,'
Michel concluded with a sigh, 'a very beautiful ceremony. It never
fails to move me.'

'And someone has to ...'

'Make sure that the oil flows at the right time and in the right
quantity. It is not as easy as it sounds. The oil must not come out
all at once, that would be too crude. On the other hand, if it is
too slow and sticky, it is a bad omen for the harvest. There are
angles to be calculated and even then it takes practice.'

'And your brother doesn't want to.'

'He is clumsy and afraid of failure. I expect he will get the
abbot to take it on. That will be the end of a proud tradition. We
used to sign ourselves with this grand title, Michaelus Liquidator,
Antonius Liquidator, and so on. Strictly speaking, it should have
been Liquefactor, but we Maronites were never much good at
Latin. Anyway, the title was rather nearer the mark than it was
intended.'

'You must be sad to be leaving all that.'

'*All that*.' He turned to look at her, his anger moderated only
by his surprise. 'But all that is precisely why I am leaving, to get
away from all this horrible superstition and deceit, these vile
devices to keep the peasants in their state of idiocy. I hated being
liquidator the only time I have had to do it so far, sneaking into
church at night with my bag of tricks: the crowbar for the lid of
the tomb, and the little wooden funnel and the airtight container
so that none of the fragrance escapes until it is time to fill the
church with that appalling smell. I felt like a thief. I *was* a thief,
thieving their minds from them.'

'Do you need to be quite so melodramatic? It's only a tradition, isn't it? Probably three-quarters of the congregation don't believe in the miracle, not really in their heart of hearts.'

'That is irrelevant. It is the liquidator's task to make them believe, to convince them that the supernatural is a daily possibility, that this physical world is not the only reality. And the way he does it is by the crudest mechanical trick. What could be a more repulsive, unholy enterprise? Whether or not he succeeds in the enterprise is unimportant.'

He stopped and he seemed purged by his outburst and an affable mood came over him. They were beyond the cedars now and over the pass and through the dark winding gorge and back in the dappled sunlight of the pines. Below them they could see the great plain and the sun white and bright on the city.

'I feel like a sightseer returning from a visit to the desert fathers,' she dared to say.

'To the fleshpots of the city.' He smiled his friendly vole's smile and began to sing *Ah! Fuyez, douce image.*

'Is that song quite suitable for a priest to sing?'

'I sang it when I was a Maronite, I shall sing it now I am a Protestant, or does your church object to *Manon*?'

'It objects to lots of things. Probably it objects to *Manon*.'

'Well so do I, it is sentimental nonsense.'

They were overtaking carts laden with green vegetables. The donkeys brayed as they saw George's donkey and brayed again at the horses. The cart drivers caught a few splashes of Michel's good humour and waved at them or conceded a toothless grin.

'Was there, when you opened the lid, was there a skeleton? I've been meaning to ask?'

'A what?' He was twenty yards ahead of her now. Either he or the horse had caught wind of the city.

'A skeleton?' Her voice rang out in the clear morning air, absurdly languid.

'Oh yes, I expect so, but it is in a stiff gravecloth and I do not stop to look. I have seen plenty of skeletons. The hills are full of them, old battles, not so old massacres.'

'Really?' She wondered if he was teasing. 'Doesn't anyone tidy them away?'

'This is not a tidy country. Anyway, even in England, when they dig up an ancient fort, don't they find bones?' And she remembered, had it been in the *Illustrated London News*, sepia photographs of excavations somewhere in Dorset, Maiden Castle perhaps, showing the pygmy defenders of the fort crouched in their shallow chalk graves with dreadful wounds still decipherable on their skulls.

They rode through the crumbly mud gate with the remains of the classical arch behind it and down the narrow street of the shoemakers, the horses' hoofs clip-clopping out of time with the shoemakers' hammers and the smell of the leather hung up on racks for tanning sharp in their nostrils after the comely aroma of the thyme and rosemary out in the country. And a great sweet weariness overcame her and she wondered if she was going to repeat her swoon on the return. Through her weariness, she became only dimly aware of Michel's agitation.

'I think I had better leave you and George here. I cannot endure Dr McFadzean's bonhomie. When my affairs are a little bit arranged, I shall come and call.'

'Oh, well, goodbye then, and thank you,' was as much as she could manage. The smoke from the fire in the stall on the corner made her feel even weaker.

'No, thank *you* and this is only *au revoir*.' But she was too tired to explain that goodbye could mean only *au revoir* too, but he probably knew that. And she held out a limp hand which he took firmly in his and, equally firmly, kissed. Ever after, the smell of woodsmoke brought back to her that kiss and the curious languid gratitude she felt for it, unable to make up her mind whether priests, or would-be priests, kissed women's hands as a matter of course if they had been educated in a French school, or whether this was a declaration of his new liberation, or perhaps, or and perhaps (her syntax was as feeble and confused as the rest of her) a gesture of spontaneous affection. She watched him ride off down the street at right angles from them and found herself using the adjective plucky to think of him and then told herself not to

117

be so patronising.

'He says he's going to become a Protestant,' she found herself saying to Dr McFadzean rather sooner than she had meant to. Perhaps the subject was better got out of the way as soon as possible, except that Dr McFadzean showed no signs of letting it get out of the way.

'Well, I'm delighted to hear it. I was thinking it was about time we got one back. You are aware, are you not, that my predecessor Mr Waterhouse poped with indecent alacrity as soon as he got out here. To add insult to injury, he joined the Jesuits down in Beirut. We wouldn't have minded so much if he had become a simple parish priest trying to save souls according to his lights, but to take up with those subtle sophisters, those –'

'But I thought all the Protestant missions had made quite a lot of converts.'

'So they have, Beatha, but not priests. A priest counts ten points in this game. You really have levelled the score for us.'

'No, no, I swear it wasn't me, he was going to anyway.'

'That's what he may say, he may even think it, but there is nothing like the proximity of delightful female company for strengthening a man's resolution.'

This was just as terrible as she had feared, and she bowed her head over the mutton stew and gazed at the pale rondels of carrot floating in the filmy broth. Mrs McFadzean came to her aid in a manner that was both sour and sisterly.

'That manner of conversation is quite unsuited to the topic, Mungo, at the dinner table or anywhere else. Elizabeth has been through a trying experience and we should not cheapen the blessing of Father Halabi's decision.'

'That was the last thing on my mind, my dear. I was simply congratulating Beatha on having seen the good father through his spiritual ordeal.'

'In that case, you should not have treated the matter as if it were a football match.'

She had to get out and get home, she knew that as she stared at the brass ornaments on the sideboard opposite and the engraving of King Cophetua and the Beggarmaid which hung above it and then at the picture of Salisbury Cathedral after rain, which hung above the fireplace, anything to avoid looking at Dr McFadzean's beaming, chewing face in front of her. Suddenly she longed for green lawns and watermeadows and the rain falling softly on the roses outside her bedroom window.

In the evening, she said goodbye to her Ladies English class. They seemed sad, desperately sad to see her go. She had made them learn Hail to thee, blithe spirit! and they chanted it back to her in a spiritless funereal tone. She must not go before they had brought her their presents, they always gave presents to departing teachers, and to her they wanted to give something special. But the train to Istanbul was leaving in the morning. So they could only give what they had with them. The dark noisy girl gave her a red and black silk headscarf, her friend handed Beatha a cut-glass scent bottle – in loving memory, she said, as though Beatha had passed over – and the plump girl with the beginnings of a moustache who had sat at the back of the class and said scarcely a word the whole time Beatha had been there pulled a gold ring off her plump finger and put it on Beatha's.

In fact, there was another train two days later via Berlin which would have done almost as well, but she was anxious to avoid saying a proper goodbye to Michel. She knew her hurried departure would cause comment, might be linked to her trip over the mountain, and even to his conversion. But for the moment she did not care what they made of it. Her feelings were too jumbled, her nerves too strung.

She stared in wonder and relief at the steam engine as it snorted into the pretty little station with the marigolds watered in the flower beds just as in France. How huge it was, the great locomotive with WINTERTHUR embossed on its gleaming green boiler. Perhaps it was the same one the Kaiser rode when he steamed over the mountains to Baalbek. In another mood, she would have resented this alien monster shunting and hooting its way into the silence of the desert and the ruins, her silence. But now she was in a fret to board and take her first sip of mint tea and watch the tawny hills slip away behind her and disappear in the haze that she thought of as *bleuâtre*, which was somehow much more evocative than blueish.

All the way home, she snuggled down into the pleasures of solitude, read *Jude the Obscure*, which she had been saving for the return journey, and somewhere between Belgrade and Zagreb cried at the suicide of the children, but also with relief at her own escape. She would spend a month with her parents, then go to London and look for a little flat near the Army & Navy Stores and enrol in a college and become a qualified, serious woman.

Since she already was a serious woman, this was what she did. As the dogcart brought her from the station round the bend in the drive, she found her father clipping the hedge with his pipe in his mouth, looking deplorably English.

'Hallo, Beatha, back early, aren't you? We only got your telegram this morning.' At least he took the pipe out of his mouth to kiss her. 'Mother's upstairs airing your bed.' And a flushed anxious face poked out of the wide-open window and shrieked at her in that frantic way her mother had of greeting people.

A fortnight of them was more than enough, especially since they insisted on inviting the Whittingstall brother who wasn't marrying her sister but was now also engaged over to hear her traveller's tales. He was not stupid, being a lawyer of whom much was said to be hoped, but his indifference to the Levant was awe-inspiring. And he was wearing a silk muffler of paisley design which was a painful reminder of Michel. Indeed, he had the same nervous trick of fluffing it out round his adam's apple, as though that bony boss were some rare jewel to be showed off.

Still, to Beatha too the Levant quickly became no more than a romantic memory like some watercolour of the Pyramids at sunset. She remembered the cold clear dawns, the smell of the herbs in the country, the cough of the camels in the narrow street outside her attic bedroom, the view of the creamy little domes and the vineyards below the Church of the Second Repentance, the Halabi girls giggling on the sofa while their mother played a gavotte on the piano, and Michel's vole teeth gleaming in the sunset as he raised the little cup of murky coffee to his lips. But it was remarkable how quickly it ceased to feel like part of her real life, which was now to be lived in her narrow little rooms with the high ceilings just off Victoria Street or sitting on the top deck of the bus carrying her up Regent Street to the teachers' college. She liked the routine. Even her pleasures were regular, the weekly visit to the Queen's Hall concert with her fellow tenant Rowena, the fortnightly dinner with her sister and the other Whittingstall brother, the lectures at the Royal Anthropological Institute in which grizzled explorers stammered their way through their adventures in the few remaining untrodden regions of the globe.

It was well into the following autumn when she came back late from an evening class and found Rowena sitting in front of the gas fire with a knowing grin on her broad cherub's face.

'A part of your past called this afternoon.'

'What do you mean?'

'A neat little chap in a bowler hat with perfect manners. But Unmistakably An Oriental.'

'Oh *no*, what sort of teeth did he have?'

'What a strange question. I'm not sure, but yes, quite big and curved, like, like a beaver.'

'Or a vole.'

'All right then, a vole, I'm not a zoologist. So that's Michel.'

'Yes, must be, didn't he leave his name?'

'He left his card,' and with a grand flourish she produced a card, nicely printed, which said: Rev. Michael Allenby, M.A. – and then below, in handwriting, 'at the Thursby Hotel, South Kensington, S.W.'

'He really has gone native, hasn't he.'

'Rowena, what am I to do?'

'More a question of what is he to do I should think, or of what has he come here for.'

The sight of this little card with its raised engraving and the address scrawled in royal-blue ink in an educated, even professional hand was unnerving, utterly disorienting, charged as it was with such intention. He had so clearly staked everything on it.

121

When he called again, at least he called hatless.

'The bowler hat? Rowena said you wore a bowler hat.'

'On reflection, my reflection in the mirror to be precise, I thought the bowler was excessive. I looked like a chimpanzee.'

'Or a vole?'

'I have never seen a vole.'

'It's a sort of field rat.'

'You pay such delicate compliments, Beatha.'

'But you really are an Anglican parson?'

'A pale young curate in fact, well, not so pale or so young perhaps but certainly a curate. I know the Thirty-Nine Articles by heart and believe every one of them. The Bishop of Rome hath no jurisdiction in this Realm of England. The Romish Doctrine concerning Purgatory, Pardons, Worshipping and Adoration, as well of Images as of Reliques, and also invocation of Saints, is a fond thing vainly invented. So much for my poor leaking Magdalen.'

'I wish you wouldn't say leaking.'

'Isn't it the right word?'

'Well, it sounds like a leaky tap.'

'But Beatha, you at least know that that is what it is.'

He was hectic in his gaiety. If he had brought his bowler, he would probably have twirled it and caught it on his walking stick like a music-hall star.

'And the Allenby?'

'That was the nearest equivalent I could find. They are a stout family from the North of England. One of them is a general in the Army. Perhaps he will make me his private chaplain.'

'I don't think that's very likely.'

'You are disapproving. You aren't pleased to see me. You wish I had not come. You would prefer I stayed in my own backwoods muttering in my dead language.' He tossed these accusations in a series of pitiful little mews of disappointment, half comic and half seriously forlorn. And she found his whole act so endearing, it fed her hunger for playfulness so gracefully, that she reached out her hand to him and then, seeing how stiff and miserly this was, she

122

embraced him with her strong arms and kissed him with a sporting innocence on the cheek – later to be recalled as the happiest moment of her life and identified as such at the time too, she thought.

At any rate, it was certainly the beginning of the happiest period, a courtship which ambled through the dusty, sun-gentled days of September, and then on through the dripping fogs which turned your handkerchief black in an hour. All through the winter, they took wet walks together under the bare-dappled plane tree up to his church in Camden Town, an indiscriminately Gothic building, not forty years old but with the grime already deep-engrained in the Kentish ragstone and the pitch-pine pews well greased by the congregation, a close-fisted and standoffish collection of City clerks and tradesmen. Mr Allenby has come to us from overseas, they would say and then after a pause, but I'm sure he's very welcome. They liked it best, he thought, when he told them little stories of life in the desert to teach some homely moral of general application. They were, after all, familiar with the milieu from their Bible classes as children. When he ventured on to their own ground, he felt a chill in the air. They did not care to be taught their duty to the poor, at least not by him. And when he turned to more controversial themes, the chill became arctic.

'What is it that distinguished Christianity from all the other faiths of the deserts (and there were many of them, believe me)? It is surely that Christ came to save all men equally, without regard to their tribe, or the colour of their skin, or their caste or their sex, for women and children too were equal citizens in His kingdom, where there is neither Greek nor Jew, circumcision nor uncircumcision, Barbarian, Scythian, bond nor free. The mercy and loving kindness of God was to flow over us all like that wonderful precious oil with which Mary Magdalen anointed our Lord, without distinction of persons, from the highest to the lowest and from the lowest to the highest.'

Beatha was proud of him as his harsh-liquid voice spoke its now virtually perfect English from the fake-tudor pulpit above her.

123

The sides of the pulpit were high, so that Michel had to raise his elbows to the level of his ears to rest them on the parapet. He looked like a naughty schoolboy, as with ever-growing eloquence he preached his message of racial concord and class reconciliation. There was a strike looming down in the docks and two of his parishioners worked in the offices of the employers and took it amiss when Michel included Ben Tillett and Will Thorn and the other dockers' leaders in his prayer that harmony and wisdom might prevail.

There were words after matins and talk of an extraordinary meeting in the vestry, even of a complaint to the Archdeacon, perhaps the Bishop.

'They think I'm a socialist,' he said proudly.

'I think you're going to get into trouble. Would you like to come and meet my parents?'

'Well, you have met my family, and when we were scarcely acquainted, too.'

'We are better acquainted now.'

'I think we are.'

His brown hand (so warm and smooth, not like the sweating palms of the Whittingstall brothers) stroked her freckled cheek and pulled a stray frizzy curl back behind her ear. This was all bliss, but when, the following spring, they sat side by side in a railway carriage staring at a brown photograph of Sidmouth, she had to admit to a certain apprehension, or frunt as it was known in the family cant. That private language was itself not the least of her apprehensions. She had told Michel about it when she was trying to describe her parents to him. He had listened to her carefully, now and then giving a brisk little nod, which he often did when he was not quite sure of his ground. Her parents were, she explained, not odd exactly. If you saw them in the street, you would not give them a second glance. But they were unusual in a way she could not quite describe, since she supposed she must be like that too.

When her father advanced to meet them across the lawn, cro-quet-mallet in hand, his straw hat matching his light summer waistcoat, she could feel Michel feeling that she had exaggerated. What could be more ordinary than the way he smiled and held out his hand and said, 'How good of you to come all this way.'

'How very good of you to have me,' Michel replied. 'I hope I shan't be too much of a pringle.'

There was a glacial pause, which froze among other things her father's keen thin face till it might have been an image on a silver coin.

'Ah,' he said, and then after a further pause, 'We use pringle as an adjective.'

'I'm afraid I am a damned foreigner,' Michel said, pretending not to be taken aback.

'You seem,' said her father, 'you seem to be picking up our lingo very quickly.'

'Beatha is an excellent teacher.'

'She is very good with, ah, people from overseas. If you have any trouble with us, she will interpret.'

Michel grinned and nodded, further enhancing, she thought, the impression of a greasy levantine.

'Tea,' her father said, 'you will want some tea.' Without a word, he walked off with his quick short steps towards the french windows at the end of the house. A tortoiseshell cat was sunning itself on the terrace just outside the windows. To Michel's amazement, Beatha's father broke into a run and gave the cat a huge kick so that it sailed into the rosemary bush at the end of the terrace.

'I thought the English loved animals.'

'Poor Cheshire. Papa doesn't really like cats at all,' Beatha sighed.

'Will it be all right?'

'Go and see if you like.'

Michel sauntered across the lawn, as though not going anywhere in particular. As he walked past the rosemary bush, he gave it a sidelong glance, but there was no sign of the cat.

They walked down the slope through a shrubbery of laurel and rhododendron to the great cedar tree on the piece of flat ground at the bottom. The criss-cross wooden seat encircling the trunk

125

was a little more broken now than when she had gone away and the view across the valley seemed meaner than she remembered. Weybridge seemed to have crept a little closer too. The red roofs of the new houses on the hill looked raw as beef in the teatime sun. Below she could trace the curve of the lane through the hollow. The lane was so narrow that the cow parsley whipped the sides of the dogcart coming back from shopping in Weybridge, and she could reach out her chubby nine-year-old arms and pick the bluebells and red campion, and going over the little bridge at the bottom the stench of the wild garlic made her nose wrinkle and she would hold up a bar of the rose geranium soap her mother had bought at Mr Budgen's and sniff its bland fragrance until the garlic was gone. At gaps in the lane, steep flights of brick steps would lead up to the cottages hidden in the hawthorn bushes above them. Occasionally, an old man in a waistcoat with no collar to his shirt would peer down the steps at them, his attention caught by the clip-clop of the pony. Her mother sitting beside her would give a jerky nod of greeting but too late for it to be acknowledged or even seen. She was never at ease with the local people (never at ease with anyone much, come to that) and she was taken to be standoffish. Now Beatha remembered how powerfully she had longed to get away from this place.

'My aunts were always proposed to on this bench.'

'And did they accept?'

'Always, even if they had only met the man at luncheon that day.'

'Even if he was a curate.'

'Especially if he was a curate.'

'Well, I do not want to disappoint you. Will you Elizabeth –'

'Oh yes, of course I will.'

And that was that. Weybridge too had its rite of passage, just like any South Sea Island, and she had obscurely known that they had to come to this place to plight their troth. An engagement sealed in Paterson Mansions or even over tea at Gunter's or Rumpelmayer's would not have been the same thing at all.

'It would be best', she said firmly, after his soft lips had met hers and so on, 'to tell them straight away. They will be thinking we are anyway, and when couples return from the shrubbery walk, something is expected of them.'

But when they sat down in the chilly drawing room – it seemed chillier here than outside in the warm Surrey sunshine – Michel found himself unable to start off the subject.

'Have a rock cake. Despite appearances, they're rather goobly,' Beatha's mother said. She was a fine, strong-boned woman, not unlike her daughter but with a curious thin-lipped smile like Voltaire's.

'They need some honey on them,' her father said. 'And so – you are engaged, I trust. You returned from the shrubbery and in this house guests are not permitted to return from the shrubbery unless they are engaged to be married. Milko Cheshire, where is that damned cat?'

'I think he's –' Michel began as he saw the tortoiseshell cat come in through the french windows and then broke off as he saw the string attached to the animal's forelegs and saw also that Beatha's father was reeling the string in under the tea table. Seen close up, the cat was not even very lifelike.

'She'll have no money, you know, not a bean. I'm a hop-broker, you know, *pour la bière, vous comprenez*, and prices have been terribly depressed for the last two or three years, utterly scraffed, in fact.'

'We were –'

'Too frunt to sing out, I expect. I was the same. We were married for several weeks before I proposed.'

'We would –'

'Whatever you do, don't ask my permission. I'd only have to give it. After all, there's nobody else in the running, now that both the Whittingstall boys are spoken for. Of course, if the hop market picked up, it might be a different story. The carriage drive might be blocked with suitors, under the cedar would be like Piccadilly Circus. But as matters stand ...'

He seemed near tears, and when Michel shook his hand, it was quivering.

'Come ... come and see the paperweights.' He led Michel to the glass-topped table. Above the table hung a grimy swirling oil painting in a massy gold frame whose galumphing arabesques and foliations continued the motion of the painting's theme, an uncertain one, a shipwreck, a sunrise, a massacre, it was hard to say. Set out on the table were dozens of paperweights, transparent little globes with their infolded motifs of flowers and coloured patterns. Was there any object which had less to say than a paperweight, Michel wondered. Could there be any more frigid hobby than the collection of these null things?

'They're beautiful,' he said.

'You think so, you really think so?' Michel could not tell whether Beatha's father was interested in his opinion. It was hard to pick out his ironies, his manner was so dry and febrile, so peppered with dry little snorts and clicks that nothing he said seemed quite safe to be taken at face value. And yet his distress, that was palpable and true.

'Oh, just losing a daughter, don't you think?' Beatha said later to reassure him. 'He is a distressed person, you know, always has been. Whenever I see an appeal for distressed gentlefolk, I think of him.'

'But why? He has you, your mother, that house, that view, the cedar tree, finer than anything I could show you, even those paperweights.'

'He has no faith. He believes in nothing, nothing I can discover at any rate.'

'Such men are often very happy, my dear.'

'... as I will discover when I have reached your advanced years. Also there are the hops.'

There had been a time, but that was in her childhood, when they would all go up to London brimming with expectation to visit the offices where all the brokers were, grouped round the Exchange in the grimy alleys just south of Southwark Bridge. Even as the narrow door was answered by the porter in the green apron, the smell of the hops would come leaping down the stairs, and go straight to the top of her head. Out in the fields the hops smelled sweet and heavy, but here in the long low partners' sampling room, their potency had a sour, almost menacing 'finish', as her father called it. Whenever she looked at his long thin nose, she thought of it probing the rows of hops on the green tin trays, as though, like some anteater's proboscis, that quivering organ was doing all the work, seeing, smelling, even nuzzling the pretty green bobbins which all looked the same to her. And then afterwards, the white wine and oysters across the river at Sweeting's, and her mother all pink and laughing and her father with his top waistcoat button undone tossing his dry nods to business acquaintances as they passed up and down the crowded passage between the tables. This little world had its own pleasant self-confidence – a Dickensian outing her mother could not help calling it, she had an addiction to the obvious when it came to comparisons – but now all that had fractured, at least for her father. He took the same train up to Town as he had always done, but he returned a little earlier, and then a little earlier still, and always looking paler, paler yet and his mouth thinner.

'They're cutting the margins to the bone,' was all he would say. She did not dare to ask who they were, or why her father could do nothing to stop them. In any case, there was the business of the wedding to be attended to. It was to be a modest, even austere affair in view of The Situation. Even so, there was still the question of The Dress, which required endless fittings, and The Caterers which provoked a painful dither between the ruinous expense of London and the humiliation of Weybridge. During this period her mother spoke almost entirely in capital letters, addressing Beatha in the third person as The Bride.

Far from being reconciled to the prospect of Michel, her parents seemed to recoil more openly as The Day drew nearer. He, The Groom, was being a total lamb, in Beatha's eyes, helpful, amiable, not standing out at all. Even his clothes seemed to have settled on him. You might be a rather dark Englishman, she said to him one day, one with perhaps a dash of Welsh blood. No hint of the tarbrush, really? Certainly not, she said.

But none of this did him any good. Her parents spoke to him

in curt little sentences, and when he answered with the utmost good humour they seemed not to listen and their features resumed a shared despair which seemed to be becoming natural.

'Do, well, do cheer up,' Beatha said, watching her mother sewing with stony-faced concentration. 'It's not my funeral.'

'I hope not, I very much hope not. But weddings are always sad occasions, in our family at all events. I cried for twenty-four hours before mine, and how right I was.'

'Oh, Mother.'

By the second Sunday in May, when Beatha actually walked down the aisle of St Monica's, Winkhill Green, they were all exhausted. Even their despair had been drained from them. When her father joined her mother in the front pew, they were a couple of bony spectres, and contrary to prediction her mother remained dry-eyed all day. And through the bleak hospitality extended at the reception – a chilly spring breeze from the shrubbery was ruffling the refreshments – through the general air of retrenchment which communicated itself to the small number of invited guests, a thin, hesitant ray of happiness insisted on making its presence felt.

'There's nothing like the married state,' Teddy Whittingstall said, squeezing her hand with his great damp paw, 'you'll be as happy as larks, I know it.' And although Beatha knew herself to be deficient in larky qualities even at her best, which she wasn't at on this Day of Days, her spirits rose and she tugged her veil off her face where the wind had blown it and said with an extravagant gesture, 'Look, Teddy, the dance of the one veil, perhaps I'll change my name to Salome while I'm about it.' He retreated, keeping his nervous eyes on her like a lion-tamer backing out of the cage.

But then perhaps the austerity was a necessary prelude to the honeymoon (not a subject proper for modern writers, I know, not the newly married aspect of it at any rate but modern readers are hardened to other embarrassments and I see no reason why they should be spared this one). The word unbridled came to her several times as they were under the damp cotton sheets in the Old

Church Hotel at Ambleside, with the tower of the Old Church right outside their bedroom window and striking the hours with a bong which they fancied coincided with their moments, as she thought of them to herself. She had not imagined anything so delicious, had not dared to imagine very much, in fact. But it was delicious, deeply so, and there was such a lot of it too. She had not imagined the sweetness or the fatigue.

'Do you think,' he said (he seemed quite unabashed about talking about these things), 'that we have conceived the last of the Allenbys?'

'You mustn't tempt Providence,' she said.

'Why not? Providence tempts us. Such an ancient line ought not to be allowed to die out.'

'No, no, but I don't want to become anxious about it. It's so nice not being anxious.'

That was the last thing she was as she tucked in (there was no other word for it, except possibly the family verb which was grunched, or rather grunched up) to the northern breakfast – egg, bacon and sausage, of course, but also devilled kidneys, and heavenly succulent black pudding, although once or twice they missed the black pudding because the other guests, mostly well-covered clergymen and their wives, had finished it.

'Did we meet at the St David's diocesan conference?' said one sturdy priest with a high colour in his cheeks.

'No, no, I fear not,' Michel said smiling, flattered by the imputation.

'There was a fellow there from Lampeter, had much your look, an excellent golfer.'

'Alas, I am a stranger to the game.'

'Can't have been you then. Look, I'm standing in for old Heathcliffe this Sunday. There'll be a fearful press with all the visitors. Any hope of your assisting at the eight o'clock? Then we could take breakfast back here and go for a tramp together.'

Michel accepted with an alacrity which irritated Beatha. She knew they had to take Communion, of course, although on holiday, but she had looked forward to a languid stroll along the shores of Grasmere, rather than the arduous trek over the Riggs which Archdeacon Sutton James outlined. And yet there was something marvellous, a mixture of the sensual and the divine, about rising from their bed and letting that delicious faintness she always felt afterwards meet the chill edge of the mist coming up from the lake through the open window and then putting on her churchgoing clothes and her perky little black straw hat which was so uncrushable it didn't need a hatbox, and tripping down the steps to cross the path of the walkers coming up from the little town, the men in their moleskin waistcoats, corduroy trousers, stout fell boots and soft hats. She didn't even mind Mrs Sutton James talking about her new house in London in a voice which seemed too loud for the quiet early morning. Michel looked grave and fine as he handed her the cup and the sickly ruby-red wine trickled down her dry throat. It was the first time she had received Communion from his hands and, although she was as she had frankly told him not a very devout Christian, it did seem a fitting culmination to the strange journey they had taken together.

On their return as they came into the hall of the Old Church Hotel, the proprietor met them with a blue saucer on which he had placed a telegram which said: *Gravely regret inform you your father died last night Margesson.*

'How terrible. Who's Margesson?'

'The solicitor, I think.' She stood in the dark hall, numb, unable to think of anything to say, feeling a great avalanche of grief coming towards her from a long way off to suffocate her. She cried out, a single awkward howl, slipped through the outstretched arms of Mrs Sutton James and ran upstairs.

Her father had shot himself under the cedar with an old twelve-bore which he used for rabbits, often as dusk was falling. The single shot ringing low across the valley was thus a known sound, friendly almost, like the firing of a gun to mark the hours in some eastern colony. His liabilities exceeded his assets by £87,000 and that at a charitable valuation. Another month and he would have been declared bankrupt. His fellow hop-brokers did what they could, but times were hard and they said to one another

132

she could always sell the house, which she did and removed to a small apartment near Beatha's old flat in a newly built block convenient for Victoria Station. This convenience was of small value to her since she had no desire to travel, but the closeness of the line on which her husband had gone up and down every day reminded her of the irremediably departed time when she had possessed something of a life to live.

After the funeral, Beatha noticed that Michel had become restless, and, by his standards, irritable. He still paid compliments to her, compliments which had that flowery foreign excess about them she liked so much, but now they seemed slightly forced from him. She was conscious of having displeased him, but in some general way she did not know how to ask about. They continued to have their moments as regularly as ever, but his approach was fiercer now. She was excited by his fierceness, she could not deny that, but alarmed too. At the same time, she noticed how assiduous he had become in cultivating the acquaintance of influential clergymen, especially those in his own diocese. He had always made himself agreeable, well, she was the beneficiary of that, but now he was positively courtly.

'Do we really have to entertain the Sutton Jameses again?'

'Indeed we do, my dear, except that this is to be not so much an entertainment as a celebration.'

'Oh, why?'

'It is partly through the Archdeacon's good offices that I am to be appointed the Rector of St Wulfstan's.'

'You sound like someone out of *Barchester Towers*.'

She had never seen the church, had only dimly heard (for like many sensible clergy wives she kept clear of ecclesiastical gossip) of its fame as 'the cathedral of the docks'. But as soon as she saw its great white profile sailing like a ship through the tangle of rusty cranes and dingy brick warehouses, she saw what he meant. There was a heroism about its soaring twin bell-towers, the spiralling crockets and finials which topped off its dizzy spire, its great, light heart-lifting interior. But its reputation was just as noble. For forty years Dr Milroy had been the spiritual dynamo of the whole sad shabby quarter. He had marched with Ben Tillett, stood up for the Russian Jews against the local roughs and against the employers who sweated them in the workshops and cutting rooms, he had given sanctuary to seamen who jumped ship. And his tongue was as silver as his heart was golden. Fashionable carriages made the perilous journey from the West End to hear him, an hour or more's journey for fifteen minutes of his simple direct sermons, adorned only by the sincerity of the speaker and the very faintest hint of a brogue. The arrival of the internal combustion engine shortened the journey by half, unless the motor car broke down on the treacherous Stepney cobbles and left well-dressed couples sitting stranded until help could be procured, having to pretend not to notice the mockery of the natives. When a pulmonary embolism finally did for Dr Milroy (with his weak chest, he had been frequently but vainly begged to exchange St Wulfstan's for a less testing, more salubrious cure on the South Coast or in some Alpine resort), all this rich spiritual inheritance was Michel's – or Michael's, for now his Englishing was complete. Only now and then in the rounding of an *r* or the rolling of a diphthong was there a tremor of levantine passion, and a highly attractive tremor too. It was not long, a month at most, before the whisper was out that Dr Milroy had been honoured by a worthy successor, one no less eloquent and just as diligent in his mission to the poor.

It was a hot summer, the hottest, some older parishioners claimed, since 1888 or was it 1892, when the cranes had been too hot to touch and the newly laid tarmacadam in Commercial Street had turned to porridge so that everyone said what a mistake it had been to dig up the cobbles. A hot summer in London was not like a hot summer in old Surrey before the turn of the century, when everyone slowed to a crawl and leant on their pitchforks and listened to the bees. July in the docks was a grim uneasy swelter of a month. The long political crisis rumbling five miles up river had its ripples at St Wulfstan's. There was talk of being prepared to make a stand for democracy, of socialism and syndicalism and other isms which seemed to Beatha a clumsy way of expressing anger and concern on behalf of the casual men

134

lounging on the wharves and street corners with dull and furtive eyes. She was pregnant now and felt awkward and fugitive as she waddled over to the Highway to catch the omnibus for the long trip to the West End to buy cretonnes and the little clubfooted brass lamps for the bedrooms like the ones she had had as a child, and of course a bassinet. At the Army & Navy Stores too, she would place her orders to be delivered (St Wulfstan's was only just within their delivery area and the delivery man looked white and scared when she answered the doorbell herself because the maid was so slow). There also she would place Michael's orders in the Wines & Spirits Department, since there was no decent wine merchant nearer than the City. She was amazed by the quantity of claret they got through, and not the shilling variety, either, but the half-crown article which had been bottled in France and tasted like heavy blackcurrant juice. I thought, she said by way of a joke, that Arabs didn't drink. You mean Moslems don't, he answered; we Christians have our Mediterranean inheritance to think of. He spoke of the beautiful differences in the varieties of grape, the subtle art of their blending, the tragedy of the outbreak of phyl-loxera which had devastated the noblest vines of Europe. And she wished she had not raised the subject. But she did notice that, although the unusual fierceness of the sun that summer had burned his face a fine leather-brown, now and then there was a reddish flush in his cheeks as well. Still, these were times that tried men's patience. Michael had a congregation, almost a constituency to speak for. He could be forgiven his occasional relaxation.

Strung out and irritable days: politics shouldered its way into what had been the easy waltz of their conversation. Michael thought little of Asquith – old Squiffy, as he called him (how had he found out this nickname? His antennae were still magical). Lloyd George was a Welsh thief and the Tories too stupid even for the Army class. Now and then, his talk had disturbing echoes of Surrey neighbours, the sort of people her parents had not been at home to.

But then the baby came, delivered (because it was her first baby and there were complications) in the Princess Beatrice Ward of the Seamen's Hospital by a doctor who was the spitting image of Lloyd George though in fact Scottish, and when she came round from the longest sleep of her life and the nurse brought her the red squalling bundle to the clucks and cheers of the noisy sailors' wives along the ward (but they always asked her to pardon their French seeing she was a vicar's lady) she opened her arms with a consciousness of unbounded happiness. They called him George after St George of England and Cappadocia, and also after George alias Mohammed who had been the chaperon or gooseberry on their first trip together. Since the baby had somewhat goggling eyes into the bargain, he soon came to be known as the Gooseberry, or Goosy for short.

Overnight, the summer was transformed for her. The hubbub of the outside world faded, and when she rose exhausted after the night feeds, all she longed to do was tell the monthly nurse to put her feet up and herself very slowly push the high-sprung perambulator with its imitation coachwork scrolls down the path behind the graveyard and on to the little raised terrace with the three tall plane trees and watch the ships pass up and down the river with their drowsy hooting and chugging. Sometimes she herself would begin to drowse and wake with a start to the cry of the starved Gooseberry and see that the sun was already off the oily shimmering water, blocked by the tall wharves opposite with their rusty cranes already beginning to look like sinister black gibbets as they did at night.

She saw less, a great deal less, of Michael now. The radiance of his reputation reached her dimly in her Gooseberry-centred world, but it was undoubtedly a reputation. When Princess Louise visited the Docklands Mission, not only was she received by Michael but she said, quite truthfully, how much she had heard about him. And the few City people who still kept houses in the neighbourhood asked them to dine, and not out of a sense of duty. The neighbourhood was going downhill fast, what with the Russians and the Poles and the sailors who had jumped ship and were doing the Lord knows what, but at least they weren't anarchists like the pale tailors' boys who were always marching and congregating and frightening decent people from what had once been a desirable quarter, not smart, of course, but refined with its rusticated porticoes and Coade-stone lions on either side and fine hooped lanterns. At least Beatha was spared all this elegiac conversation because she was too tired to go out to dinner and was furious if Michael broke into her precious sleep when he slid into bed beside her.

But they were friendly to her after matins, identifying her as a kindred spirit in what was fast becoming hostile territory. 'You must admit, we are a little besieged. Sometimes Stepney feels uncomfortably like Mafeking.'

Mrs Teazle with her sharp laughing eyes and her jaunty feathered hats had a way of putting things which was much admired. How beautifully Michael dealt with what Beatha called 'your feathered friends'. He laughed at their acid witticisms without committing himself to the acidity, flattered their vanity without himself seeming to become their lapdog. And when he was in the pulpit, his homilies about the simple virtues – patience, honesty, fidelity – seemed to pierce, but gently pierce, their painted carapaces and reach through to the common humanity which must surely lie beneath like some infinite subterranean sea.

It was accordingly a brutal shock when Michael one morning, having broken open the seal on one bulky envelope, retired to his little dark study overlooking the graveyard and returned a few minutes later, as pale as when she had first known him.

'I have some disagreeable news.'

She looked up at him, continuing to stroke the fluffy back of the Gooseberry's head (he had grown into a sturdy toddler, taciturn and broody – she thought he needed company and hoped for a second child soon).

'Mr Teazle is suing his wife for divorce.'

'Oh,' she said. 'They seemed a quite devoted couple to me, but then you know them so much better.'

'He is citing a number of co-respondents.'

'A number? How many? How extraordinary – I know she has that look in her eye, but even so –'

'One of the co-respondents is myself.'

'You? But –'

'It is, of course, a foul untruth. I shall contest it with the utmost vigour. But the mud will stick, it will stick like glue. It is a lie, a lie,' he repeated.

She burst into tears, ran from the room, lay sobbing on her bed for hours, refused to let him in, then let him in, listened to his endless protestations of innocence, became practical and lucid for an interval: what was the evidence against him, how exactly would they contest the allegation, could they afford a proper lawyer and so on. Then she collapsed again, and retreated into mute isolation – or isolation with the Gooseberry, concentrating solely on his welfare, treating her husband as though he were a representative of the Gas Board come to read the meter. The trust was broken, irreparably broken, that much she knew. Perhaps the allegation was false, perhaps Mr Teazle had just tossed Michael's name in to add lustre to an otherwise squalid list, but she could never be sure of it. And even if the allegation was technically false, which three-quarters of the time she doubted, there must have been a flirtatious friendship or at least the appearance of one, enough to prick the husband's jealousy. At the very least Michael had been, no, not indiscreet, that was an awful stuffy word, but thoughtless of her in his conversations with Mrs Teazle. And a clergyman of all people must know how close thoughtlessness was to faithlessness. Whosoever looketh on a woman to lust after her hath committed adultery with her already in his heart. Conversations could, after all, be criminal, crim con, the lawyers called it, and intercourse could be physical, the dividing line was as thin as a membrane. She lay crying on her bed for another day while Michael went over to St Paul's Churchyard to consult her family solicitors, who had dealt with the winding up of the hop-brokers and found that sort of affair much more plain sailing than these contaminated waters. Dissatisfied and anxious, Michael switched to a specialist in divorce law who proposed to hire a silk. It was not simply the extra expense but also the evergrowing alien gravity of the case that made Beatha more miserable still. The

138

Gooseberry absorbed the atmosphere around him and became even more stolid and silent. Hitherto Michael had fondled and dandled the child with an unappeasable gentleness every minute of the day. Now he only gave the Gooseberry a brisk hug morning and evening and could scarcely contain his annoyance when the child upset a cup or swept a piece of cutlery clattering on to the floor. He began to seem distracted, he who was always so alert, so present.

Yet to her surprise, as the date of the hearing came nearer, Beatha found her mood changing. She remained distrustful of him, continued to believe him guilty of some kind of faithlessness, but she began to feel indignant against the outside world. She wanted to defend her hunted vole, not because she was convinced of his innocence but because he was being hunted. She volunteered to give evidence on his behalf, offered to bring the Gooseberry along with her and stage the most affecting scene imaginable.

'I hope it won't come to that, madam,' Mr Arthur Jacques KC said in his dry, savouring voice. 'Too much of that sort of thing might suggest that we have something to hide. Your presence in the witness box will be more than enough. Your husband could wish, if I may say so, for no more eloquent testimony.'

'Because of my honest English face, you mean.'

Mr Jacques inclined his lean greyhound head.

'Well, it is pleasant to think that plainness may have its advantages.'

'Mrs Allenby, please. I meant quite the reverse, that a husband blessed with such a wife would not dream of looking elsewhere.'

She was suddenly sickened by the facility of his courtesy and had an irrational hankering for old-fashioned English inarticulacy of the Whittingstall variety.

The hearing made a stir in the papers, and assisted the sales of a slender volume which an ecclesiastical publisher had persuaded Michael to put together: *Sermons and Addresses* by the Rev. Michael Allenby M.A. To a modern reader, it seems almost incredible that so many copies of this little sky-blue book should have been sold (they turn up in second-hand bookshops in cathedral closes to this day). The images and sentiments in them seem so banal, and a modern scholar would instantly recognise the arguments, which sounded daring then, as feeble provincial eddies of the mighty waves of modernist theology that were beginning to break. Michael delighted in taking the words of some well-loved hymn – 'God is working His purpose out, as year succeeds to year', for example – and demonstrating that they did not, could not mean what the congregation had taken them to mean; God could not have a purpose in the human sense, otherwise His purpose would inevitably be realised and He would then be purposeless; God simply was, as He was in all great religions. And he might go further and mention some common denominator between the theologies of Judaism and Islam and Christianity, and his flock would forgive him because he did it so gracefully and feel flattered to be included on these excursions.

'Mr Allenby, you were a frequent guest at Mr Teazle's mansion, were you not?'

'They were kind enough to invite me to dine on several occasions.'

'You came without your wife on those occasions?'

'My wife was recovering from the birth of our son. Later on, she had to stay at home to feed him.'

'Quite so. You came alone, as a bachelor gay. And you became a favourite of Mrs Teazle's.'

'Both Mr and Mrs Teazle were most agreeable to me.'

'You are interested in flowers, are you not?'

'Yes.'

'Quite an accomplished botanist, I understand. And, knowing of your interest, Mrs Teazle asked if you would care to see her conservatory which is attached to the saloon – on the floor above the drawing room.'

'Yes, she had an excellent collection of delicate plants, orchids in particular.'

'And you went alone with her to see these delicate plants?'

'I did.'

'That trip upstairs did not strike you as unwise for a man in your position, a man of the cloth alone in a conservatory with a highly attractive married woman?'

'It is precisely because of my position that there was nothing compromising or indiscreet about it. I am often alone with married women in the course of my pastoral duties.'

'You are often alone with married women?'

'Would you insist, sir, that I take a chaperon whenever I go to console a female in distress, say, a lady who has recently been widowed?'

'I insist on nothing, sir, I merely enquire. Were you consoling Mrs Teazle?'

'Certainly not. I had previously expressed an interest in seeing her delicate plants. She was merely responding to my interest.'

'I put it to you that she was responding to another kind of interest, and responding with a good deal of ardour too. I put it to you that once protected by the foliage of these delicate plants you lost no time in embracing Mrs Teazle and kissing her passionately on the lips.'

'That is a foul lie.'

'I put it to you further that the following afternoon when Mr Teazle was at his place of business and the servants had been given the day off, you paid a second visit to No. 7 Albion Square and there had intimate relations with Mrs Teazle, defiling the sacred purity of your friend's marriage bed.'

'That is an even fouler lie, there is not a word of truth in it.'

'Mr Allenby, you are not a native of this country, are you?'

'No, I was born in the Levant.'

'You are, in fact, of Arab extraction?'

'Yes.'

'You changed your name to Allenby, one of the most distinguished in the North of England and presently carried by a Major-General in His Majesty's Armed Forces.'

'I took the name when I converted to the Church of England. I did so as a courtesy to that Church and its adherents.'

'I am sure that we are all most grateful for the courtesy. Now, in your part of the world, would I be right in assuming that the attitude of men towards women is rather different from the attitude of decent people in this country?'

'I am not quite sure what you mean.'

'Well then, let me spell it out for you in plain English, Mr Allenby. When you see a woman in your country, you automatically assume that she is fair game. If you can get her, you can have her. No matter who she is or what her station in life may be, she is yours for the possessing.'

'That is an abominable thing to say. I am amazed to hear such things said in an English court. In my native land, we are infinitely solicitous of a woman's reputation, and the woman for her part will be more careful still, since the penalties for losing her reputation are more severe.'

'*More* severe? More severe than in this country, you mean? So now we have it. Arab women are to be protected with the utmost solicitousness, because if their reputation should be sullied or smirched, they will suffer the direst penalties. They may be stoned, I have heard tell, my lord, or have their hands cut off.'

'What you may hear tell, Mr Kendrew, matters not to me. Pray proceed with the cross examination.'

'As your lordship pleases. So Arab women are to be protected, most solicitously protected. It is British women who are fair game. In our free society, any man is free to seduce his neighbour's wife, that's what you meant to say, isn't it?'

'You know it is not.'

'Well, you may not have meant to say it, but say it you did.'

'No, I did not, Mr Kendrew. You speak as if I spring from some godless harem. In fact, I was born into one of the oldest branches of the Christian church. I was studying for the priesthood in that Church which, as you know very well, cherishes precisely the same respect for the chastity of women as does the Church of England. While studying, I met my wife who was engaged in missionary work in that country. After my conversion to the Church of England and a curacy in the West End, I became rector of St Wulfstan's, in which capacity I have sought to serve the poor and sick of the parish. I know both Mr and Mrs Teazle solely as parishioners and − until these miserable proceedings − I had thought as friends too. There is not a word of truth in any of the allegations against me, and I must beg to be discharged from the case so that I may resume my parochial duties.'

The public gallery, packed as it had been all week, broke out into hysterical cheers. The judge, who had been wearying of Mr Kendrew's overblown advocacy for the previous forty-eight hours, seized the opportunity to enquire whether Mr Kendrew had any further questions to ask or any further witnesses or evidence to offer in relation to Mr Allenby. The answer being no, the judge discharged Michael with a fulsome apology for the baseless slur upon the character of such an admirable servant of God and minister to the poor.

All this was fine and dandy. Mrs Teazle denied everything. Mr Teazle in the witness box revealed himself to be insane with jealousy but unable to produce independent corroboration of his wife's amours. The divorce was refused and Mr Teazle was last heard of in Dieppe, living in considerable poverty while his wife moved to a small house in Chelsea and entertained with unabashed elan.

And Beatha, who had sat upright and expressionless throughout, feeling the sweat run down her spine, remained upright and expressionless as her husband led her from the court without a stain on him. She never mentioned, not on that day nor on any day that followed as long as he lived, that he had told her, quite explicitly, that he had never seen Mrs Teazle's orchids.

'Never?' I interjected, unable to stop myself, although still wanting to hear the story rounded off. I had heard some of the story already from my cousin Theo, but to find out the rest, I had got in touch with a more reliable source: my old companion Richard Shay, Rickshaw the legendary traveller and still more legendary storyteller, who added to Theo's family gossip a broader sweep, firmer historical background and, it had to be admitted, a touch of romance, so that our corner table in the shabby little pub behind the British Museum seemed to be lifted out of ordinary time by the narrator's magic. Shay was drinking mineral water, whether because of some old tropical complaint or his instinctively ascetic nature, and his pale face shone with the effort and pleasure of the telling.

'Never,' he affirmed. 'I asked her that several times. She knew he must remember he had told her he hadn't, but she couldn't bring herself to ask him about it because she knew he would tell her another lie.'

'He might have lied to her in the first place because it was in fact all quite innocent but he didn't want her to get the wrong idea.'

'You really believe that?'

'No.'

'Well, anyway, subsequent events proved that her instinct had been correct. She counted three, possibly four mistresses after Mrs Teazle, until Michael died in his late fifties between the Wars.'

'What did he die of?'

'Oh, drink. Arab livers aren't as strong as ours, you know. It was covered up quite nicely, a rare tropical disease that he'd picked up from one of the sailors.'

'That doesn't sound like much of a cover-up to me.'

'Not picked up in that way. At least nobody ever accused Michel – I prefer to think of him as Michel – nobody accused him of being a pederast. In fact, after the Teazle affair, no one accused him of anything. In the eyes of the world, he remained a preacher uniquely endowed with spiritual grace, charismatic in the proper sense of the word, a man who had been unjustly accused because his charisma had exposed him to the envy of meaner spirits.'

'But my cousin Theo said that his branch of the family called themselves Hale rather than Allenby when they came over because they didn't want to be tarred by being associated with Michel.'

'Your cousin is a great gossip. If they did think like that, they were wrong. Michel's public reputation remained quite intact. He grew a little tubby later on. Beatha showed me one of the last

144

photographs she had of him, in a straw hat in the early thirties. It was their Silver Wedding. They had gone back to the Lake District to celebrate – she herself put inverted commas round the word. It rained the whole time and they barely spoke a civil word to one another. In the photograph, he looked like a rather broken-down member of the Crazy Gang, squat and grinning. But he kept his eloquence to the end. My own mother heard him preach in St George's, Hanover Square, shortly before he died. Like a nightingale, she said it was.'

'And the son, George?'

'The Gooseberry grew up to look like one. He quarrelled with both his parents as soon as he was grown up. Became something in the City, I mean something really unmemorable, a discount broker perhaps, and, more to the point, became remorselessly English, with a grinding English wife. Beatha hasn't seen either of them for years, not since their son, her grandson, was a boy.' He paused, savouring the length of the estrangement. His conversation had once been exhaustless, effervescent as a moorland spring greeting the turf around it. Now there were pauses, sometimes long ones which needed to be broken into. The years of solitary travel among taciturn tribes had accustomed him to silence in company. His fine pale features were an enamel silhouette, the famous blue eyes seemed not to blink. He had to be snapped out of it.

'And the son, George's son?'

'Your friend.'

'Well, we don't know it is. All you know for sure is that George had a son.'

'I'm sure it's him.' Rickshaw enjoyed certainty. Perhaps that too he had learnt from the taciturn tribesmen. The stories which beguiled their vigils on stony hillsides needed to be brightened by the certainty of the storyteller. To those clinging to life's narrower ledges, the ambiguity we prize so much must seem less charming.

But there was no denying he could still tell a story. Even the little sketch, a vignette no more, of his mother having tea with the old woman in the next-door flat was as vivid as most people's narratives of epic adventure. 'They had been living next door to one another for thirty years, divided by the thickness of a Victorian jerry-builder's partition wall, the widow of a colonial officer and the widow of a clergyman. Never more than a stiff Good morning Mrs Shay, Good morning Mrs Allenby, not even a smile, my mother despises smiling, she regards it as a sign of weakness, a futile attempt to ingratiate oneself with fate. They would wait for the lift, side by side, without a word.'

'But when the lift broke down, for example, then surely –'

'The lift would not dare break down. I have never known any mechanical device oppose my mother's will. Anyway, then suddenly there she was, large as life – if anything a little larger – sitting square and upright as a frigidaire in my mother's sitting room opposite Mother, the two of them demolishing a Fuller's walnut cake and discussing the past with positively morbid enthusiasm: the Abdication with particular reference to the role of the Bishop of Bradford, the Rector of Stiffkey and the manner of his end in the lion's cage, T. E. Lawrence and the manner of *his* end on the motorbike, not much mourned by either of them. All our yesterdays whizzed past while the Fuller's cake dwindled before one's eyes as in one of those speeded-up nature films where they show a flower opening or a bird hatching. By the way, my mother is desperately sorry she won't be there to introduce you. I don't know what her previous engagement could possibly be. I suspect she simply doesn't want to play second fiddle in this particular recital. Here we are.' He led me down some litter-strewn steps towards a green door in the area. Pinned to the door there was a hand-drawn poster for the bazaar, showing some balloons and the spire of the church in the square behind us. The door opened before we got to it to reveal a large woman with untidy grey hair crouching on all fours in an effort to wedge a piece of cardboard under the door to keep it open. It was only when she staggered into an upright position again that I realised how old she was.

'You're early,' she said.

'I'm sorry, Beatha,' Rickshaw said. I was startled to hear him use her name, partly because he had met her so recently, met her properly, that is: he had passed her in that airless, dusty passage with the ginger carpet often enough. Or was I startled in the way one is always startled to meet a legend, especially a legend grown old? In my mind, she was still the pale girl saddle-sore in the desert, feeling the shade of the cedars creep over her.

We sat down on the folding plastic chairs and Rickshaw brought us some strong tea from the urn steaming on the long trestle table at the end of the church hall. And she began to talk, my third source after Theo's malice and Rickshaw's romancing. Much of what she said I have incorporated in the foregoing pages. Any life there may be in those pages comes from the clear, direct way she had of speaking. (Her voice was so clear as to be almost beautiful. How strange to think of a couple both gifted with beautiful voices. Yet one expects lovely faces to marry one another, why not lovely voices too?) But if the pages seem stale and second-hand – a hackneyed tale about an English girl in the mysterious East, or Near East anyway – then mine is the second hand that has staled them. For, to tell the truth, there was also something offputting about Beatha, or Mrs Allenby as I certainly called her. She was undeniably splendid and would have attracted the kind of men like Rickshaw who simply adored splendid old women, if she had not been so modest, so disdainful of showing off. Yet I had to admit it, I found her daunting, even as she responded, cheerfully and without embarrassment, to the questions I put to her.

Around us, the bazaar helpers were drifting in, sorting out the home-made jams, bickering about whether some of the cuddly toys were too grubby to put on sale, rigging up a clothes line to hang some second-hand suits on. The smell of mothball and ancient sweat wandered down the high-beamed hall, easily overpowering the fainter fragrance of the home-made pot-pourris.

'Dead men's clothes,' she said, waving a bony freckled hand at the rack of suits twisting slightly in the draught from the open door. The suits were sad to look at: greasy pinstripes of a chocolate brown and violent blue that you no longer saw on living shoulders; the outmoded shoulder padding on them made it seem

147

as if these dangling ghosts were jostling one another like men in a restless crowd.

'Did I come to hate him? No, never that. He was like a strange mistake I had to live with, like when you have made a mistake in a knitting pattern but have gone much too far to start again. I was very distrustful of him. I realised that I couldn't really believe a word he said, and not just about that sort of thing either. He was most unreliable about money. One always had to see the bank statement for oneself. Yet of course he was utterly charming to the end, there was never a bird left on the trees by the end of the evening.'

'But that must have been infuriating, wasn't it?'

'Not really, well, not after I had got over the first shock – which only took about ten years.' She gave a harsh laugh and I began, at one remove so to speak, to imagine how Michel's voice must have sounded, how it broke from liquid to harsh, from honeyflow to jagged edge, and then reformed and flowed on again. 'No, it was like taking some delightful performing animal around with one. You know how naughty he can be at home, how he drives you mad with his barking and the messes he makes, but you're still pleased when he gives pleasure to others, too much pleasure sometimes, alas.'

'I don't think I've ever heard a widow talk about her late husband quite like that,' Rickshaw said.

'Oh dear, I don't think I'm very good at being a widow. Your mother speaks of your father rather more politely, but then she perhaps has a politer marriage to look back on. We were not polite to one another, not at all. I can't blame my son for not wishing to have anything more to do with us. I regret it of course, but I can't blame him.'

'And your grandson?'

'I regret not seeing him since he was a child. I used to teach him the songs Michel had sung. And now I don't suppose I ever shall.'

'Are you sure it's him, my friend I mean?' I could not help interrupting.

'Oh yes, of course, that's why you came, isn't it? People always come to see one for a purpose, don't they? It's him all right, doing that ghastly job out in Essex. I know because the solicitor had to get in touch with him the other day. About the inheritance.'

'The inheritance?' Rickshaw and I chorused like bad actors in a pantomime.

'His cousin, I suppose it must be, Michel's nephew, died out there, unmarried, had made a lot of money as a banker, left it all, lock, stock and barrel, to my long-lost grandson. *Quelle histoire.*' She raised her eyebrows.

'A lot of money?'

'Oh yes, a lot. There you see, the whirligig of time. What do I get from the Halabi family? Poverty, betrayal, neglect. And my grandson whom I haven't seen for years cops the lot.' Her sudden rough, vulgar tone was appealing, more so than her earlier detachment.

'Well,' I said. 'So Tony comes into his own.'

'And now,' she said, 'the home produce stall beckons, though what people can produce in a window box in Battersea, I have absolutely no idea.'

She rose from the plastic chair, stately, straight as a pillar, with damp grey curls playing around her long pale neck.

The news of Tony's legacy was electric, romantic, a proper story. I felt conscripted, I had a part to play. The estranged grandmother, the wonderful dignified being from another age, she too must be brought on to the set and reunited. True, she had not asked to see Tony, let alone Josie. She was too stiff and proud to bring up the subject, and I was too timid. In any case, Tony's news ought to be checked first. He might have taken his father's side, although I had never heard him talk of his father or indeed of his family at all (modern men don't). They had no telephone, the government had abolished telegrams and the post was too slow, so once again a dirty green train snaked out of Liverpool Street with me in the corner of the carriage gazing at the Essex fields and hedges turning brown, but now all charged with meaning and hope, not as on my last trip looking featureless and desolate.

I walked up the cement path with a high skipping feeling in my legs, as though I was the one who was bringing the legacy news. Only after knocking on the front door did I notice the neglected garden, the grass growing in the cracks of the path, the Michaelmas daisies unstaked and flattened, the sticky sweetheart and bindweed scrambling over the rosebushes. I peered through the grubby half-drawn curtains. The living room contained only the cheap furniture and the rickety table we had had our tea off. The shelves were empty, the walls bare, except for the outlines of where the picture frames had been.

'They've gone.' The other side of the concrete posts and green wire netting which divided the gardens of the cottages, an elderly woman in a dirty pinafore and wellingtons was weeding around her runner beans. 'Oh yes, they've gone.' Her withered head poked out between the beansticks. 'They came into money and they went. Well, you would, wouldn't you. There's nothing here for anybody.' She had one of those East Anglian voices which sound depleted yet not complaining, as though the speaker is suffering from a serious, possibly fatal disease, but is trying to keep it from you.

'Do you know where?'

'Oh east, east. They didn't leave no address, said there wouldn't be nothing to be forwarded. And they were right, there hasn't been, not even a postcard.' She seemed pleased, almost admiring at this lack of correspondence.

It was fitting that they should have vanished like this. They had, after all, been the subject of divine intervention. A golden shower had been unleashed upon them and it would have been a comedown if one had glimpsed them deciding what to pack for the Middle East or going in to make arrangements with their bank managers. Curiously, I envied them more when they had been poor and unhappy. I had not wished to be with them then, their striving made me feel uncomfortable. Now they had served their time and resumed their rightful place. I felt a strong, no, an overpowering urge to see them, almost literally to touch their golden limbs again now that they were once more gilded and moving as easily about the court as they used to. There is an inconsistency about all this, since I have a priggish side and normally regard inherited wealth as bad for people. Honest sweat-dewed achievement is what I profess to respect, and actually do respect. But then in this case there was no question of respect. It was more a matter of love, and in such matters achievement is a clumsy interloper. I wanted to see them come into their own, watch the world acknowledge their unique grace. The fact that what they had come into had been someone else's, the property of this no doubt sleek unappetising banker cousin, that was neither here nor there. Their grace too had been unearned, after all, and it is the unearned that one falls in love with. The golden shower had fallen in the right place.

Yet I did not seek them out. A certain embarrassment held me back. Besides, in a way I preferred to dwell on the thought of their romantic opulence, rather than chase after them at the risk of being an irksome reminder of their earlier ups and downs. They so clearly wanted to get away from everything that might remind them of their low period, and that must surely include me. So I resigned myself to following their starry tracks from a distance, through glossy magazines and the occasional newspaper feature about their amazing luck. I was not preparing to bump into them, and so, of course, bump into them was what I did, although bump is too jocular a verb to cover the disturbing aspects of our meeting.

Now

'Less blackcurrant, more gooseberry,' said the man in the bow tie.

'Gooseberry?'

'Oh yes, gooseberry.'

'Nobody else has spotted the gooseberry.' The other man's sad red face was screwed up with anxiety. His companion bent forward and despatched a low-looping glob of red spit. The spit just cleared the bow tie and crept over the edge of the gleaming silver bucket. 'Gooseberry, I'll put that in our tasting notes if you don't mind, I'm most awfully grateful.'

'And chewy too.'

'Chewy. You are kind, it's only an ordinary Gamay, but we do like to think it's got something.'

'If you drank too much of it, you could ...' The man in the bow tie paused. '... get quite drunk.' The light from the street shone in through the arched cellar windows, shedding a dusty aura upon the heads of the connoisseurs raised in gargle, their adam's apples bobbing like billiard balls, their shoes shining beetle black on the sawdust floor. A priestly chill in the air.

'Of course, we can't quite manage the body.'

'No, the body, of course not.'

'Not without the sun.'

'You need a lot of sun.'

'You can say that again. I mean, take him, lucky bugger, his stuff just puts on weight like I do. Only two years old, and every mouthful's simply bulging with muscle already.'

'Amazing.'

'But still we've got the nose. They can't compete there.'

'The nose ...'

'Even when they're a bit thin, our wines have a nose on them that you simply don't get out there.'

I dipped my nostrils in the winking blood, but the sinuses were keeping vigil and only a musty tinny smell came through and even that was more likely to be left over from the gilder's shop on the corner. Through the gilder's door and windows flung open (on a raw enough day) to get rid of the odour, you could see ornate mirrors and picture frames and cherubs holding up light fittings and wall-mounted eagles all doused in a Midas shower. That was the smell that always came to me when I thought of this part of London, acrid at first then bellying out into a sickly sweet odour, then thin and acrid again, unpleasant but compelling and drawing you on to some other connection that was not quite placeable. But it was unfair to link the smell to the quarter which was still a beguiling district, with its left-over trades and craftsmen, shabby and ageing but with a bit of life in them still: jewellers' sundries, Gustave Langweil Artificial Flowers, milliners' requisites – ostrich feathers a speciality, weights and measures, optical instruments, colourmen, engravers' tools, olive oil importers, brewing equipment, moulders and diecasters; some boarded up now, the rings and watches and scalpels and burins and brass weights now only outlines of dust in the empty display cases, but others still humming with the noise of lathes and drills, and the traffic of dealers, delivery boys and sundries men not much changed since Mayhew's day. And setting up shop in the peeling premises were the sundries men of the new age: graphic designers and avant-garde shopfitters and landscape architects and software programmers. Girls with folded arms in long black split skirts nipping across to the sandwich bars for diet yogurts and vegetable spring rolls to be heated up on the office microwave would bump into pale orthodox Jews in long black flapping gaberdines with briefcases full of gold and silver chains and wedding rings. It was all, not picturesque exactly, but nicely tucked away.

'There he is over there, I really must congratulate him on his eighty-sixes.'

'Would he have come over specially for this?'

'I don't know about specially, I think he comes over to Claridge's a couple of times a year, for this and that.'

'And a bit of the other perhaps?'

'No, no, he brings his wife.'

I followed the nodding head of the man with the bow tie and there, standing amid the garglers at the far end of the room, was Tony. He had no glass in his hand and he was as pale and slim as ever, so that he could not help standing out from the ruddy garglers around him, and yet there was something profoundly unsurprising about the sight of him. I had no idea that he made wine now, still less that his wine was something to be talked about. But his popping up did not seem weird precisely because he was so detached from his surroundings, just as we are told that religious people are not at all taken aback to see the Virgin appear at a football match or the supermarket check-out.

'This is the presiding genius of Château des Palmes.'

'I'm afraid not. All the credit goes to my vigneron. I know virtually nothing about wine, I just help stick on the labels.'

'The eighty-sixes are wonderful, they really are.'

'Oh, thank you, we were so worried about them to start with, but they have come on nicely.' He spoke in the soft concerned tones of a parent, and with what sounded like a faint French accent. When he spotted me, he embraced me in the French style, but somehow did not embarrass me nor seem to be brushing aside the men he had just been talking to.

'Tony, you –'

'Antoine, now, I have reverted, I am a throwback. And Josie is Joséphine with an *accent aigu*, at least when I remember she is. You must try some palm wine.'

The wine was everything they were saying about it, and as it began its majestic progress down my throat, fumes of pleasure lost no time in fogging my brain.

'What do you think?' Tony/Antoine said.

'Wonderful, quite wonderful.'

'You're supposed to make some intelligent comment about the stuff, you know, use your imagination a bit. We desperately need a few fresh adjectives.'

'I'm already delirious. I can't spell.'

As it happened, by some quirk of the synapses, what did percolate the fog at the moment was what the gilding smell reminded me of. That acrid-sweet-acrid coming-and-going was in its potency, its unpleasantness, its annoying compulsiveness like, in fact very like, the smell of spikenard. All that was lacking was the spikenard's vegetable oiliness. What a peculiar destiny Tony had embraced, it seemed, with the same unflurried grace as he had embraced me here in Bludger's *the* Wine Bar, with the golden light flowing over him through the windows in the pavement.

'You must come back and see Josie.'

'Oh, I'd love to.' An unwanted caressing tone had got into my voice.

'It sounds as if you've met Madame Halabi before, my friend,' said the man in the bow tie.

'Yes, I have.'

'She's a magnificent woman.' He dipped his bow tie in reverence to Tony, who riposted with a courtly nod.

'She certainly is,' I said, slowish on my cue, not because I wished to disagree but because that wasn't quite how I had thought of her.

Yet when we came out of the lift into the breathless silence of the hotel corridor, against my will a certain awe did take hold of me. My noiseless feet on the thick cherry-and-gold carpet seemed to be carrying me towards a daunting interview with some legendary princess. The sensible side of my brain which had not yet been taken over by the Château des Palmes told me not to be so silly. I was on my way to see an old tennis partner who had knocked about a good deal since leaving north London. But the sensible side of my brain was wrong. To the first blink of my blurred eyes, as we came in, the room seemed to be empty as well as deathly silent, the silence broken only by the tick of the big Boulle clock on the chocolate-and-white marble mantelpiece. Then something stirred on the big brocade sofa and Josie rose from the tasselled tapestry cushions like the goddess from the foam. One of the tapestry cushions turned into a small Pekinese dog the colour of grainy honey.

'Oh, how shaming. To be caught asleep in the middle of the day.' She kissed me on the lips, kneading my face between her hands, the gentlest of bakers. She was still warm and milky-smelling from her sleep and my knees gave under me. An irritable noise from the peke, halfway between a yawn and a bark, stiffened my sinews a little.

'How did you find him?' she asked, patting me here and there as though Tony had picked up the most unusual and quite charming small piece of statuary.

'I was out drinking for my country, and there he was . . .'

'Sozzled, I suppose.'

'Certainly not,' I said. 'Just sipping.'

'Ah, those sips.' She turned to get a cigarette out of the sandalwood box on the little marquetry table by the sofa and in her turning, the silky peignoir – there seemed no other word for this flowing garment of bruised peach – swirled about her haunches and I became aware that her body had taken on a new sumptuousness, to be computed by colder brains than mine at an extra twenty pounds or so, which had transformed her whole style and personality. She seemed to speak and move more slowly, her voice sounded lower, duskier.

'See how fat I have got.'

'You look wonderful, like an odalisque.'

'Exactly, fat. We lead such a sedentary life, don't we, Antoine?'

'Nonsense, *chérie*. We have just had a fortnight's skiing at Gstaad, and then before that we were snorkelling in the Virgin Islands.'

'You were skiing, I was drinking hot chocolate with masses of cream and in the West Indies I just sat on the beach and soaked up all those complicated drinks.'

157

'She exaggerates.'

'No, I don't. Since I have had the babies, I have become a dozy cow and the awful thing is I don't give a shit.'

She subsided back on the sofa, despatching a couple of smoke rings with a lazy moue.

'It's a strange life we've fallen into,' he said, 'like winning the pools, I suppose, but the thing is, so far we're ridiculously happy, aren't we, *chérie*?'

'Oh, totally utterly fabulously,' she said raising her eyes to the ceiling. I noticed that, unlike Tony, her voice had remained quite English, almost truculently so.

How long were they here for, had they seen their parents, been to the club?

'Antoine's grandmother died as we were just getting settled out there. Such a pity, we would love to have shown her round. Otherwise, we're both on non-speaks with our aged p's. Antoine hasn't spoken to his since he left school practically, and since P-J and Iris have made it so clear they think he's beyond the pale, they're out too. It's their own silly fault. They should never have encouraged him in the first place. I suppose they might have thought differently if he'd been a duke or had a lot of dosh but as he was only a penniless scrap merchant he wasn't good enough for yours truly otherwise known as the Princess of Muswell Hill and so he had to be given his cards. Unfortunately for them, ha ha ha, our hero does become a millionaire and practically a duke –'

'Don't talk nonsense, darling.'

'Practically a duke in his own country, but it's too late. They have sealed their own fate. And they won't even see little Michel and Beatha, so tough tits.'

'*Chérie.*'

'Don't keep saying *chérie*. There's no point in not facing facts. The truth is, if you've behaved in an unforgivable way you're not likely to be forgiven. People don't like to think about that, they much prefer imagining that somehow Father Time will do his healing bit and all sides will begin to forget and then begin to

158

forgive. But in most families it isn't like that, is it? People remember terribly clearly and they go on remembering.'

She had never spoken at such length before, at least not when I was around, and, put down in writing, her words must sound bitter and slightly desperate. Yet in practice she sounded quite cheerful and matter-of-fact.

'He's become a Maronite, did you know that? It wasn't exactly something he had to do to lay hands on the inheritance, not legally anyway, but it seemed like a convenient wheeze, you know, showing that you mean to fit in with the locals.'

'It's a peculiar feeling,' Tony said, looking fractionally nettled at this lightweight explanation of his conversion, 'like coming home. You can't help being moved at rejoining the Church your ancestors belonged to for so many centuries.'

'And Josie?'

'She supports me very loyally.'

'I'm glad you think so. I must say, though, that as mumbo-jumbo goes, it's all rather sweet. You must come and stay, you absolutely must. Oh John, you are sweet. On the table, I think.'

A waiter had brought in a huge pannier of fruit and patisseries with a posy of flowers nestling on top of it. Josie leant forward and inhaled the posy, then exhaled a sensuous mmm as though she had never smelled such flowers. 'Oh John, you do spoil us. Just look at the freesias. Do thank darling Mr da Silva, won't you?' The waiter, a slender quizzical dark young man with something of Tony's style, took all this in his stride: a faint smile, a few murmured words of thanks, and he was off, trousering the tip without breaking stride.

Josie picked an apple from the pannier and attacked it with her white teeth. The scrunch sounded very crisp in the carpeted silence of the suite.

'You eat like a peasant, *chérie*.'

'I am a peasant, a Welsh peasant, and you can't get more peasanty than that, don't you agree?' She appealed to me with a wave of the half-eaten apple. 'What about the way Arabs eat? That cousin of yours, Camille, he eats like a horse, literally, snorting

159

and chomping, it's disgusting. Anyway, I don't have to sit here and listen to you criticise my table manners.'

'You don't have to sit here at all. I thought you were going to take the children to the park.'

'Milou said she didn't mind. I thought she was looking a little pasty and needed some fresh air.'

'You thought *she* was looking a little pasty.'

'Oh shut up.'

He went to the window and looked out of it. I could see his brown hand playing with the acorn of the blind-cord, up and down as though it were a yoyo.

'The most extraordinary thing', I said, to break the silence, 'is that it turns out we're related, connected anyway. Your cousin Theo Hale, well he's my cousin too, on his mother's side, distant, of course, but there is a link.' My voice began to trail away at the end of the sentence as I sensed a galloping frost.

'You're interested in that kind of thing, are you?' Josie said. 'I'm surprised, I didn't realise you were so old-fashioned. Do you know this Hale person, Antoine?'

'Yes, he is a cousin.'

'. . . they were originally Halabis too,' I put in, unwilling to go down without a fight.

'I believe they were. He is a fat old solicitor who lives in the backwoods somewhere, a homosexual, I think'.

'Oh,' I said, 'I'm not sure . . .'

'Why the fuck hasn't Milou brought the children back yet?'

'I can't see why you're so impatient for their return. You don't seem to take much notice of them when they're here.'

A heavy melancholy settled over me, a kind of brooding pervasive dullness like mid-afternoon indigestion. All the shine had gone off them, not in the physical sense, of course. Tony had changed down into a fluffy jersey of the exquisitely muzzled shade of amber and a pair of cream linen trousers, and Josie was so *soignée* that the sofa and the fruit and the flowers and the patisseries all seemed to be conspiring to cosset her.

But all this made the bickering more squalid. Their spiritual coats had gone dull and mangy, and a certain repugnance began to well up inside me, much against my will, for I wanted to love and admire them still, I wanted to go on enjoying the fairy tale.

The key turned in the lock, and a chunky Arab-looking girl in a grey nanny's uniform came into the room followed by two toddlers with bright round faces and dark eyes. Their mouths were lapped in jammy smears and they looked tired and on the verge of turning truculent.

'Darlings, what filthy faces.' Josie swept them into her arms, and they hoicked themselves up on to the sofa and nested up against her, their jammy faces burrowing into the bruised peach. This came as a distinct relief. In my gloom, I had half fancied they might recoil from her or respond with stiffness and distrust. 'This is Michel and this is Elizabeth, Beatha, and this is an old friend of Papa's who's going to come and see us when we get home, isn't he?'

'Yes he certainly is,' I said. The two children looked at me without speaking, their dark eyes unblinking, their jammy faces expressionless. Then they began punching their mother in the ribs.

'Stop it, stop it.'

Josie's plump arms fended them off, but the children went on pummelling, crying and chuckling at the same time to start with, then relapsing into a tired moan as they stopped punching and clutched at their mother with fierce little fists.

'I hate grizzling children. Milou's kept them out much too long. Don't rub there, Michel, it isn't nice.'

'It is nice.'

'No, it isn't. Oh, what have you – you are a horrible little boy.' The spurt of his pee across her thigh left a dark parabola on the bruised peach. She slapped him with a crisp ringing slap and his yowl filled the whole suite. She jumped off the sofa, all languor gone, and marched off into the bedroom to change, shouting for Milou as she went. The little boy sat on the sofa, his wet legs not reaching the carpet. His sister sat at the other end of the sofa, sucking her thumb, looking at him with scientific curiosity, now

161

and then stealing a glance at me to see how I was taking it. The nanny came and took Michel off to clean him up. From the next - door room, the yowling continued.

'Miche dirty,' Beatha said as soon as he was safely out of the room.

'No, he's just had an accident,' Tony said.

Tony seemed unable to muster his old grace to cope with the incident. He got up and began to walk irritably round the room. Beatha swivelled her head to monitor his reactions. For my part, I felt terrible – profound pitch-black lake of despair, at the stomach's bottom, head of sour sludge, lungs choked with dust, to name but a few symptoms, so why should he be expected to feel much better?

Yet I could not forgive him, or Josie either, for so quickly dis-illusioning me. In their troubles, they had displayed a certain imperviousness, they had been noble. How humiliating to have glamorised a second-rate couple who happened to have fallen on their feet without in any way deserving to. It was pitiful to see them cave in without a fight to the petty failings of the rich. What could be more dispiriting than to think that we were puppets of our bank balance, all our principles and qualities liable to be blown away by a financial blast or windfall. To see people as they really were was not to see them at all, it was the beginning of death. Without a certain shimmer the world was as dull as a car park, as lifeless as the surface of the moon. Glamour was, after all, originally the same word as grammar, both were ways of describing language, that strange obsessive business of giving names to things which had brought us to our present pass but without which there would be no pass to be present at. When the scales fall from our eyes, when all the shimmer and the squinting is gone, we see nothing worth seeing. In any case, our world is the world we have made up and we don't let go of it so easily. When Josie slopped back into the room on a fresh pair of mules, my cra-pulous annoyance was not much abated (if anything it was sharp-ened by the purple cocktail dress with sequin swirls across the bosom which she had climbed into). But I could not help think-

162

ing too of her lovely astronautical gambolling on the tennis court in the old north London days, and my melancholy took on a softer tinge.

'You'll come, won't you?' she said. 'I promise you Michel will be housetrained and I shan't be so ratty.'

'Oh yes I will, of course I will.'

'You must, Gus, you really must.' The sound of my name on her plummy lips was almost unbearable, caressing yet painful, a sudden stab of unattainable delight. I find it strange when other people seem quite unmoved by the mention of their name but perhaps that is how I too look to the observer in such circumstances, quite stolid, frozen.

'He's called disgusting! He's called disgusting,' Beatha crowed, bouncing up and down. 'Disgusting people can't come to our house.' This, the longest sentence she had so far uttered, was exquisitely articulated.

Michel took up the cry, a little less securely. 'Gusting people can't come to our house.' He was better at it when he joined in the refrain with his elder sister.

'Shut up, shut up. He's coming, so there,' their mother shouted.

But I didn't. Perhaps in time it might have come about, but events took a different course — I think that is the right phrase, although a ponderous one. What happened seemed so little intended, the sequence had so little logic to it, that I could not help thinking of 'the events' as so many bedraggled schoolboys milling about at the start of a compulsory paperchase before jogging off in a dismal gaggle without much idea about the route. But in the end the events were brought together, tidied up, placed in something resembling a course.

I came upon Richard Shay loitering palely at the Smoked Meats and Fish counter. His gaze seemed locked upon a piece of white plastic cut in the shape of a thistle which said Rannoch Smoked Venison Is Also Excellent Served With A Creamy Avocado Sauce. His eyes had that unblinking fixity they always had, alert yet also distant, so that he never looked at all inquisitive.

'Rickshaw,' I said.

'Ah.' He turned to me with his unfailing enthusiasm but without the faintest affectation of being taken aback. It would have been the same had we bumped into one another in a shebeen in County Kerry or a dance hall in Paraguay. The world was so full of wonders that everything was equally surprising and must be welcomed with the same delight but without any suggestion of what-are-you-doing-here, for to stress either the you or the here would have been to condescend to the circumstances. 'Don't you adore smoked venison?'

'Never had it,' I said.

'The best I ever had,' he said, 'was in northern Norway. We used to lie out in the meadows stark naked in the endless summer days and an old boy with huge moustaches would come out of the smoking huts with the smoked roe-deer sliced thin on caraway seed bread and little horn cups of aquavit.'

'Whatcha want?' said the girl behind the counter.

'My dear, could you let me have half a pound of that marvellous-looking smoked venison?'

'It's seventeen pounds a pound, you know.'

The tiniest twitch of pain made a lightning transit across his noble features, and he reduced the order to a quarter of a pound. This glimpse of bachelor economies was embarrassing but it was over in a second. 'You'll want to hear the whole story, about Tony, won't you?' he said. 'You must come back to my mother's flat for a cup of tea. I'm just starting to clear the place up a bit, you know she died two months ago.'

'Oh no, I'm so sorry. You sure you want −?'

'I feel the need of company when I'm there. So many memories, often ones I'd prefer to forget.'

'Well, if you're sure, I'd love to. I need to hear the story. I only know what was in the papers.'

We took the bus down a long avenue of dusty red-brick flats with their iron balconies empty except for the odd bicycle or forgotten flowerpot, their tall windows darkened by the overgrown plane trees, the once gay bands of cream stucco turned to a muddy beige. As the bus drew into each stop, the trees would brush its roof with a slithery rattling noise.

'I like this area,' he said. 'It's so mysterious.'

It was hard to see what he had done so far about clearing up the flat. When he turned the Yale key in the door, the dust seemed to rise to greet us. The china ornaments and the photographs on the old walnut keyboard instrument looked quite untouched, and the heavy green brocade curtains with their scalloped pelmets might never have been drawn.

'It's a harpsichord,' he said. 'Mother used to play, not well, her fingers were too big, Scarlatti mostly.'

Melancholy began to mingle with the dust in a thick choking fog. I began to wish I had not come, although I had to hear the story.

'Sit down, sit down while I make the tea, and then I'll begin.' He was all alert, nose twitching like a hound on the scent, his pale driftwood body tense as a catapult. I settled back in the green brocade wing chair which matched the curtains. Mrs Shay's flat now seemed like the most comfortable place in the world. The laggard tick of the gilt clock on the mantelpiece, the ghostly tingle from the harpsichord as his foot set a floorboard creaking, even the lingering smell of cat, all induced contentment and attention.

'I took the bus,' he began. 'Do you like that mint tea, oh good, I took the bus. I had no car, in any case I was told that the authorities did not welcome private motorists, but I like buses. It was the route Alexander must have taken, you know, there isn't any other pass they could have gone over. It must have been lovely when Beatha rode that way with Michel – the flowers and the olive trees and then the cedars up in the hills – but I'm afraid it's all guard posts now, and utterly pointless bits of barbed wire in the middle of nowhere, and rushing trucks and jeeps overturned by the side of the road and then the usual fearsome civilian litter as well. The view from the top is still marvellous, of course, when you look down into that unspeakably lush valley and see the olives and the vines shimmering and the other mountains beyond glittering like shards of mica ...'

'And the little creamy domes of the church? I always liked the idea of them.'

Richard Shay looked at me with a second's worth of impatience: he painted the pictures, the listener listened, that was the division of labour and he insisted in the most amicable way possible that this was how it should stay.

'Entrancing, but, of course, the village has grown. That gently winding track down to the stream is now a tarmac road with breeze-block bungalows and shops and then, as you go further on, there are half-finished high-rise concrete skeletons of apartment blocks along the hillside with the ground floors already occupied and bricks piled neatly at the side ready for when the owner can afford the next load of cement. And then as you come closer to the Château des Palmes – there is a dear little sign to the house with a green palm tree on it – you are really in a town. But it's not just the little provincial sort of Arab town you can find all over that part of the world – with a couple of greengrocers and a place where you can get retread tyres and another place which has bits of old pipes. Here there are boutiques, jewellers with branches in Paris and Palm Beach, people selling glamorous matching luggage and silk scarves, there was a discotheque too, and a restaurant with little bay trees outside it and an awning. The woman sitting next to me in the bus clucked in amazement or disapproval, I'm not sure which, and the two hens she had on her lap with their legs tied together clucked too. I clucked a bit myself, it was the most amazing sight, a mirage if you like, and the people were kitted out to match, the men in smart cream suits and the women in shimmering gauzy dresses which made them look as if they were floating along the street. Down the side streets you could see some rather smart villas with bougainvillea dripping over their high walls and dogs barking behind the walls. I stopped and asked a man the way outside the Benetton branch and he told me to stay on the sidewalk and hang a right when I got to the drugstore, *and* he told me to have a nice day.'

'But the house, was that changed too?'

'Not a bit, it looked just as I imagined, the charming old farmhouse with the green doors round the courtyard and the hens pecking.'

'And Tony?'

'He was nowhere to be seen, to start with. So I was taken inside to wait, and that was the most extraordinary shock too, because I'd expected that the inside would be like the outside with wooden beams and the quaint little doors with painted wooden arches, and it wasn't like that at all, it was much, much bigger than it looked from the outside. I was taken into a huge hall with a high vaulted ceiling and a chandelier and a shiny floor which looked like marble. The chairs were all set against the wall, and there were several Arabs sitting in them. They mostly looked elderly and a bit run down, not at all boutique folk. Like me, they seemed to be waiting. It seemed to be an official audience chamber, in the modern ministerial style you find in offices everywhere in the Middle East.

'Then, after a bit, Tony appeared in a rather smart sweater and cream slacks, looking as if he'd just stepped out of a knitwear catalogue, and all the old men got up and bowed. He gave them quite a polite nod back, I suppose, but that was all, and then he took me off into his study, which had modern squashy leather sofas and a Dufy of the Casino at Nice, and a whole lot of glossy magazines from London and New York. And he sat me down and fixed me a Martini and said how great it was being a Christian in Wogland because it meant you could drink all you wanted and there was no competition.'

'He sounds terribly smooth.'

'He was and he wasn't. He kept on saying how happy he was to have come out as a wog – every time he used the word my little liberal heart skipped a beat – and it's true he did seem much readier to talk about himself. I asked him did he feel different and when did he know. "I was twenty-one. My father called me into his poky little study. He looked terribly embarrassed, well, he always looked embarrassed when he was talking to me, embarrassed and bad tempered, but now he looked ashamed, as if he was going to tell me he had to go to jail. And he told me about this mysterious grandfather they'd never spoken about, but he thought

167

I ought to know now I was grown up and of course it didn't make one any less English, there was no need to worry about it. I asked him about Theo Hale, who'd always been described as a sort of distant relation, how did he fit in, and my father said in fact he was quite a close cousin and was also a Halabi. They'd taken a different surname because at the time his parents had come over, my grandfather's name was in all the papers with the Mrs Teazle case. Well, I was furious and disgusted. I can't describe the contempt I felt for the lot of them. My mother was just as bad – in fact, it was probably she who had insisted on the secrecy. I moved out as soon as I could and never spoke to either of them again, except about practical arrangements." "But", I began, and he interrupted me, "Yes, I know, the awful thing was that I did exactly as they wanted as far as the family secret was concerned: never told a soul, never made any further enquiries, looked bored whenever anyone started talking about the Middle East, pretended I was from nowhere and had no relations, as though I was England's answer to the Virgin Birth. Oddly enough, I rather enjoyed the whole thing, I liked being terribly British and at the same time thinking to myself that I had hidden depths. But I suppose it must have been a strain – at least, looking back it does seem a very peculiar way to live, at least compared with the way we live now."

'And I suppose he was relaxed and I believed it when he said he felt he had really come home, I really did. But then, of course, as we all know, coming home isn't always an utter bed of roses. There was still something restless about him, I thought, I don't quite know why I thought that, the way he moved or something. I felt it more when he took me over to the church. "I'm the Liquidator here, you know," he said, "that's my official title. I'm in charge of the Miraculous Liquefaction of the Magdalen. I have to keep it up, it's quite a source of local income. There's no harm in it. *Credo quia impossibile*. One believes in more impossible things than that, after all. I think one ought to believe in impossible things, don't you? Keeps one from getting too cocky." "Yes, I quite agree," I said. "Oh, thank you," he said, rather oddly. He also told me that when he told the locals that it was a funny thing but he'd also been a liquidator back in England, they all assumed he'd been some sort of a gangster because they knew perfectly well there would be no miraculous liquefactions in our poor dull country. Of course, he explained to them that his duties had been entirely legal and above board, to do with winding up companies, and so on, but they didn't really believe him, it seemed such an implausible cover story. Clearly, what he'd been doing was running a sort of armed protection racket, putting the squeeze on debtors. As a result, he acquired an instant reputation as a man to be reckoned with, which was partly why all those poor old fellows would wait for hours to plead for his help. So from one point of view, overnight he'd become a kind of Mafia chieftain, the ultimate hard man, but then he also seemed to have a gentler kind of role, more like the curator of a National Trust property. In fact, as we were standing in the porch, with him in his Ralph Lauren polo shirt and his Gucci loafers, he suddenly noticed some litter which had blown into the corner – crumpled fag packets, cellophane, leaves – and slipped behind the curtain and brought out an old straw broom and began sweeping away. It reminded me of something, this elegant pale figure – it's extraordinary how quite untanned he was – sweeping away in the dim religious gloom, with all the light and heat and dust pulsating outside. I couldn't quite think what it was, something in a film or a book, something rather sad. "Perhaps, on second thoughts," he said after he'd put the broom away, "it's not a question of belief, really, more a matter of keeping things tidy." Who sweeps a room as for thy laws, I said, but he didn't respond. Even after coming out, as he called it, he's a silent sort of chap, Tony. Then we went out on the terrace and sat on the wall and looked across at the blossom on the other side, the white apple and the pink peach and I suppose the redder pink must have been cherry. There were no breeze-block bungalows on that side, just the traditional old houses with their green shutters and red roofs and snow on the peaks behind them. Immediately below us the sheep were grazing and amusing themselves by jumping over the little boundary walls.'

'Sounds wonderful.'

'It was. As we were looking at the view, a little old man with one arm came up and gave me a card for *Le Como – Grand Nightclub Select*. How nice, I thought, that they should think the Italian lakes as romantic as we do. But on the card there was a muddy photograph of Perry Como in the nineteen forties. Don't come before midnight, he said, the horniest chicks only come late. Then he saw it was Tony I was talking to and he bowed and made himself scarce. Then we went back to the house and had the most delicious mezze, the stuffed vine leaves were brilliant and so were the very light pastries with melted cheese inside. It was a huge party at a vast glass-topped table, several cousins and their wives and a priest in full fig and a couple of local functionaries in double-breasted suits. I sat opposite a young cousin, couldn't have been more than eighteen, with the most enormous black eyes you ever saw. He ate like a peasant. Although he wasn't very tall, he had these big hands which seemed to claw at the food like a vulture. He didn't say much. I asked him whether he was studying and he laughed a vulture-ish sort of laugh and turned to his neighbour, a fat boy of about the same age who couldn't speak any English, and presumably translated my question to him and they both nearly ruptured themselves laughing. I asked Tony about him afterwards and he said, oh that's Pierre, no, he's not exactly an intellectual, he's captain of our football team. And he laughed, too, rather grimly I thought.'

'And what about Josie?'

'Well, she wasn't there, she'd taken the children up into the mountains to teach them how to ski, but she was coming back the next day. Anyway, in the afternoon Tony went off to attend to some business and I had the sleep of a lifetime, I'd been on the road for days. The mountain air, the blossom on the hillside, the couple of delicious glasses of arak I'd had for lunch, the dear little room, not tarted up like the main reception rooms, with its painted wooden bedstead and cotton coverlet and little ivory crucifix hanging on the wall, it was a sort of monkish heaven. It was quite dark when I woke up (blink and you miss the twilight in those parts anyway) and there was quite a commotion going on

170

outside the room, running feet, a good deal of fierce muttering and the sound of car doors slamming and engines starting up. I got up and walked along the passage to the hall, and there was Tony standing there in a high state of agitation, his immaculate casuals looking really quite rumpled. There was a transistor radio on the octagonal table beside him blaring out what sounded like a news programme of some kind. What happened, I asked. There was a fight at the football match, the one Pierre was playing in, against the next-door village. And it's on the news? I said in foolish surprise. The other people shot our goalkeeper's brother, Tony said, that fat boy opposite you at lunch. He's a bit of an idiot. Every time we scored, he insisted on firing his gun in the air to celebrate and the home spectators got fed up, so they confiscated his car. Wouldn't it have been better to confiscate his gun, I asked. I suppose they didn't think of that, Tony said. Anyway at half-time, he fetched his brother the goalkeeper and a couple of other team mates, including Pierre, and they went to get the car back from the shed it had been taken to, and then they all started blazing away and the bullets started rattling round the shed like hail, Pierre said, and the goalkeeper's brother's dead and two of the other clan are in the Christian Brothers Hospital and will be lucky to pull through. Small massacre, not many dead, so far, he said bitterly. Couldn't Pierre have stopped it at all, I asked. In this part of the world, captains aren't expected to stop fights, and Pierre's a captain all right. He himself got away with a chipped bone in the forearm, he's having it dressed now, should be back any minute. Tony was in a queer mood, I thought, agitated and worried, of course, distracted by trying to think what he ought to do, but also elated in a way, with a glitter in his eye, not at all that laid-back character we used to know.'

'And what did he do?' This picture of Tony fired up by the prospect of action was itself curiously elating.

'In fact, nobody got back from the hospital until it was time to dine and all we had to go on till then was the earlier reports and the quacking radio. So there we were again sitting down at the huge glass table and eating more delicious food, and there was

Pierre again with his arm in a sling, but without the fat boy, and his enormous black eyes went up and down the table checking who was against him, who was blaming him. He told us what had happened, well, reported to Tony, would be a more accurate way of putting it, not quite like a junior officer reporting to a general, more like a commanding officer explaining to a politician who could not be expected to understand what fighting was like. You got the impression that the Liquidator, for all his fearsome past, was generally regarded as a non-combatant, a civilian. But the whole thing did seem extremely military, despite the fact that Pierre was still wearing his shiny Benetton tracksuit and trainers. Two of "our men" had been injured as well as himself, but not seriously. One of the other clan was not expected to survive. Tony said he had already spoken to – but they were speaking in Arabic now, much too fast for me to follow – I assumed it must be the head of the other clan and they had promised that the matter should end there, there should be no further bloodshed. Would the deal stick, I asked Tony when he explained it to me. He shrugged his shoulders. Did anything ever stick in that part of the world? He had rung the hotel in the mountains. Josie and the children were already on their way back. This was a time to be at home. What would –'

Mrs Shay's doorbell rang, a sharp screeching reproof to these outlandish goings-on.

'Oh God, the tuner. That's why I was coming here in the first place.'

He brought in a tall bald man with dark glasses, stooped with a blind man's stillness. Behind them, a small fat woman was jangling car keys. 'I'll be back in forty minutes on the dot,' she announced and clumped off down the stairs again.

'Sorry about the blindness,' the bald man said. 'It's a bit of a cliché, I'm afraid. Still, it helps to get you accepted in this job. There's one bloke I know has got no ear at all but gets a lot of work because he's got such a lovely guide dog. But then the dog can't drive, and you need to cover a fair bit of ground these days to earn a crust. Harpsichord innit, fiddly little things to deal with but I love the tone.'

'It was my mother's. I like to keep it in tune.'

'Quite right too – but then I would say that, wouldn't I?'

Shay led the tuner to the stool where he sat in a vulture's hunch over the keys, first rippling up and down the scale, then going back to try out a dubious note, requesting our help to hitch up the lid, then plunging down into the bowels of the instrument, seeming less and less blind as he found his way around and began adjusting the strings.

'Don't mind me,' he called out. 'Please talk amongst yourselves.'

Tentatively at first, then growing accustomed to the sound of his voice through the tinny twangling, Rickshaw resumed. To me, the thin erratic notes of the harpsichord accompaniment made his tale more outlandish still.

'What would the attitude of the police be, I asked. Tony seemed barely interested. Oh I expect they've taken statements, he said, in fact I think Pierre said they had, the station's quite near the football ground, but you know with so many guns around – he spread out his hands, not so much in despair, I thought, as to convey the utter irrelevance of the police in such matters. Father Bedui has appealed for calm, he's much respected in those villages. He stopped the last incident turning into a war. When was that, I asked. About six months ago Tony said. That time the quarrel broke out in the church down in the valley, so Father Bedui was in a strong position to scold them – two more dead that time, maybe three, one was an old man who had a heart attack. Father Bedui preached the most wonderful sermon in our church. When I came here, I thought his name must mean he was descended from some wild-eyed Bedouin, but in fact it's a corruption of Padua, after St Anthony of Padua. Funny old place this, isn't it, he said.'

'This thing really needs a total overhaul. The dampers are gone on half the keys and you've got a nasty bit of woodworm on the frame, if my fingers aren't telling me porkies.'

'You couldn't play something for us, could you? I'd love to hear the old instrument again.'

'You're the boss, squire. What's your fancy?'

'Could you play a little Scarlatti? My mother was so fond of Scarlatti.'

'Bit early for me, but I can do you the Sonata in C. Kirkpatrick 657, if I'm not mistaken.'

He played with what seemed to my dull ear a marvellous nimble sprightly quality which set off the sadness of the piece. I particularly liked the utter stillness of his head and shoulders. As he played, a spurt of envy went through me, surprising me by its force – envy for Tony, not simply for the rich and glamorous destiny that had been thrust upon him but for the intense and passionate quality of that destiny and the ineluctable force with which it had been thrust on him. To be strictly accurate, of course, it was not ineluctable at all. He could, I suppose, simply have pocketed the cash element of the inheritance and let the rest of it flow to whichever mafioso cousin had the best title to it or would fight hardest for it. Then he could have bought a rectory with six bedrooms just outside Saffron Walden and bred miniature sheep. But he had not slunk off in that direction, and part of my envy was really admiration that he had not, and irritation too that I had understood him so little. He had never seemed like a venturer, the sort of person who would instinctively volunteer for an assignment in Vietnam, or risk all his money on a single card or accept a bet that he could drink a whole bottle of tequila non-stop. But then I suppose there are what might be called polite venturers, who wait until fate issues a formal invitation. Usually it takes the outbreak of war to identify such people. Tony's invitation had come by a different route.

'What do you think of the Scarlatti? Some wise guy said I overdid the legato, but I like to keep it moving.'

'It was very beautiful, thank you,' Shay said. The tears must have been in his eyes for some time. One teardrop was already halfway down his pale cheek.

'Thank you squire. It's not often the punters ask the old blind tuner to play, and I hope it does you as much good as it does me. I could have a bash at some Lully if you fancied it.'

174

Once again the long fingers stretched over the discoloured ivory keys, their splayings more sedate this time. Shay too resumed.

'Tony was called over by one of the officials in double-breasted suits. I wandered out into the courtyard. It was pitch dark now, a wonderful night for the stars. You know how the sky suddenly seems crowded – no, positively encrusted with stars on a clear night out there. There must have been a dozen men or more not so much strolling around as prowling. Every now and then the slits of light through the shutters caught them or caught their gun barrels and you realised they were armed to the teeth: rifles, shotguns – I think I saw one or maybe two automatic weapons but I may have been seeing the same one twice. It took me a few moments to register something else: we were shut in. In the daytime, the place had seemed like a pleasantly rundown farmyard. I hadn't been aware of gates, but now high doors blotted out the road. There was even a sentry posted on the roof of the stable building next to the doors; I could see his outline quite clearly against the stars. The centurions prowling in the darkness made me nervous. It was so peculiar, this ramshackle medieval garrison protecting the chandeliers and the Dufy and the copies of *Cosmopolitan* and *Vogue* on the tapestry firestool, and Tony in his boutique casuals as the janissary directing operations. I wanted to get inside and go and bury myself in my little monkish room, but just as I was turning towards the steps, the sentry on the stable-roof stood upright and shouted something I couldn't understand, and there was the sound of running feet and then the grinding noise of a large beam being drawn back and the clanking of great rusty hinges, and the high doors were drawn open, showing for a moment the street lights and the road running away down the hill, before these too were blotted out as a large vehicle roared through the gateway into the yard and the doors were shut again behind it. The vehicle seemed huge, reducing the yard to its modest actual size, not more than forty or fifty feet square, I suppose. It came to me with a shock of patriotic recognition that it was a Range Rover, and out of it tumbled Josie, the children and what

175

must have been the nanny, while the driver got the luggage out of the back. "Christ, what a journey! Oh, there you are Rickshaw, Tony said you were here, though I don't know what on earth you're doing out of doors on a night like this. *Où est monsieur Antoine?*" she yelled to the servants who had come tumbling out through the green doors. "*Prenez les enfants, vite, vite.*" The children ran in with the laggard scamper of dormice just out of hibernation, rubbing their eyes as they came into the bright light of the reception chamber. I followed Josie inside. Her rich chestnut leather shoulder bag bounced on her dark-blue blazer like a soldier's bandolier, and the Hermès scarf loosely knotted round her head fluttered like a pennant. Tony was already kissing the children, then he took her in his arms while the old men sat along the walls under the dimmed chandeliers. His embrace seemed somehow formal, the embrace of foreign potentates at the foot of the aircraft steps. She began talking while he was still holding her and he appeared almost to pull her after him into the little sitting room with the Dufy and the glossy magazines. Since the children and the nanny followed them in, I saw no reason not to do the same, although I soon wished I hadn't. Thank you, that was beautiful too.'

'Well, that's my lot for today, squire. I hear fairy footsteps in the dell.' The bell rang as he spoke, and Shay went down to let in the small fat woman who was still jangling her keys. After they had gone, I began to feel uncomfortable. I wasn't quite sure why. Shay's legendary narrative powers were just as charming as ever, but I began to wish to be somewhere else, although I also wanted to hear the end of the story.

'On my way down the passage to the little sitting room – the passage was in total darkness – I suddenly became aware of hands feeling me up and down, first down my front and along the outside of my legs, and a voice was saying, "*Pardon, m'sieur, c'est nécessaire,*" and I realised I was being searched and then, as the door at the end of the passage opened and let in the light, I saw that it was Pierre who was searching me. His huge black eyes were staring up at me and there was something like a grin on his sulky face, and so I couldn't resist giving him a friendly pat in return and then he stroked me I won't tell you where, and I was hopelessly in love with him, well, I probably had been from the moment I saw him but the violence had confused me so I didn't know whether I was coming or going. Later that night he came to my little room and stayed for an hour or two. He left when he heard the sound of gunfire in the town, but we had had time enough. He managed so well, despite the sling.'

I felt certain that Shay had not originally intended to tell me this bit but somehow the rush of the story had carried him away and he had then felt honour bound to push on to the end. Certainly some sort of extra stress – perhaps the Scarlatti being played in his mother's room – must have stirred him to talk in this way, for although he was dedicated to a single life, he had never before let drop any hint of such affections. It was true that his experiences with women – what few glimpses I had had of them – sounded fleeting and unsatisfactory. His real passions were solitude and liberty, but perhaps his hour or two with Pierre was brief enough not to count.

'Anyway, by the time I got into the little sitting room, there was a full-scale row in progress. I absolutely hate rows, they make me curl up inside and I rather prefer to pretend they haven't happened, but the circumstances were so peculiar – the Range Rover snorting outside, the sentries on the rooftops, the gunfire down in the town, and Pierre, and the little Dufy on the wall with its gay green domes and palm trees and horsedrawn carriages trotting along the Promenade des Anglais drawn as a child would draw them, and standing behind Tony one of the heavies in his shiny double-breasted suit. The whole thing was so odd that it didn't seem quite real. "I tried to telephone all afternoon," Josie said. "First there was no answer, then they said the line was down, then they said our phone was out of order. I made such an embarrassing nuisance of myself that we can't ever go back to the Hôtel de la Neige. And where was the bloody driver? There was that huge great thing sitting outside the hotel, but you know I hate driving it – anyway, he'd got the keys. And every five minutes the radio was giving more and more horrific bulletins, though I suppose it was really the same bulletin over and over again. *Where were you?*" "I was down in the town, there were several things to attend to at the office, the shippers –" "Don't give me that bullshit. You were swapping tracksuit bottoms with that hairy dwarf in Benetton." "Oh Josie, please." "You'd think he'd have better taste. I mean he fancies himself rotten, but out of all the women in this godforsaken country he chooses the most physically repulsive bitch you've ever set eyes on. Have you been into Benetton yet, Rickshaw, you'll pick her out straight away, she's the only one of the assistants whose moustache and bottom both sweep the floor. And her parents chose to call her Angélique, that wasn't kind was it, not kind at all. Why didn't they call her Groucho, that would have been much better." "Josie, Josie, I was talking to the German about the new casks." "You know what they say about old wine in new bottles, Rickshaw, turns sour in no time. Well, that's what happened to our marriage. We put up with quite a lot together, I wouldn't say we were happy exactly, that would be overdoing it, but we were together, you know. Even when we were really down on our luck and Tony was working for the social security in East Anglia, we were still properly together. But as soon as he hits the jackpot and turns into Antoine the lord of all he surveys, then phut!" Her hands made a kind of exploding gesture and the children who were cowering round her ankles huddled deeper into the shelter of her tartan skirt. "The frog turns into a prince and a prince has to behave like a prince and his women, well, they're just women, aren't they? I mean, I suppose I'm number one wife so I'm entitled to custody of the Range Rover, but as for any affection or loyalty or common decent feeling – forget it." She sat down and began to sob, her head still wrapped in the Hermès headscarf with those stirrups and saddles round the edge. The heavy in the shimmering double-breasted suit whispered something in Tony's ear. I half thought he was asking whether Tony wanted her disposed of. But he must have been merely asking permission to leave the room. Tony nodded and he slipped out of the door at the back. I suggested to Tony that I too might slip away. "No, no, stay. You'll get a bad impression if you leave now. Josie is very tired, we are all a bit on edge. We must stay together a little longer and have a drink and we'll all feel better." "A bit on edge," she snorted through her handkerchief, "that's a nice way of putting it. That creepy little cousin of yours starts a small civil war and here we are besieged in this dump like something in the Middle Ages. On edge! At least you haven't lost your gift for English understatement." "Josie, Josie. Not now." "Why not now?" she screamed. "We're obviously going to be shut up here for fifteen years so we might as well have it all out." "Look, I really am going to bed," I said. "No, you're not, Rickshaw, you're going to sit down beside me —" she patted a space on the pink-and-green chintz sofa and I limply obeyed – "and you're going to listen to every single nasty word." Oh, she's changed so much, Gus, she's quite different from that sweet leggy girl you introduced me to at that enchanting party you gave a million years ago. She used to be so fresh and so *thin*. Now I could feel her thigh bulging against mine, and her bosom was a positive cliff. She's still a handsome woman, perhaps more handsome in some ways, she's got a kind of sensuous dignity now, but it's not the same.'

'I know, she was already like that when I saw her at Claridge's,' I said, but I was thinking much further back to the little drinks party in my bedsitting room with two dour colleagues from work sitting on the bed all evening not speaking to anyone else and Richard Shay charming the other dozen guests with his curiosity and his anecdotes (I scarcely knew him, scarcely knew anyone come to that, it had been bold enough to give this party, sheer mad courage to invite him). And then, making the party, if it came anywhere near being made, Josie and Tony standing loosely in the middle of the room, their heads nearly touching the ceiling, shedding grace, dispelling anxiety, just being there and making there seem the place to be.

'Then suddenly, Tony had had enough of us all. We were, well, dismissed, there's no other word for it, quite calmly and pleasantly dismissed. Sleep well, I hope we'll all feel better in the morning and so on – but dismissed all the same.'

179

'Josie too?'

'Yes, she got up, stretched herself in a languorous sort of way and said how tired she was and thought it was time to go to bed, as if she'd thought of it all by herself. But she certainly obeyed. In fact, I noticed that she usually did when Tony issued any practical instruction, not out of respect for him exactly, more as though it was something mechanical which simply had to be done, like filling a car with petrol.

'Then in the morning, all the horrors seemed to have been washed away. It had rained later in the night – there was a gentle drumming on the window when Pierre was with me – and everything looked so fresh and green and silvery. Down the corridor I could hear the sound of news bulletins on the radio, but I slipped out past the sitting room. The Range Rover was still out in the courtyard, its olive-green flanks spattered with mud. In the daylight it seemed reassuring, like a reminder of the Cotswolds. There was still a boy with a gun mooching about in the gateway but he took no notice of me and I wandered out into the tightly shuttered town. There was a track leading down to the river between scrubby olive trees, old women on donkeys off to forage. It was a scene of total tranquillity. There was nobody about down by the stream. I stripped off behind a tree and gave my aching limbs the bathe of a lifetime. He was so gentle, you know, so tactful, so patient with my clumsiness, for him it was all such a matter of course, that's what made it so exquisite.'

'Yes, quite,' I said.

'As I came back into the courtyard, to my surprise I met Josie just about to get into the Range Rover. She was in a gleaming white tennis dress. Come on, she said, come down to the club and get away from all this. As it happens, I hate tennis and anything to do with tennis, but bachelor guests have to do what they are told, and I hopped in and she drove me a couple of miles out of town to a country club surrounded by fine old trees. The clubhouse was in a fake Arab style but awfully charming, with chocolate and cream turrets like a building in Celesteville, and there were girls in jodhpurs hitching horses to white wooden rails and immaculate red clay tennis courts with little chairs for the umpires and ballboys in white shorts and eyeshades. A wiry young man with the face of a handsome lizard rushed out to embrace her and asked effusively whether she was all right. I couldn't make out whether he was the tennis pro or Josie's lover, or a bit of both. They sat me down with a cup of mint tea and I pretended to watch them playing, but I was really gazing at the mountains and thinking about Pierre. I had no illusions, I knew it was just a single, glorious, unrepeatable thing, but I wanted to keep it as fresh as possible in my mind for as long as possible. In fact, I think that half-hour by the tennis courts was one of the pleasantest I have ever spent in my life.

'Then Michel appeared with his nanny, for his tennis lesson, and Josie came and sat down beside me and sucked a glass of freshly squeezed orange juice through a straw. Michel was obviously going to be good at the game. He still needed both of his skinny arms to lift the racquet, but he was a charming sight with his stick legs scampering across the court and his big black eyes like sucked toffees totally concentrated on the ball. His gestures were completely French, all shoulder-shrugging and little oufs of disgust when he messed up a shot. I think I began to fall in love with him a little too, or perhaps it was just the wonderful morning freshness of the sun and the glitter of the snow in the mountains.'

'And that's when you heard?'

'Yes, just as they had finished and little Michel was scurrying round collecting the balls for the pro and placing them in little clusters around the court. A man in a dark suit – the manager, I suppose, but he looked like a messenger of death – came out with a mobile phone in his hand. Bad news, he said, Monsieur Pierre has some bad news for you. She took the call sitting there in the white wooden chair. With her dark glasses and her long legs under her tennis skirt, she looked the epitome of luxury and leisure, like Cleopatra in her barge almost.

'Pierre spoke to her like an officer reporting to his colonel-in-chief, she told me later. She didn't mind that, she couldn't have borne it if he'd been sweet and sugary. Perhaps he was being matter-of-fact to cover up his emotion, perhaps he was just like that by nature. Madame, he said, he'd never called her madame in her life before, I regret to have to inform you of a tragic outrage which occurred earlier this morning. Masked gunmen broke into the Château des Palmes and murdered your husband and your daughter. They were standing side by side in the doorway waiting for the car to come back to take them to the club. They died instantly. There were many bullets. I am desolated that we failed to offer them better protection. I shall blame myself to the end of my days.

'Of course the truth was, it was Pierre they were really after, but he happened to be out in the fields at the time. No doubt they were quite pleased to have got Tony, never mind about the little girl, but he was really only a non-playing captain.

'She insisted on driving us back to the house. She was crying, of course, but in a quiet stifled sort of way and her hands were very firm on the steering wheel. I said all the useless things one says on such occasions – not that I've ever been through an occasion quite like that – how she must not be ashamed to grieve, she must let herself go, how much I admired Tony for the way he had taken up the challenge he had inherited, how one would never be able to think of him in the past tense. She barely responded, her gaze fixed on the winding road back up to the town.

'They had left him and the little girl lying there, his tall thin body beside her plump little body, both covered with blood. The blood was spreading and curdling all over the dark shiny floor. They seemed to be hand in hand, but that may just have been the way they had fallen. The flies were already beginning to gather. I have never seen anything so horrible. Never.' His voice trailed away into a sob, and I was moved by his brokenness and found myself on the edge of tears and then over the edge. I had grieved for Tony and his daughter when I had read the news in the paper, but my tears now were for the horror of the scene and for those who had to witness it.

'Couldn't someone get a cloth to cover them up, I said, and

someone went to get one, but they wanted Josie to see for herself. They expected something of her, I suppose, they wanted her to throw herself upon the two bodies and hug them and kiss them and howl and howl for hours and hours. And I think if I had been in her place, that's what I'd have done. But she didn't exactly. She knelt down beside them and kissed each of them once, on the only part of their faces which wasn't covered with blood. Then she got up and screamed once, a long hoarse scream which I shall never forget, and went off down the passage to her room. A moment or two after she had gone, a woman came with two blankets and put them over Tony and Beatha, and I went out into the yard to get some air.'

'And afterwards?'

'She stayed in her room, didn't come out for two days. You could hear her crying, especially at night, but she didn't come out. They were a nightmarish two days for me, not that that matters. I couldn't leave her, yet I wasn't allowed in to speak to her and I couldn't leave the compound because we were besieged, or, to put it more exactly, chose to regard ourselves as besieged. In fact, the murderers had got clean away and obviously hadn't the slightest intention of coming back because they'd done the business, as the saying goes. Then after two days, out she came, very smartly dressed in black, very Parisian, with her suitcases all packed and little Michel and the nanny all packed too. We're off, she said. Off where, I said. To London. We'll stay with my father to start with. You mean off for good? Yes of course. What about the funerals and so on? I want them to be buried in London, would you mind awfully staying behind to arrange that for me, Rickshaw, I really would appreciate it. But will there be time for that, I said, meaning ... If you're worried about decomposition, she said, at least there are two things this ghastly country knows about – one's embalming and the other's refrigeration. It was then I realised I had rather underestimated her.

'As I feared, it took ages to arrange. Even after the official post-mortem examination, there were about six different departments to deal with, all of whom seemed to think I was some unlicensed

183

bodysnatcher, not to mention the airline people who were not helpful at all. So we only managed to get here last Friday.'

'You mean the funeral hasn't happened yet.'

'It's tomorrow, actually. Golders Green at eleven. There's no announcement, because Josie wants no fuss at all and certainly no press, but I'm sure you'd be very welcome. Look for the name of Tallboy on the notice board.'

'What?'

'Tallboy's the name we're using to put the press off the scent. Apparently the vultures comb through the day's list and they all want a picture of the widow of the romantic British sheikh gunned down by terrorists.'

'Tallboy,' I repeated, half to myself. Even in death, Tony's name was an unstable thing, twisted out of shape to meet the needs of the moment.

The dark brick buildings were hidden in the trees. The groups of mourners standing outside the sturdy chapels looked lost and oppressed by being so little removed from one another, as though the crematorium was determined to press home the fact that they weren't the only ones that had lost a loved one. Death was a mass activity and so was disposal. Nothing privileged or special about yours, don't think that. Please stand well back to let the preceding congregation leave the chapel.

Richard Shay was almost alone outside Chapel H, except for the undertaker's men taking a coffin in. After a minute or two, they came out again, looked around rather warily and took out of the hearse a large cardboard box which they also carried into the chapel.

'What's in that?'

'Beatha's coffin. They thought a child's coffin would attract attention. There are some flowers inside the chapel. Ah, here they are.'

A dark green Rover, not in its youth, came through the gates and drew up outside the chapel. Josie and her parents, dressed in ordinary office clothes, no mourning, got out and went straight

184

into the chapel. We followed on their heels.

The preliminaries had been so desolate that I was surprised to find as many as a dozen people already seated in the pews. Gradually, their faces came into focus, and names too. There was old Ted Boddington, the groundsman from the club (I half expected to see his old sneakers on under his pinstripe trousers as usual) and, good Lord, there was Roger Stott from Trotter's Corner and, no, not possible but yes, the unspeakable Norris Elegant had somehow found his way in, and that nice man behind the counter in Timothy White's who had such a peculiar back-hand, and two or three more regulars from the club, including Sten Svensson, the laughing Swede, sombre now in black like a figure of death in a Bergman film, and Evan Grumbar, the charm-ing American banker with the drunk wife who seldom appeared but had this morning. The whole world Tony and Josie had left behind had been recreated for this occasion.

The maimed little service got under way without much pre-amble. The vicar sounded out of breath, perhaps because he had a streaming cold, but to start with I did not really listen to what he was saying. My whole attention was clutched by the two var-nished gleaming pine coffins side by side on the platform, the lit-tle one half the size of the other.

'... sympathy in this cruel tragedy. I must tell you quite hon-estly that I never had the privilege of meeting Tony or Elizabeth, but I know what a lot I missed. Tony was a well-respected mem-ber of the community, by all accounts, always had a cheery word for one and all. And in remembering him we remember also his beloved daughter Elizabeth who I'm told was specially keen on dancing and swimming and looked like a chip off the old block. Tony, as many of you will know, was a keen tennis player himself and a prominent member of the local club before he went over-seas. I'm not a player myself but I understand that he could hit the ball a pretty fair old wallop. In asking God to take extra special care of two of His precious creatures who have been so cruelly taken from us into His mercy, we give thanks for all the gifts of youth and physical strength and sporting ability that He enriched

185

them with. And Tony and Elizabeth, we'll miss you, but we'll never forget how lucky we were to know you both.'

Enriched, well, yes, he was certainly enriched, and missed, yes, he would be missed, including by me. I suppose he had not left a great deal behind. It seemed that the misery of his parents and grandparents had flowed through him, after all, but not visibly, like a stream which flows underground for a mile or two and then comes out again much the same as it went in. Only now that he was dead did I begin to guess how much effort must have gone into his gracefulness. The grace had been manufactured under pressure and when the pressure was off he had looked ordinary again. Perhaps true grace was always manufactured like that, perhaps grace was really a moral quality but cunningly disguised so it deceived everyone into thinking it wasn't. For those of us who remembered him in the dim quietness of the club his early death helped to keep his memory green. I did not like to think of him in middle age, pursuing his mechanical little love affair in the back room of a boutique, investing in some dubious property development, growing fat.

'Sorry about the vicar,' I said to Josie afterwards.

'He was just what I wanted,' she said, with a fierce look in her eye. 'I didn't want anyone who knew Tony or Beatha, or who knew anything about us at all. I've had enough of all that.'

We were standing out under a pleasant colonnade, only lightly dusted with urban soot. Behind us little votive tablets recorded the names and dates of those who had passed through these furnaces. In front, a lawn with rosebushes studded with more tablets, for customers whose families had been prepared to spend a little more. By some trick of the slope, the lawn appeared to stretch away to eternity, so that the columns of black and white tablets marched away from us until they hit the fleecy sky.

'Glad I managed to gather some of the troops together.' Geoffrey Pagan-Jones only seemed to come up to my elbow now. Illness had shrunk him further still so that the glitter of his eye, the narrowness of his head, the folds of skin at the neck gave him the aspect of a tortoise whose evident great age only enhanced its

186

further life expectancy. 'Josie didn't want anyone to come outside the family, but I'd already put up a notice at the club and of course the boys all wanted to come and pay their respects. Anyway, you need a bit of company at a funeral.'

Perhaps he was right about that. For all his efforts, though, the pews had still been half-empty, and the chill stealing in from the side doors made us tremble, and not just at the moment when the two coffins slid through the automatic doors and were gone.

'You remember Rhona, don't you?' The tall woman beside him, tall compared to him, anyway, gave me a hearty handshake and an uneasy smile. Of course. I had not remembered her at all, had assumed as P-J scuttled in the chapel that it was Iris he was with, my mind's eye automatically looking for the widow's parents. But in any case my recollection of Ron would have been dim. I had only seen her in her long pleated tennis dress, not in this severe navy-blue suit with a silver brooch in the shape of an aeroplane. And besides, there was a certain likeness between the two women: the bristly dyed-chestnut hair, the strong features, handsome and querulous at the same time, an upright, umbrageous look.

'Poor Iris wasn't well enough to come. We're just a couple of crocks now. Ron's keeping house for us at the moment. I don't know what we'd do without her.'

His daughter's gaze – stony, contemptuous, unconcealed – revealed the state of affairs clearly enough. The gaze went stonier still as Ron overcame the unease and began to talk. 'It's a big house to keep clean, much bigger than you'd think to look at it. Mrs Davidge is a treasure, an absolute trezh, but she only comes once a week, and the laundry is a total farce, so I'm doing my Mrs Tiggywinkle bit *and* trying to make sense of P-J's accounts, so it's quite a scramble, but I love it. Iris is so good about everything and I'm just glad to be able to help out. The doctor's very pleased with her, but she does get tired, I don't know whether it's the drugs or what. It's a real blessing to have Josie and Michel back, I mean, in spite of the tragic circumstances. Iris absolutely dotes on Michel, you know, well, he is an adorable child, such a terrible pity she

187

never had a chance to get to know Beatha, isn't it?'

By now Josie had left our little group and was walking back towards the archway at the end of the arcade. When she reached the arch, she kept on walking until she disappeared round the corner.

'No, P-J, don't try to drag her back. The poor girl's had enough for one day. We'll catch up with her later.' But Pagan-Jones continued to stare at the archway, unable to contain his aggravation.

'She could have stayed and said thank you to the people from the club.'

'Geoffrey, don't hassle her.'

'No, I suppose you're right.' He subsided into glum acceptance, but now and then still darted tortoise glances towards the archway. Although the day was mild enough, a kind of thin mist lurked in the far recesses of the colonnade. A fancy began to gather in my head that we too had half passed away and were hovering, our feet not quite touching the ground, in some waiting room or assembly area for the next stage. The lines of tablets marching up the lawn drew us forward over the brow; the roses stirred by the light breeze seemed to be waving us on.

'They're so early, aren't they?'

'What?'

'The roses, I saw you looking at them,' Rhona said. 'They're awfully early this year.'

'Oh yes.'

'But they plant them beautifully here, don't they? I wish we would get ours to grow like that. I sometimes think Iris plants a bit too closely.'

'Does she?' No, this was hell, and not much improved when Norris Elegant came towards us. He was making bizarre swishing motions with his right arm which I did not immediately recognise as an imitation of a person playing tennis, though in his case possibly a quite accurate imitation.

'Long time no play.'

'No indeed.'

'I'll give you a bell.'

'Great,' I said.

It was late June, July perhaps, before I found myself ducking along the little path under the full-bosomed privet. It was surprising that the hedge was still unpruned. In earlier days, ten years earlier I realised with a jolt, one would already have had to squeeze past Ted Boddington perched on his paint-splashed stepladder, his filthy size thirteen tennis shoes sticking out at head height, with his electric clippers singing away above. The clipping was one of the few tasks that appealed to his idle curiosity because it meant he could see over the hedges and down into the neighbours' gardens. From several gardens away, you could see his rheumy prurient head moving along the top of the privet.

But now the hedge lolled out over our heads and flicked at our bare legs. The gate at the far end had to be pushed hard to open against the weight of the overgrown branches. The club, always tucked away, now seemed to be actively resisting visitors.

The edges of the path, normally scorched ginger by some death-dealing herbicide of Boddington's, were mossy and weed-infested now. The court netting had rusted, the holes in it only patched up roughly. The green paint had flaked off the corrugated-iron roof of the clubhouse, and the wooden pillars were no longer white. That calculated refusal to smarten the place up had degenerated into unconcealed decay. For me, though, there was something beyond the sadness of the spectacle. The whole place seemed utterly remote, as though my mind was dimly imagining it rather than it being there before my eyes. It was not, as people usually say of such revisitings, that the place seemed smaller, rather that it was a place I used to know and to which there could be no real going back.

'He's let the club go to pot,' Norris Elegant said.

'Yes, it's a pity.'

'He's up to something, don't you worry. Never does anything without a reason, old P-J, you'll find. There's been a bit of a hooha here about Tony.'

'About Tony?'

'On the noticeboard. You know what these old club chaps are

189

like.'

He led me to the green baize board in the draughty passage outside the gents changing room. The little notice was typed on the secretary's old typewriter which hopped about the page and could no longer do *es*.

We regret to announce the tragic death of A. M. Allenby (Gent's Ladder 7). He was a keen and popular member of the club for many years and represented us in the gent's doubles at Beckenham five years running.

Underneath, someone had scrawled in red biro 'see suggestions book'. I flipped through the suggestions book, an old cash register tied to a nail on the wall by a piece of string. Inside, the same red biro had written: *Surely it is tasteless and out of place to refer to a member's position on the ladder when he's just been murdered. Also was the name correctly spelled, see attached cutting JPS.* The writer had painstakingly sellotaped to the page a newspaper cutting about the murders, with a blurred photo of M. Antoine Halaby, in an open-necked shirt, looking carefree.

Below, a neater hand had written in blue ink, *I disagree. The Hon. Sec. provided a fitting tribute to a great gentleman. I for one will never forget his volleying the year we reached the Middlesex semis. WRG.*

Hear, hear. We'll no look upon his like again. PQde S – a shaking hand in purple felt-tip.

In fact, this was a clerical error resulting from direct copying from the membership list. Profound apologies to all those to whom distress may have been caused. Hon. Sec.

'I thought of adding something,' Norris said. 'But then I thought too many cooks.'

'Quite right.'

'After all, between you and me we didn't get on all that well. The chemistry wasn't right.'

'No.'

'Nice bloke and all that, but if the chemistry isn't right, a rela-

190

tionship won't gell, will it?'

'No.'

'Well then, shall we get cracking?'

The plunk of the balls resounded with a viscous melancholy across the empty court. The slither of our soles suggested flight from some unnameable enemy. The place was so empty. In the old days, even on a midweek morning there would be a few women's doubles chattering away or a couple of journalists sweating off their hangovers. But now Norris and I had the place to ourselves. He took the first set.

'What are you up to these days?' I said as we were pausing to take a slurp of Lucozade.

'Freelancing mainly.' He shot me a glance of gloomy hatred. 'Working from home is the name of the game now.'

'Ah,' I said, trying to think of something to say which would not imply compassion.

'It's great to be out of the rat race. I can't say I envy young John Edward.'

'John Edward Davies you mean, the boy who used to be barman here?'

'Well, we all have to start somewhere,' Norris said, relieved to find an opening for reproach. 'Yes, the lad's come a long way. He's in my old stamping ground, Disposals, and right on the inside track in every sense of the word, so my spies tell me.'

'How do you mean?'

'We never bandy a woman's name in the mess.'

'Don't we?'

'Well then, use your imagination. Where would you most want to be in, if you were on your way to the top in the great firm of Pagan, Jones and Company?'

'Oh,' I said. 'Really. Are you sure?'

'Yes, I have my proofs.' His use of the plural, typical Norris in its misplaced pedantry, was at the same time unconvincing. I was too fastidious to question him further, but I was confident that he would not be able to resist telling me. Halfway through the next set I broke his serve by a couple of floating dabs which left him concrete-footed at the net. As we changed ends, the sweet musk of his after-shave tickling my nostrils, he stopped and said, 'She goes to his flat in the afternoon after work. She doesn't want her father to know, but everyone else does so it's only a question of time. It's in Crouch End, the flat,' he added, as though this detail would finally defeat my disbelief.

I could not think how to respond. My whole body was choked with nausea, sadness and, what else? Rage, I suppose. Norris Elegant stood there, the black hairs sprouting out of his Lacoste shirt and out of his nose. The hairs were visible too through the sweat-soaked shirt, running in flattened whorls across his chest. He was panting too; ill-fortune had shortened his wind.

John Edward Davies's revenge was fierce and squalid enough, but to have it relayed to me by such a messenger drained the world of grace. It did not occur to me for one moment that John Edward had the slightest affection for Josie. She was simply the climax to his programme of haunting the witnesses to his father's execution. Perhaps the thought had come to him quite late on, months after he had come to the club. The sight of her long limbs had touched off a flicker of lust in him and the primitive circuits in his evil little brain had made the connections. Mere haunting was, after all, a bloodless occupation, but to shaft one's victim in the most intimate style like this was a vengeance on the Jacobean scale, next best thing to drinking his blood out of his skull.

Yet a puzzle remained, a puzzle which made nonsense of the rest of the story. How had John Edward Davies got anywhere at all in Pagan-Jones's business in the first place? For what conceivable reason could P-J have taken him on as a partner after getting rid of him as a barman? These tangled speculations took my mind off the game, and Norris Elegant won the second set too quite easily. Something approaching pleasure creased his features, but with difficulty, like a rusty metal shutter which it takes a crowbar to open.

We walked back through the car park. The Michaelmas daisies were bursting through the asphalt, their dusty blue flowers seeming to gulp for air. The white lines marking the spaces for the secretary, treasurer and chairman had quite faded. Mine was the only car on the lot.

'You didn't bring your car then?'

'No,' Norris said. 'I've given up driving – on doctor's orders.'

For the first time I became aware how shabby he had become. His teeth were blackish-yellow and there was a fetid smell about him. His shorts were discoloured at the crotch and the shirt had foodstains down the front. He was still breathing heavily.

Our conversation limped on as we changed. How dank and desolate the changing room was. When I offered him a lift, he declined. The offer accelerated his changing, so that he seemed to be tying his tie and combing his black thatch at the same time. With a grunt of farewell he was gone.

About half a mile down the High Road, just after the little parade of shops where I had once been mocked in my Edwardian fancy dress, I caught sight of him several hundred yards ahead walking fast with an exaggerated hip-roll like a man in a walking race, his blazer tail flapping behind him. Beyond some bushes, he disappeared into the gravel driveway of a large institutional red-brick block. I slowed down to read the little wooden sign stuck in the black earth of the flower bed – Prospect House Hostel – and drove on.

For weeks, perhaps months, that was the last word I had even indirectly about Josie. She seemed to have slipped too far away from me, she had seen too much. I felt I could be no use to her, though that was not normally my criterion for keeping in touch with someone. It would be kind to say that I was too shy to ring her up; nearer the mark to admit that I had become a little bit frightened of her.

But my heart leapt all the same when I heard her voice on the telephone late one night that autumn.

'Well, you aren't much of a friend, are you? Not a word since the funeral. No, no, I didn't mean that. I know what it's like, what I'm like, rather. But I'm better now. I'd love to see you.'

'So would I,' I said. 'I'm sorry I didn't get in touch. How's it been?'

'How's it been,' she pondered. 'Rather exciting really.'

'Exciting? I thought that's the last thing it would be. I mean, I know your old life had its drawbacks, but surely that was exciting, wasn't it?'

'In a kitschy, desert-song way, yes I suppose it was, but it was the wrong sort of exciting, for us anyway, particularly for Tony. He wasn't the sort of person who needs to spread his wings. He was better off keeping his potential latent, if you see what I mean. I think quite a lot of people are like that, you know. They are happier when they can keep their reserves strictly in reserve.'

'Yes, but you –'

'My dear, let's face it, I became a bitch. I still am, a hard-faced bitch, in fact. It wasn't good for me at all. You never recover from being special, you know. It's different from being spoilt, you can recover from that, I think, if you're given a real hard shock when you're young enough. But being special – ah, once you've thought of yourself in that way, you're destroyed as a person. That's what happened to this whole bloody country, can't get over not being special any more.'

'So why do you find it so exciting to come back to?'

'It's not the country, it's the work. That's what I really love. Funny, when you think how keen I used to be to get away and become a doctor, only I hadn't got the A-levels, so I had to train as an anaesthetist. Yet here I am, closing down businesses right and left – it's a wonderful time for chartered accountants.'

'But you aren't even a chartered accountant.'

'Oh yes, I am. You never bothered to ask, but all those years I was hanging around with Tony, I was taking the course. Because deep down I always knew my vocation – like a nun.' She gave one of her great gurgly laughs that had stopped my heart fifteen years earlier and stopped it still. 'So every day in every way I get more like P-J, which is a bit grotesque in a woman, I suppose. Which reminds me why I rang you up was to have you round to a birthday tea for the old fart. He's eighty on Tuesday.'

In contrast to the club, the hedges were clipped, the rhododendrons cut hard back so that their elephant-coloured branches stood bare. In the island beds, late summer flowers cowered in the raked and weeded earth, the Michaelmas daisies staked in disciplined clumps. Ron had been taking a grip on the place, I had heard. The front door had been painted a lively cream and even the boot-scraper had been cleaned and burnished. As the door opened, the whiff of some fragrant cleaning fluid came at me. It was like entering an expensive nursing home.

The hall seemed lighter. For the first time, I noticed the Chinese rug with the contorted leaping horse on it and the bulgy sidetable made of assorted veneers and the matching pictures of girls in Kate Greenway bonnets sitting by the edge of rushy ponds. And there was Rhona, looking clean and bright herself in a white linen dress like a nurse's uniform, but also worn, her face grey rather than pink and the light in her green-grey eyes mostly gone.

'It's quite a party,' she said. 'Daddy's in wonderful form.' I could not remember whether she had always referred to P-J in this way to me, or whether this was a recent recognition of his senility.

'He always is,' I said.

'When he's in company, yes, but between you and me he does get a bit down in the dumps now and then and it's quite hard work keeping his pecker up.'

'I'm sure it is. You do a wonderful –'

'Oh don't be silly, I'm not fishing. It's a labour of love. It's really Iris I'm more worried about at the moment. She's going downhill fast.'

'I'm so sorry.'

'Last week I thought she might be slipping away from us. But she's doing awfully well today.'

'Good.'

'It would be so kind if you could manage to have a little chat with her. I'm afraid it will be a bit one-sided, but I know she'll really appreciate it, although she may not be able to express it.'

The door between the two pictures of girls in bonnets was thrown open, and Josie came through it at a rush with a kettle. 'More tea, more tea,' she shouted as she passed on into the

195

kitchen. 'I don't know how their bladders cope.'

The sight of her struck me dumb. She had somehow become young and lollopy again, moved with the old awkward grace. Her face seemed eager and small and delicate. The sensual weight had melted off her, had vanished as swiftly as a holiday tan.

'Doesn't she look marvellous?' Rhona said.

'Yes.'

'Quite recovered. There's no tonic like getting back to one's own country, is there? I mean, home's home when all's said and done. Pity about the little boy, though.'

'Oh, what ...'

'Can't settle at all. Doesn't like school, won't play tennis, doesn't make friends.'

'Well, I suppose it's not surprising when you think what he's been through.'

'Mm,' she said, unconvinced. Clearly she felt that little boys ought to be made of less sensitive stuff.

At that moment, Michel came out into the hall. He was taller now and with Tony's pallor and stillness he might have been a page in a renaissance banqueting scene, the one whose lack of animation and negligent stance half-turned away from the viewer suggests that despite appearances the whole business is really a bit vulgar.

'It's quite a scrum in there, isn't it?' Rhona said to him. He looked at her, nodded and passed on through to the kitchen.

'You see?' she said.

'Well, perhaps I'd better join the scrum,' I said, suddenly anxious to be away from her pulsating resentment.

At first, I could scarcely see anything in the crowded sitting room with its low ceiling and small leaded windows. It was hard to find a break in the wall of blazers and flower-printed dresses. One or two of the taller guests, such as the egg-domed former treasurer with the wild eyebrows, found their heads brushing against the bulbous slightly judaic brass chandelier, which had always seemed too devotional for the Pagan-Joneses.

'Here, take those.' Rhona's voice fierce behind me. And her

196

bony hands thrust into mine a hot tray of miniature pizzas, some-what blackened. It was now impossible to move at all. I tried to slide the tray round the woman in front of me but only succeeded in sawing at her hip which she clutched at with her free hand before moving an inch or two sideways. Round the corner of her singed haunch, I could at least now see our hosts. They were seated in the broad wing chairs, which had been dragged from their normal positions either side of the fireplace and placed up against the little windows at the far end of the room. There they sat enthroned, both with a little square of lawn and island beds and rhododendrons visible through the window behind their shoul-ders – figures in another sort of painting, earlier, one in which the intense stillness of the figure of the Virgin or some saint or other is intensified by the contrast with the gentle landscape behind them (not that the Pagan-Jones's garden could be described as relaxed after Rhona had been at it). Iris had shrunk right back and moved scarcely at all, except for an occasional wag of her hair, now a pinkish-chestnut colour. Her husband by comparison looked much the same as ever (after all, his tortoise head had always seemed infinitely ancient to me).

Gradually, I scythed my way through with the pizza tray and greeted Geoffrey.

'Well I never. You are kind to come and see a poor old sod. My hard old heart is deeply touched. The boys are all here, you know, including several I had kicked out of the club years ago and one or two of their wives who kicked *me* out when I went a bit too far. Still, at our time of life you have to let all that wash over you. Tell you who's here too, that chap who used to be bartender, you probably won't remember, John Edward Davies. He works for me now in Disposals, exceptionally bright lad.'

'I didn't even know he was an accountant.'

'There's a lot you don't know, cocky. Passed the exams in no time, quicker even than my Josie. You've seen Josie, haven't you? Looking a picture, isn't she? So much better since – well, I know it was a ghastly thing to happen, but he was never right for her, young Tony wasn't. I felt that from the beginning, didn't say a

197

dickybird, mark you, not my place. But he just wasn't right, nice chap, of course, beautiful tennis player, but not right for her and not right for the business either, made a real horlicks up at Trotter's Corner. I sent him up there to give him a chance to make a name for himself but he fluffed it. When you get to the bottom line, he was a fluffer was Tony, a real fluffer.'

Not for the first time, I marvelled at P-J's ability to sweep away the past, to toss into oblivion old statements, actions, loyalties. There was something magnificent about the way he seized the instant – alert, slippery, indefatigable.

'Funny thing about John Edward, extraordinary thing really. When I was High Sheriff for my sins, way back this was, part of my official duties was to attend a hanging, dreadful business, but you had to see the thing was done properly. And the man they were hanging was one John Edward Davies, our friend's father. Squalid little crime, murdered the manager when he was robbing an off-licence. His son was born posthumously and his mother gave him the same name, see, to show she didn't care what the world thought. Quite a touching story, really. I didn't click with the name at first, it was so long ago, but then when I remembered and told him the tale, he didn't seem to bear a grudge. Had no idea at all of my part in the business, of course.'

'No, of course not.'

'So we became fast friends as a result. Curious link really when you come to think of it, that I should have seen his dad hanged.'

'Very curious.'

'There he is over there, look. Remember him now?'

As a matter of fact, I wouldn't if I had not been expecting to see him. He looked neater, smaller, the rawness sanded off him. As he stood talking to a woman in a purple suit, he was tamed, almost toyboyish. You would not have suspected a molecule of vengeance in him. The youth who had stared that cold wolfish stare as Geoffrey Pagan-Jones was being shovelled off to hospital was altogether someone else.

'Isn't he a sweet boy? Really dishy.' Rhona's whisper in my ear was less than welcome.

'Who do you mean?' I fenced.

'Oh don't be silly. I heard Geoffrey pointing him out to you. Young J.E.D. over there. The new golden boy. Don't say you weren't staring at him too. There's something about his eyes.'

Initials already. This transformation was going too fast for me. I had a sudden impulse to shout: this boy's out for vengeance, he won't be content until he's broken you, he's a monster like his father, only worse. But sudden impulses are used to being repressed under my roof, and this one was snuffed without difficulty.

And John Edward Davies went on chatting, taking the odd well-bred sip from one of Iris's best china teacups and generally seeming totally sortable and sweet. The room, airless at the best of times, was becoming very hot. Even when fit, the Pagan-Joneses had never opened their little leaded windows, and now in their decay they stayed dedicated to frowst.

'Hot, isn't it?' The voice was sonorous and remote, not unpleasing.

'It certainly is.'

He was tall (I had seen his head knocking against the chandelier a minute or so earlier) with a big pockmarked face which was both puffy and aquiline. Unlike the other men, he was dressed for the City in a heavy pinstripe. His fairish frizzy hair was scraped back and tied in a little ponytail. His manner could have been described as confident, though unease gnawed at the fringes of it, and a certain menace too. At first, I felt I had seen him before, a long time ago, then the feeling went away and it was his strangeness that struck me more.

'Do you know many people here? I'm a bit of a newcomer myself.'

One or two, I said. How had he come to know the Pagan-Joneses?

'Business,' he said. There was a nasal, dragging sadness about his voice, so that he seemed to wish each word unspoken as soon as he had uttered it.

'Not another accountant, I hope.'

My jocularity dribbled away into the stoniest ground known to geology.

'No,' he said in a voice of infinite gloom. 'I'm an entrepreneur.'

'Good for you,' I said, my jocularity spurting into frenzy. 'You actually start businesses instead of closing them down. And what are you working on at the moment?'

'The club,' he said.

'The club?'

'The tennis club. Geoffrey's club.'

'Ah.'

'It's quite a project. We're going to put in a new clubhouse and a couple of squash courts and a pool.'

'You're going to do *that* in collaboration with P-J?'

'Right. He's going to keep a slice of the new company, although he's made it clear he doesn't want to have any part of the management. Well, at his age ...'

'You mean he's *selling* the club? But I didn't even know he owned it.'

My puzzlement seemed to cheer up the man with the ponytail. He began to use his big hands to illustrate points. Entrepreneurial animal spirits suffused his puffy cheeks.

'Let me bring you up to date. The club became effectively bankrupt as of November last year. Falling membership rolls, big bank loan with interest rates going up all the time, it's a familiar tale. So Geoffrey offered to take it off the members' hands before it actually went into liquidation. As of January, he became effectively sole proprietor, and when I came along, well, it was a marriage made in heaven, because I had set my heart on this club, oh, donkey's years ago. I always thought it had mega potential.'

'Lucky for Geoffrey you came along when you did. Otherwise he'd just be landed with an empty club and a gigantic debt.'

The man with the ponytail smiled. My innocence was like a pick-me-up to him.

'Yeah well, these things happen sometimes. As you say, we were lucky. Of course, the planning permission helped. I wouldn't deny that.'

'Planning permission?'

200

'It's going to be a really delightful little close of executive homes. I want it to have the feeling of an Oxbridge quadrangle.'

'Where ...'

'You know that little patch of waste ground just behind the roller sheds. Well, running from there to Court No. 3. I'm thinking of keeping one back for myself. I can put you down for one, if you like. It's a great prospect, take a dip or play a quick set before work, or watch the game from your own terrace.'

As he spoke, the feeling that I had seen him somewhere before grew on me. Even now that he had become bonhomous, the initial combination of menace and unease still hung about him like a lifting fog.

'You've known the club for a long time?'

'Yes, I have. I was never actually a member, though. You'd have to say that I admired it from a distance.'

'I see,' I said, without seeing. And then I did see. 'Oh *yes*. You were one of the squatters.'

He was quite unabashed, in fact proud.

'That's right. You've got a great memory for faces. We were younger then, of course, thought we were going to change the world.'

'You organised a petition.'

'That was me. I was the solicitor. Well, articled clerk at that moment in time, actually. Remember Scraps, that mongrel we had?'

'Yes, of course.'

'Well, I've got a gorgeous golden labrador now, pure bred from Mrs Bellingham down in Kent. And, we've given him the same name. I know Scraps doesn't sound like much of a name for a labrador, but I was fond of that mangy old thing.'

'That's nice.'

'I do hope you'll join. Sten Svensson's already taken out family membership. Fantastic news about him being acquitted, isn't it? The club's officially closed at the moment because the builders are starting next week, but we're keeping a couple of courts going for the use of old friends. Come along any time. We've changed the

201

locks, so you'll need a key. Here.'

He pressed into my hand a little gold Yale key, newly cut. It sat in my palm, winking up at me. I stared back at it in wonder.

'Don't feel embarrassed,' the ponytail man said. 'It's no skin off my nose. We won't be touching those courts for months yet and anyway we like to keep the goodwill going.'

Still I could not answer. My breath had been knocked out of me by this final coup of Geoffrey Pagan-Jones. He had liquidated his own lifelong love and at a profit too. Even I could see that the deal was no happy accident. Geoffrey and Ponytail must have been in cahoots for months. As the club dwindled and the paint peeled off the clubhouse and the privet grew unchecked, P-J's bright immortal eye was casting around and found Ponytail, waiting, staring behind the netting as he had been years earlier.

Go with the flow, everything flows, nothing stays, you can't step into the same river twice, all business problems are basically problems of liquidity – tags old and new whirled and flapped around my head.

'Are you all right? You look a bit pale,' said Ponytail.

'No, I'm fine, really.'

'So you've met our saviour,' Josie's voice came sweet and girl-ish from behind my left shoulder.

'Well, we haven't actually introduced ourselves properly. I'm Todd Pelican.' The man with the ponytail put out a large clean hand and I grasped it with limp fervour.

'Has Todd told you all about his exciting plans for the club?'

'Yes, he's –'

'Isn't it all going to be brilliant? It'll be really marvellous for kids. Of course, Michel isn't back into tennis again yet, but the pool he'll love.'

On, on relentless, the rush of life with the shredder working overtime on the remnants of the past. No pause, no let-up, no exemption for anything just because it had once been loved, or for anyone, come to that.

'On second thoughts, I do feel a bit wobbly. Would you mind if I slipped away?'

'I said he was looking pale, you know, like someone who's seen a ghost.'

Todd Pelican gave me a firm farewell handshake.

'Remember to bring the key,' he said. 'See you on site.'

'You poor thing,' Josie said. 'I'll see you out.'

She took my arm, and steered me through the blazers and flowery dresses out into the hall. We walked slowly across the garden. Dusk was on us and the grass was already wet beneath our feet.

'Are you feeling well enough to hear a secret?'

'Of course.'

'I'm going to get married again. You'll never guess who to, though it's someone you know or used to.'

'Congratulations. As a matter of fact, I think I do know.'

'Really, how – oh I suppose you saw him there today. Well, what do you think of John Edward? Dada loves him.'

'Well, he's a bright lad. I hope you'll be tremendously happy.'

'You don't sound very enthusiastic. I shouldn't have sprung it on you like that in your enfeebled state.'

'No, I mean it. He is bright.'

'I know *that*. But you obviously don't like him.'

'Perhaps he isn't that easy to get to know, for a man anyway.'

'Why not?'

'Look, Josie, I really don't know him properly.'

'I should have thought he was easier to get to know than Tony. I mean, we were married for years and I never really knew what he was thinking.'

'And you're sure you know what John Edward is thinking?'

'What on earth do you mean by that?'

She was angry and puzzled. I had gone too far.

'I'm sorry, I'm feeling lousy, I don't know what I'm saying.'

She swallowed my apologies with relief, almost pleasure. We stood at the gate under the savage rhododendrons. It was dark now. The street light in the lane threw a pale orange glow on her face, and she looked as she always had.

'You'll see,' she said. 'We're like partners.'

'Partners?' For some reason it seemed an odd word.

'We can really work together, as well as, oh you know – the other stuff,' and she gave the old giggle, the little gurgling linnet's chuckle she used to give when she missed an easy forehand. An indecipherable dread took hold of me as we were kissing good-night, and I shuddered as our cheeks met.

'You're shivering,' she said. 'You must hurry home and go to bed with a hot toddy.'

There was no reason for me to go anywhere near the area now, since I had moved several miles away a year or two earlier. Even the old tennis link had been broken, since I had been afflicted with some minor but occasionally agonising shoulder complaint. But once a year I still visited my old dentist, in his little bow-win-dowed surgery shaken by the heavy traffic taking a short cut to the North Circular. There was a certain contrary satisfaction to be had from walking along the parade and noting the changes: Dewhurst the butchers gone, Timothy White's gone through sev-eral changes before settling down as Cushy World The Sofa People, North London's Finest Pet Store now displaced by a great grey lump of meat turning slowly in the window, now and then basted by a sombre Turk, only Gloyne the Undertaker unmoved and unaltered except for a fresh sign along the bottom of the black window offering Twenty-Four Hour Service.

But this time I knew that I had another, final call to make, and I took the little gold key off the bookshelf where it had been sit-ting for weeks in front of *The Satanic Verses* and the *RAC Hotel Guide* for 1989.

Boscastle Avenue looked just the same as I had always known it: the high gables with their ridged and scalloped tiles half hidden by overgrown branches of laburnum and acacia and the glossy leaves of much prized magnolias, the little gravel semicircles in front of the house with the wife's runabout snoozing in the silent afternoon, the occasional whimper of a cooped-up puppy or the drone of a rotary mower, but not, not any more, the oldest song of the suburbs, the plunk of tennis balls from an unseen game, that erratic, irritating music of the bourgeoisie which bears an embarrassing resemblance to some modern music (I had a fogey friend who was an oboeist and who claimed that *all* music after Schoenberg sounded like a mixed doubles in which nobody ever said sorry).

Just beyond the house with the ginger and purple crazy paving, I turned right intending to take the privet path to the club, but there were three strands of barbed wire strung across it, with a red No Entry sign dangling from one of them. Even if there hadn't been, the two sides of the hedge had grown so much that they had met and blotted out the path.

For some reason that closing off seemed fitting, decent almost. A little breeze wandered down what gap remained and ruffled the privet tops and set the No Entry sign twisting gently on the wire. The faintness of the breeze was fitting too. It matched the effacing of the path, a reminder of how weak the past could be, how tenuous the grip of our imagination.

At the road entrance round the corner, I had to jump into the hedge as an empty lorry came out at speed. The dwarfish brick pillars had been knocked down to widen the entrance and now lay in broken lumps in the hedge. One of the grey cement balls which had topped them was lying in the long grass beyond. The car park was a wasteland of rubble and orange mud. Beyond, the foundations of some of the executive homes had already been laid; the surprisingly small rectangles of cement looked hardly dry. Further on again, men with pneumatic drills were churning up Court No. 3, favoured by our Sunday morning doubles because of its seclusion and now doomed for the same reason. Watching or supervising this activity was a figure in a hard hat seated in what appeared from a distance to be some kind of miniature fork-lift truck. Only when I got closer did I realise that the man was in fact sitting in a wheelchair which had been stationed next to two surveyors' poles stuck in the ground to mark some boundary or other.

'This is a hard hat site, you know.'

Geoffrey Pagan-Jones tossed the rebuke at me with a chortle. He seemed delighted by the bustle of the site, the noise of the

205

drills and the cement mixers and the two site managers in suits and green wellingtons studying their clipboards with that strange lost look which suggested that they had mistaken the site altogether and ought to be conducting operations at least half a mile to the east.

'I like to come and see how it's all getting along. It's only seven minutes from home in this contraption. First-rate machine, used to be Iris's, but of course she's got no use for it now in the hospice. Rhona always wants to push me, but I like to travel under my own steam. They'll be pulling the clubhouse down next week. Amazing what a pace they go at when they're on piece-work, these lads.'

A few yards away, a workman levelling off a cement floor looked up at us sharply although the gravelly rumble of the mixer was too loud for him to have heard. Even so, the slap of his trowel on the soft khaki slush suggested that somehow he suspected he was being got at. Geoffrey's presence had lost none of its power to disconcert. His unconcealed relish for change, demolition, liquidation, unsettled even those, perhaps particularly those, who were paid to carry out the tasks involved. They, after all, might well be inveterate haters of alteration, conservative sticklers who simply happened to do this kind of work for a living and saw no glory in it. The workman, a short red-faced man in his forties with a shock of white hair, wiped his brow and looked up at us again. Perhaps he was just wondering why this man in the wheelchair came and watched him.

'You've met Todd? Todd Pelican, my partner in this great venture. Terrific chap, got a real eye for a business opportunity.'

'Yes, I've met him, we all met him years ago.'

'Did we? I don't remember, but then my memory's a goner these days. No, I ran into him just the other day when the club was in financial difficulties and I was at my wits' end, and he instantly spotted the way forward. That's where we'll put the pool for starters, he said straight off, just like that, before I'd even put a proposition to him.' He chuckled at the thought, or perhaps at the delicate ingenuity of his version of events. 'It's wonderful to have a new interest in life at my age, see the old place coming to life again. Lot of people retire without leaving themselves anything to achieve, think it's all going to be fun and games in the sunset. But you always need to leave yourself a challenge.' He gripped the arms of his wife's wheelchair more fiercely and pushed out his jaw in a challenge-meeting sort of way, looking strangely uncomfortable, rather like Churchill in the Graham Sutherland portrait.

'But you aren't properly retired anyway, are you? You're still the eminence grise at Pagan, Jones, after all.'

The Churchillian effect dissolved into another chuckle, this one rather stagey, like a villain being accused of murder in a bad play.

'Oh dear me, you are behind the times. Just off to book your ticket on the *Titanic*, I expect you are. No, look, there's an interesting thing. You see over there that chap with the black hair sticking out from under his hat. That's another piece of young Todd's smart thinking. Instead of having to make do with the scum of the bogs all the time – pardon me, my good sir –' he doffed an imaginary cap to the red-faced man with the white hair who was luckily now out of earshot – 'he takes on some of the chaps from the hostel down the road as labourers, half the price, and no trouble with the union. And some of them really take to the work. Of course, you'd expect it with that fellow there, wouldn't you? You remember him, of course.' And I already had remembered him, a good deal quicker than I had recognised Todd Pelican.

'Poor old Norris,' Geoffrey Pagan-Jones sighed. 'Never really looked the executive part. I gave him his chance. They all get their chance, you know, it's up to them, that's what I always tell them.'

I squinted through the hazy air at the figure of Norris Elegant, sturdy as ever yet woebegone now as he stumped back to the cement-mixer with his shovel carried in front of him like an offensive weapon. His powers of application seemed undimmed by misfortune. I felt an overpowering desire not to hear one word more about Norris Elegant, and hazarded, a little impertinently, I suppose, 'And John Edward Davies, is he going to get his chance too?'

P-J stared at me in amazement (I'm not sure whether genuine or put on). 'You still haven't got it, have you?'

'Got what?'

'That's what I'm trying to tell you. About the business. I've wound it up.'

'Wound it up?'

'Thought I was getting too old to keep a proper eye on things. With these big firms amalgamating all the time there's not much room left for the little chap. Mark you, their costs are twice as high as ours and they move about as quickly as a three-legged elephant, but that seems to be the way of the world, so I'm off. Dissolved it, just like that, pouff!'

And his old brown tortoise hands flew up above his head and apart, wide apart, scattering the firm's dust into the haze, the Prospero of chartered accountancy closing the show and magicking all its trappings away into thin air. He had sucked up the shower of gold as nonchalantly as he had showered it in the first place. He was better in this guise than as the wheelchair Churchill, for the essence of his will was that it should remain hidden and not exhaust itself in a show of defiance. What he had to offer was, after all, a show of magic: perpetually a dissolving, glittering, liquescent kaleidoscope of unexpected effects, presented with innocence and bonhomie so that you could not see any harm coming to anyone as a result, at least not until the harm hit you smack between the eyes.

'But what about Josie?'

'My darling daughter?'

'I mean she's trained specially and ...'

'She's a wonderful girl, you know that and I know that, but I don't want her to waste her life trying to rescue silly sods who've made a cock of their business. No, she'll be much better off as she is with the little nest-egg I've scraped together for her. You see, to be absolutely honest, women don't really make first-class liquidators, they get too emotionally involved. And as for that fellow of hers, he may do very well as a husband but I'm not so sure how far I'd trust him with my money. You've got to remember what's in the blood. These days we're not supposed to visit the sins of the fathers, I know, but I like to take a look at the pedigree before I buy a horse.'

'But I thought you –'

'Lively enough *looking* lad, I grant you, but remember, I knew the father, not socially, of course.' He began a chuckle which was meant to sound embarrassed. 'Oh blast it, there's Stotty.'

Across the building site, with that lopsided walk which suggested that the raising of each foot was fractionally impeded by some glutinous substance, came the dark unchanging figure of Roger Stott. On the bright hazy day, he seemed to be looking for a funeral, one which was somehow not quite real, perhaps staged for a film with everyone too neatly kitted out in black. He nodded at me, that sardonic not unfriendly sideways nod, which seemed to say, I know your game but don't worry. It must have been two or three years since we had met, but from his greeting it might have been yesterday.

'He looks well, doesn't he, considering,' Stott said as he flicked off the brake on the wheelchair. 'He likes to come out here in the morning, monarch of all he surveys. I run him down here in the Granada and the lads keep an eye on him.'

P-J gave a hint of mumbled snort as though to suggest that this was not the whole truth, but he did not revive his claim that he usually came here under his own steam.

'Interesting spot, this. Used to be a Roman fort, commanded extensive views of the surrounding hilltops, you see – Highgate, Crouch End, Ally Pally, as far as Trotter's Corner probably. Then in the Middle Ages there was a Cistercian monastery over there.'

'Who cares, Stotty, who cares? We've got the lot concreted over now.' P-J seemed to have recovered his confidence.

'Wonderful people, the Romans – central heating, main drainage, roads with a proper camber, you name it they had it. And no fucking chartered accountants either. Come on, my lord, her ladyship awaits. Ron's got some nice lasagne for you today.

Turned it out of the packet with her own fair hands, she did.'

He grasped the handles of the wheelchair and put it through a smart, almost military ninety-degree turn. P-J only had time for the faintest salutation before he was being bumped along the now broken asphalt path. In my last glimpse of him, he was shrunken, frail, a pawn in other people's endgame. I think he shouted something to me, but the noise of the cement mixer drowned it and besides he had his back to me. Roger Stott wheeled him at a ruthless pace and in no time they were out of sight behind the builders' heaps of sand. Even then I expected him to reappear somehow, perhaps only as a Beckett head poking out of the sand, at once dauntless and pathetic – but of course to be dauntless was already to be a little bit pathetic. In his heyday no outside agency would have presumed to try daunting him. He was simply a sorter out by divine appointment, the archangel of necessity.

By the time he died, a few months later, he had himself been concreted over. The new club bore no mark of his years as its presiding genius. The old members had mostly fled and the new members did not want dreary old sepia photographs cluttering up the ivy-and-bamboo wallpaper. They did not want Denise, either, with her knitting and her menacing stare. Instead they got a beautiful receptionist with a tan and a way of saying Hi which made you feel instantly at home. It had to be instantly because the new members were birds of passage, alighting only for a brief workout before flying on to the Coast or the Gulf. They had neither the time nor the inclination to get to know each other, preferring to exchange tanned smiles and Hi-how-are-yous with all and sundry. Even in the sauna the intimacies were said to be businesslike. In the new bar (opulently laminated but with a little sign perched on it saying no tropical hardwoods had been used) a charming Filipino in a red bow tie mixed perfect whisky sours. There were no beer pumps.

The house? That had been left to Rhona. Perhaps he took some impish satisfaction in the thought of her reigning there, even hoped to provoke a posthumous squabble of the sort he liked hearing about in other families. But there was no argument and

Rhona sold the house without difficulty and moved smartly to a cottage on the South Coast hedged about with impenetrable sea buckthorn and a shingle beach beyond to walk the dog on. Iris lingered on in her hospice, may still be there for all I know, furious but unable to speak, and occasionally shaken by curious convulsions for which the doctors cannot find a name.

As for Josie, she too defied her father's wishes. He had sold the goodwill of Pagan, Jones to one of the new giant accountancy firms he complained about. The sale included a clause forbidding the establishment of any firm with the same or similar name within the next ten years. Josie easily circumvented this by establishing Josephine and Partners, the first known all-women firm of accountants – first in England anyway, there was rumoured to be a rigorously feminist one in southern Nevada. Josie's pitch was less exclusive. She took advantage of the new freedom to advertise by using a fetching photograph of herself with the slogan, 'Wouldn't you rather let a woman see your bottom line?' As a result, some of her father's more sporting male clients put their business her way.

'Then,' she said when she dropped in on me at the office, unexpected, unexplained, 'they're reassured by the sight of John Edward. Some are even reassured by a glimpse of Norris in the back office – he's so much better now. And we're really quite efficient anyway, I promise you we are. I only wish I didn't have to wear these shoulder pads. I look like an American footballer.'

She giggled, and then she winced.

'Oh, giggling does make my face hurt. Ran into the fridge door in case you're wondering. Don't believe me if you don't want to.'

The bruise on her cheek was brown and velvety like the mole which lay beneath it. It made her face seem even rounder, smaller, belonging to some creature whose habitat was too fragile or habits too gentle for its own good. It was darker than the brown shadow I had seen on the same cheek years ago under the bare light bulb. Here, the wall-light, a lemony whorl stuck there like a custard pie, cast the dozy vespertine glow of hospitals at night, and it gave her head that fragile look of some being that was short of a skin or shell – ah no, that was it, though I wished it hadn't been, it was a shell she lacked, she was a younger version of that questing old cross-wrinkled tortoise head we had all thought we were rid of.

'We're awfully happy, you know. I never thought I'd hear myself talking like that, but I know what you think about John Edward, and anyway we are.'

She touched the bruise lightly with her index finger, as though the touching would bring her luck. I felt an extraordinary brutal longing for her, coarser and fiercer than any I had ever admitted to myself before. Perhaps it was the thought of John Edward beating her up that made me want to have her in all the most perverse ways. I could only just see the outline of her bottom as she got up from the squashy office sofa and turned to put out her cigarette, the corner of her hip straining against the cream of her smart linen skirt.

'You mustn't look at me like that. I'm sure your secretary wouldn't like it.'

'It's lovely to see you,' I said, 'but is there any particular reason?'

'Oh you are suspicious,' she said, lighting another cigarette. 'I just wanted to keep an eye on you,' and looked at me sidelong.

'That's nice.'

Her squint had regained its old charm and lent a teasing intimacy to her faintest smile.

'You're not as thin as you were.' She bent over and patted the general area of my abdomen.

This tone annoyed me in a way that I realised she had always annoyed me. All the same, her closeness brought me near to swooning, and when she left the room the last flip of her cream skirt across the slender swell of her calf stayed in my mind for weeks afterwards. I think about her still when I see the jaunty ads for Josephine's, and I think about John Edward's raw red fist smacking into her soft cheek.

It may seem peculiar to end a story with a surge of baffled lust, but then stories ought to end with life going on because it does go on and going on means the eternal renewal of desire. The divine turncock does his rounds and up go the jets spurting merrily from every dolphin's mouth and triton's horn. That urgent, liquid, throbbing gush – Descartes's *fontainier* has a lot to answer for. But the difference here is that my desire for Josie isn't going to be satisfied, never was meant to be satisfied.

I had been in love with her ever since she had been in love with Tony, especially then, I now realise, and, all right if you insist, a little bit in love with Tony too, and now he was under the roses in the crem and she was dodging John Edward's raw red fists. And all my old longing for her had come back, but longing was all there was to it. Nothing had come of it then and nothing would come of it now. This is one of those fountains that has been cut off from the mains years ago and moulders unregarded in an over-grown part of the pleasure grounds, half hidden by the ragged box hedge.

And I saw too that I had misunderstood their gracefulness. I had marvelled at its liquidity but missed its transience. Grace will not stay with us. It is a fleeting, golden swarming, a sweet breeze on the bare skin. That, after all, was what both the story of Danae and the story of the Magdalen were trying to tell us. Serious per-sons pretend that there is such a thing as living in a state of grace. But there isn't. Grace just comes and goes.

All I can say is that this is how the story ended, for me but not for others. Josephine and Partners had a fee income of three mil-lion pounds last year. Michel is just out of the Priory and says he'll never touch drugs again, and John Edward denies that his mar-riage is in trouble, although the police have been called a couple of times.

On a cold spring night, late March or early April, Mr Wall escaped from the hospital where he had been sectioned for a decade and more, clambered over the locked gate of the farm he had once owned (the receivers had changed the locks long ago) and threw himself in the slurry pit where his body lay unnoticed for three days until someone spotted his tweed cap floating like a water lily on the dark surface.